HOT ON THE TRAIL

The light was dim in the soldiers' quarters, but Brett could make out a couple of figures. Brett could smell the scent of men in the room, and realised that both men were semi-naked – one had his neckerchief and boots on, while the other was topless. And both were playing with enormous erections.

Taylor led Brett over to the centre of the room and kissed him passionately. The two other men sat watching and masturbating as Brett and Taylor allowed their hands to wander over each other. Brett felt Taylor squeezing his rigid cock, and became overwhelmingly turned on at the thought of sex here with three soldiers, the four of them in an orgy of sex and desire. His hand grabbed on to Taylor's firm backside, and he gripped the cheeks with his large hands.

HOT ON
THE TRAIL

Lukas Scott

First published in Great Britain in 1999 by
Idol
an imprint of Virgin Publishing Ltd
Thames Wharf Studios,
Rainville Road, London W6 9HA

ISBN 0 352 33461 4

Cover photograph by Trademark

Typeset by SetSystems Ltd, Saffron Walden, Essex
Printed and bound in Great Britain by
Mackays of Chatham PLC

For Andrew

Bacon in the pan
Coffee in the pot
Get up an' get it
Get it while it's hot!

– old cowboy song

The Terrence Higgins Trust

SAFER SEX GUIDELINES

We include safer sex guidelines in every Idol book. However, while our policy is always to show safer sex in contemporary stories, we don't insist on safer sex practices in stories with historical settings – as this would be anachronistic. These books are sexual fantasies – in real life, everyone needs to think about safe sex.

While there have been major advances in the drug treatments for people with HIV and AIDS, there is still no cure for AIDS or a vaccine against HIV. Safe sex is still the only way of being sure of avoiding HIV sexually.

HIV can only be transmitted through blood, come and vaginal fluids (but no other body fluids) passing from one person (with HIV) into another person's bloodstream. It cannot get through healthy, undamaged skin. The only real risk of HIV is through anal sex without a condom – this accounts for almost all HIV transmissions between men.

Being safe
Even if you don't come inside someone, there is still a risk to both partners from blood (tiny cuts in the arse) and pre-come. Using strong condoms and water-based lubricant greatly reduces the risk of HIV. However, condoms can break or slip off, so:
* Make sure that condoms are stored away from hot or damp places.
* Check the expiry date – condoms have a limited life.
* Gently squeeze the air out of the tip.
* Check the condom is put on the right way up and unroll it down the erect cock.
* Use plenty of water-based lubricant (lube), up the arse and on the condom.
* While fucking, check occasionally to see the condom is still in one piece (you could also add more lube).

* When you withdraw, hold the condom tight to your cock as you pull out.
* Never re-use a condom or use the same condom with more than one person.
* If you're not used to condoms you might practise putting them on.
* Sex toys like dildos and plugs are safe. But if you're sharing them use a new condom each time or wash the toys well.

For the safest sex, make sure you use the strongest condoms, such as Durex Ultra Strong, Mates Super Strong, HT Specials and Rubberstuffers packs. Condoms are free in many STD (Sexually Transmitted Disease) clinics (sometimes called GUM clinics) and from many gay bars. It's also essential to use lots of water-based lube such as KY, Wet Stuff, Slik or Liquid Silk. Never use come as a lubricant.

Oral sex
Compared with fucking, sucking someone's cock is far safer. Swallowing come does not necessarily mean that HIV gets absorbed into the bloodstream. While a tiny fraction of cases of HIV infection have been linked to sucking, we know the risk is minimal. But certain factors increase the risk:
* Letting someone come in your mouth
* Throat infections such as gonorrhoea
* If you have cuts, sores or infections in your mouth and throat

So what is safe?
There are so many things you can do which are absolutely safe: wanking each other; rubbing your cocks against one another; kissing, sucking and licking all over the body; rimming – to name but a few.

If you're finding safe sex difficult, call a helpline or speak to someone you feel you can trust for support. The Terrence Higgins Trust Helpline, which is open from noon to 10pm every day, can be reached on 0171 242 1010.

Or, if you're in the United States, you can ring the Center for Disease Control toll free on 1 800 458 5231.

One

Brett grinned as he made his way towards the river. It was a real beautiful day, he thought to himself, as he looked into the blue sky. It was what today was all about for him: promise was as thick in the air as the scent of pine and the cry of the birds above. He wasn't much of a thinker, Brett McKinley; indeed, he was a man known for actions rather than words. Which, of course, was what *today* was all about. Action, the excitement of doing, changing, *making* his life. No, not much of a thinker, but he couldn't help letting thoughts and fantasies fill his head this morning.

Breathing the fresh morning air into his lungs, and feeling the crisp air on his undergarments and breeches, Brett strode ever more purposefully towards the crashing river. He could hear children playing nearby, their excited babbling matching the river's mood and sound. He remembered how he too had played around the river as a child, although there had never been much time for playing, then. Something had always needed to be done. The horses had always needed tending, crops picked, wood gathered: always he had had to watch and learn, his father and uncles telling him how and what they were doing. *A guy needs to learn these things early if he's going to get anywhere here*, they'd said. *You'll thank us for the way we raised you, boy.*

Brett had always hated the term; he'd never been a boy. He'd always been a young man, never known the freedom of childhood. He resented that, and today was the day he was going to prove to them just how much he'd learnt, back then. It wasn't what they had taught him, it was what he had learnt. He was going to prove that the boy was a man, a real man, who could make it out on his own, who could claim his own life, his inheritance. The eldest of four sons, Brett had always been the one supposed to care for and look after the others, his brothers – who had become lazy, relying on him. No more, Brett told himself. No more.

That Brett was no boy was immediately apparent in his physique. At well over six foot, he cut a strong presence with whomever he met. The long days cutting wood and chasing horses, building and farming, had honed his physique perfectly. Under the thin cotton of his undershirt, Brett's biceps swelled against the fabric, the sleeves rolled up to his elbows revealing strong forearms, decorated by short dark hairs sitting like dark snow on his bronze skin. They made their way in a teasing trail to large, masculine hands, well groomed (he had pride in his appearance, even if only for his own satisfaction). The skin on his hands was hard with wind, sun and rain, but their shape was perfect, and often dwarfed the hands of the men he shook deals with. Their grip was strong, the skin inside on his palms warm but hardy. Under his breeches, his heavy-set thighs were perfect for running against the animals he often pitched himself against, and came in useful for the wrestling bouts he sometimes had to prove his worth, and in competition. He had pinned many down with his powerful physique, had often sat victoriously on their chest and howled with laughter as they struggled underneath him. Of course, it was all good-natured fun, but secretly he liked them to feel his manly power, to succumb to his masculine prowess, and realise his dominance.

Brett felt the early morning sun hit his face anew as he passed from under the shade of a tall pine. He had striking features, a fact which the young girls attested to with fits of giggles as he walked past them. And walk past them he did, despite their obvious desire for him. Brett's features were strong and inspiring; he had always been seen as a man's man, his bones strong rather

2

than delicate, chiselled by the outdoors and his habit of cold shaving early in the mornings. His brothers preferred their lazy whiskers, but Brett liked the splash of cold water against his skin every morning: it made him feel awakened, making his face tingle and come alive.

He'd catch the twinkle in his steely grey eyes as he followed his shaving in the small mirror above the wash basin. Not a vain man, Brett was nonetheless aware of how his eyes seemed to grin out at those he looked at, his stare piercing whoever had the audacity to meet his gaze. It was not that he looked menacing; rather, it was as if he was sharing some unspoken joke, was familiar to them in a way they could not comprehend. Brett's eyes drew you into him, took you away into a private place he had created just for you. They were the eyes of a heartbreaker, but also of a man who had never been loved.

The children playing by the river called over to Brett. They all adored him, the group of three all coming from the nearby Borron family. Bill Borron had always treated Brett kindly, had always been a surrogate father to the young Brett. Often, he would sing him songs next to the fire, after Brett had worked hard all day. It had been a brief respite from the hard days Brett had suffered in his twenty-three years at St Joseph, in the mid-Western territory which would become known as Missouri. Bill had sung of the early days on the ranches, the pioneers and the crossings over, courage and bravery, and of the skirmishes against the Indian tribes round and about. Brett had loved the adventure in the songs, the tales of long journeys, riding out towards the setting sun, the hope beyond the horizon. It had been all he had dreamt of while he worked.

The Borron children ran up to him, dripping with the cold water they'd been splashing at him. He greeted them as they plied him for songs. Lately, Brett had taken to singing them some of the songs that their father had sung him. He had sung them with a different feeling, though: not the memory Borron had filled them with, but the yearning that he felt, as if the stories were his dreams. They were, of course, and his sound was the sound the children wanted to hear. He had a strong voice, a booming bass that resonated with the simple songs he sang. Brett

3

knew that the children would miss him, but maybe someone would write a song about him one day. About the trip he was beginning this morning.

A sharp sound broke Brett out of his reverie. Ma Borron was calling the children in, and he sensed that their first meal of the day was ready. He looked on as they ran laughing up to their mother. It was a perfect image of home, and one he suddenly realised he would miss. There was warmth, security and tenderness here. Beyond the few miles that he had known from childhood, Brett didn't know what 'there' was. Through the songs and the stories, and some strangers who happened by from time to time, he knew that it was an awfully big place out there. He knew that there were riches, adventures, exploits, and dangers. Not just the dangers of snakes and wolves and animals he had never seen, but the danger of men. Other men, who could hurt and steal and kill in a way that he had never experienced here, in this kind, caring, small community he had lived his whole life in.

Ma Borron waved at him as he looked on. 'I hear today's the day, Brett. Good luck to you. Though you know it breaks your Mama's heart to see you go!'

'It breaks my heart to leave her, Ma Borron. But she's got Pa and the rest of the boys. You promise to keep her company, though? She's always said what a good friend you've been to the family.'

'Be sure I will, young Master McKinley! And one day we'll all visit you over there where the gold flows. Not that I could journey so far at my age. Still, maybe, one day we'll be seeing you in your finery. God speed you!'

Brett bowed graciously as Ma Borron called in the children and waved him farewell. Gold, she'd said. His spine tingled even as he thought about the word. His eyes lit up again, and he became aware of the morning chill against his skin. Ever since the gold discovery a couple of years ago out west, the stories had become wilder and wilder. They said it was running out of the mountains like water, that it hung from the trees, that it rained gold dust. There was enough of the stuff to make whole houses and roads from it. The sun never went down, because the gold shimmered all night long.

Brett knew the stories to be exaggerated, but they also thrilled him. There was no doubt that something was out there, that there must be fire in the billowing smoke these tales produced. He could stay here no longer. He knew he had to step out, make the break with his home and family here, and trek the paths that would take him to the truth behind the stories. He had to know what was out there. Brett was going to find his own fortune: maybe it was hidden within these stories of gold, or maybe they'd just all be fool's gold. But he had to know. He had to escape.

Of course, there had been a row. His mother had cried, and his father had refused him 'permission' to set out. His lazy brothers had rolled their eyes and sneered at him. But his resolve was set: he had told them repeatedly over the weeks that it was his intention to head out west and make his fortune. If he had their blessing, they would hear from him when he arrived, and if possible he would send on for them to join him. If they continued with their carping and upset, it would be the last they would hear from him.

Brett had always been his own man. There had been a half-hearted truce, whereby his decision was accepted but not welcomed, and nothing more had been said. Even this morning, none of them had risen early to bid him farewell. Somehow, however, he had felt his mother's gaze as he left home. He wondered if she had sneaked out silently to watch him leave, or if it had been his imagination.

Standing watching the river crash and break against the rocks as it made its never-ending journey, Brett stripped off his under-shirt and then his breeches. He stood naked, then felt the thrill of the cold water against his feet as he waded in. For a moment, he stood and let the slight spray break against his hot skin. He felt the blood rushing through his veins, felt the heat of his flesh, and saw wisps of heat escaping from his hot body. He felt like one of the beasts of the country, another living creature enjoying the raw passions of life.

His frame was lightly kissed by the sun's morning greeting to the world. As he stood, legs apart, naked and wild, he laughed his deep, energised laugh. He felt a raw man now, naked, full of purpose and might. He bent down and cupped a handful of water to his already clean-shaven face. Its cold spray splashed against his skin, and he tasted its freshness as he opened his mouth and let it slide into his hot, thirsty mouth. The water broke against his perfect set of teeth, snaking a journey around his tongue and down his throat. He splashed more of the cold river against his flesh, soothing the passion and heat he felt. He lowered his head against the water, his head breaking the surface of the water so that his short, dark hair followed the pattern of the stream like moss growing on stones. He kept his face under the water for as long as he could, feeling the water flow over the back of his neck, stroking the short hairs at the nape, tickling and caressing him.

Brett brought his head up, thrusting it back and felt the water course off him, dancing into the air. A trickle of cold water ran down his strong bronzed back, trickling all the way to the tip of his backside, finding a way between his firm, hairy buttocks, and settling into his arse-crack. More water cascaded down his broad chest, through the triangular forest of hair that nestled from the top of his chest down towards his belly, where it became a slight trail broadening into the valley of pubic hair that surrounded his genitalia. The water dripped down his large cock, wetting his heavy ball sac, droplets resting on his heavy thighs, dampening the slight dark hairs on them enough to glisten.

He looked around, and saw that he could enjoy the sensations washing through him this morning with no one watching him. This early morning wash was invigorating him, preparing him for his long journey ahead. He didn't know when he would feel this secure, this safe, this *alive* again. Brett submerged himself completely under the water, letting the currents wash over him and massage his every muscle. He lay directly in the path of the stream, allowing it to bob him gently as water kissed every part of his anatomy.

A sigh escaped from his lips, and he knew that he couldn't let this moment finish with just a wash. Often, when he woke aroused in the morning, he would come to the water and let it take him in this way. When he was just discovering his own body's pleasures, as an adolescent, he had believed that the cold water would calm his passion, that the fearful passions he felt would be dissipated by the cold, the wet, the rawness of the river. He soon realised that it only helped increase his pleasure, and it soon became part of it.

Brett began to touch himself more erotically, following the path of the river down his body. It was electrifying, his hot hands travelling up and down his body as the river raged round him. The coarseness of his palms was a sharp contrast to the smooth water, and he enjoyed his coarse hands scrubbing his skin, travelling over his chest and belly, further down to the root of his passion. He closed his eyes, resting against a boulder that cradled him in its grey expanse, hard against his strong back.

Already, his growing erection was lapping against his thigh in the water. He could feel the hot excitement against his wet thigh, feeling a little juice sticking his penis slightly to his hairy leg. Brett allowed his hand to rest on the thickening shaft, moaning gently as his palm brushed against the underside of his cock. He played his hand against the erect pole, stroking but not yet gripping his ever-growing rod. His free hand began to play with his left nipple, which was already hard from the cold morning air. *Ahhhhh.* Now he could grab his burgeoning tool, and slowly, slowly, stroke up and down the hard shaft. He let his hand pull up to the top of the uncircumcised flesh, and then pull down to the hairy base where his balls were beginning to tighten in the water. Already the shaft was thickening to its full girth, as he continued his slow strokes all the way up and down his hard cock.

Meanwhile, his other hand began to play with his opposite nipple, taking its button between his thumb and first finger and gently rubbing, then tightening his grip, squeezing the tip until the pleasure forced him to stop. His hand travelled through the light hair of his chest, wet and following the pattern of his hand-movements. He traced his hair the wrong way, up towards his face, and then stroked it back down so that it no longer stood up on his chest. He let his hand move up on to his face, follow the line of his cheek and throat, over his temple, and then allowed a finger to sink into his hot, aching mouth. He sucked on it, tasting

7

the freshness of the water, and the coolness of his finger compared to the heat of his tongue as it circled around it. Another finger joined the first in his mouth, and Brett alternated the attentions of his lapping tongue between them, letting it slide up and down his skin, sucking gently on each digit.

This was so good, so pleasurable, even better than the first time Brett had come here and found these magic sensations. He hadn't understood the sudden erection he had felt in the water, or why his touching it made it grow more and more. He had only been a mere adolescent then, not possessing the fine physique he now took pleasure in. How he had taken pleasure in the way his body grew! How delighted he had been to discover the hairs that surrounded his growing genitals, that tattooed his chest and crowned his thighs and buttocks. He had loved the way he developed the manly attributes he had so admired in other grown-up men, and now he could admire them in his own special way. He could take care of his manliness in the way that he so wanted to of other men's.

Brett could feel it happening again, the way it happened that first time in the stream. His breathing was becoming quicker, and he could feel his heart jumping about in his chest, like it was doing some crazy dance inside him. Despite himself, audible groans came from him, such was the pleasure exploding inside. He quickened the long strokes of his cock, allowing them to become faster and his grip stronger and tighter. Brett could feel his face wincing, contorting with pleasure and becoming hotter against the slight breeze. He closed his eyes and felt the pressure mounting for release, the excitement he had felt since daybreak demanding expression. Opening his eyes again, Brett squinted at the bright sun, the only light in a clear blue sky, and he felt his own light beginning to rise.

He was pumping faster and faster now, knowing that any moment orgasm would rush through him and his hot sperm would rush out. He loved this moment, and looked down as he pounded faster and tighter on his hard, hot dick, feeling blood spasm through his veins and muscle, his breath gathering for one long last groan. As his booming moan broke the air, reverberating around him, Brett felt himself coming, a glorious flow shooting from his tightened balls all the way up to the tip of his underwater cock, and finally shooting into the flowing water of the river. Again and again he thrust into the water, suddenly standing so that his hot spunk shot out into the air, falling like rain into the water, a glorious storm of hot semen breaking the water. Brett let the ripples of orgasm flow straight through him, feeling them subside in his heaving body. He looked down and watched the milky white stream swirling around his penis, clinging desperately to the tip of his softening rod, thick hot cream against the clear water. Slowly, Brett watched his come being swallowed by the river, eagerly sucked into its currents and carried off like a precious trophy. He let the water lick the last vestiges of his fluid, washing his satisfied cock with a cooling kiss.

Brett lay once again against the rock, the after-effects of his orgasm leaving him slightly sleepy, but refreshed by the coolness of the water around him. His breathing began to slow down, and his temperature returned to normal as his balls gently lapped against his sleeping cock. Once more, he had proven his man-hood, his wild passions, his unknown desires. If only he could find someone else who could do this for him, who could take him to such earth-shattering pleasure. Would the river be forever his only mate, the only tongue to caress and swallow him? How could he find such wild, elemental passion in someone else?

Brett stroked his cock clean in the water, the last few drops of semen slowly escaping from his cock-hole. He brought the water close against his face, splashing his skin and mopping his brow. The water almost smelt of his own sweat, but cleaner and purer, now. It was the last time Brett would find such pleasure in the river with himself, for he knew now his journey was really beginning. He watched the river flow, and wondered whether he would be following it or escaping it. With a last look up at the promising sky, and feeling the air warming around him already, Brett dried himself off and set about his journey. If only there could be this much excitement all the time, he thought as he headed away as far west as he could.

Two

B rett McKinley strode to the banks of the Missouri, the fine
and majestic broad expanse of water that had always filled his
body with awe. As he looked at it, he imagined where it had
been before crashing through his home: down from the Rockies
way up north, past Fort Benton, and on down through North
and South Dakota, land of the Sioux Tribe, about whom he had
heard so much. Then, filled with energy and vitality, the river
wound its way further south again until it washed the banks here
near St Joseph. He knew it would go on to join the mighty
Mississippi further south. He thought of his own river and how it
flowed into the Missouri, seeing himself as part of that great
journey.

Now, there was another journey. Brett knew that this was the
easy part for him, the steam boat southwards to Fort Leavenworth, where he could rest and prepare for the major part of his
gold-seeking journey. From there, he would have to join the
Oregon-California route to get west into the new gold territories.
It was the biggest journey he would ever make and it would
demand every ounce of his strength, courage and determination
if he was to reach his goal. But when Brett wanted something,
he always got it.

There was no turning back now. Not after he had defied his
mother and father. His father had been a farmer at St Joseph for

many a year now and, although kind enough in his own way, he was a fearsome man who ruled his family with an iron will. His mother was dedicated to her family and, Brett thought, often quite lonely, there being few womenfolk round and about. That was why he knew she appreciated the small kindnesses of Ma Borron, the pastries and pies and gifts the other woman would bring round. In return, she had helped to raise the younger Borron family. In such a small community, it was important to look out for each other.

As he approached the river station, seeing the rising smoke and hearing occasionally the excitable voices of traders and soldiers moving southwards, Brett turned round to see a billowing of dust and the canter of horses. He raised his hand above his eyes and squinted ahead. The rising sun was strong on his face now, continuing to brown his already tanned skin. He swore as he realized what he was seeing: his three brothers were riding out towards him, their purpose no doubt to 'persuade' him to return home. Was this their idea? he wondered. They wouldn't – couldn't – have such thoughts of their own. He imagined his father's angry face warning them not to come home without him, his mother's tear-filled eyes begging them to plead with him.

Cursing again, Brett carried on striding towards the riverbank, ignoring the approaching men.

John, the second eldest McKinley, shouted after him. 'Brett! Hold up there! We've come to put an end to this madness.'

Brett carried on walking as the youngest brother, Al, made himself known, too. 'Ma's so upset, Brett. You can't leave her this way.'

Frank, the laziest and most manipulative of them all, chipped in his opinion. 'So what's new? The boy never thought of anyone but himself. Now he's got some fancy dream he wants to follow. Let him and, a few days from now, we'll hear tell of him face down in some stream, or his scalp'll be some native's trophy. We should never have bothered coming after him.'

Brett turned. 'You're right there, Frank, and that's the only true word any of you has spoken. You should never have come. You should have stayed back home, like you will all your lives. That's not for me, any more. I've paid my dues there. I'm heading off. Sure, Frank, you can scoff at my dreams of making it out west, but that's cos you haven't the sense to think such things!'

Frank spat his tobacco on to the floor. Although only a couple of years younger than Brett, he had already missed out on his brother's finer features. He was lean, but his muscles would never be honed the way Brett's were, and Frank never seemed to bother trying to build them up. While he could get others to do his work for him, there was no need to do such things himself. None of the brothers had Brett's good looks – they were all pale imitations, as if the cast had been broken with Brett.

Al attempted to make peace – as the youngest, he often found himself on the wrong side of the brothers' arguments. His slighter frame often meant he'd receive the loser's wrath after any of their numerous fights.

'You're just not thinking, Brett. C'mon, at least leave it 'til we know more about these stories. All this talk of gold. It's just boasts and songs. If there's anything to them, we'll hear it for definite, soon enough. We'll even see it with our own eyes.'

'Al, I don't want to pick a fight with you. But if I wait 'til I see proof of everything in this world, I'll be an old man before I step out the door again.'

'You may not be picking a fight with Al, but you've picked one with us,' Frank threatened as he and John lowered themselves from the horses. They'd come solely with the intention of beating up on him, Brett was sure. Why else would they suddenly be so concerned about his safety, or the closeness of the McKinley family? He started to rid himself wearily of the supplies for the journey, letting them drop to the ground with a thud. After unmanacling himself, he prepared for the inevitable: a trial of strength between him and his two brothers, while young Al looked on. Al was already being handed his older brothers' horses to hold while they roughed with Brett.

Frank came forward first, a rough sneer breaking the unhandsome line of his face. Brett was reminded of the time that Frank and John had come back from one of their 'adventures', one of the few times they left the safety of home in search of a thrill or two. They'd boasted that they'd been and picked themselves up a pair of whores, screwing all night long and even swapping partners as the night wore on. They boasted of the many positions they'd experimented with, how their lust had known no bounds and how the women had been pleased by their patrons over and over, begging for more from the McKinley brothers. Brett knew most of it was idle boasting, but believed his brothers had paid for the sex they'd had. They'd have to, he'd thought maliciously.

Frank threw a punch that fell wide of its mark, as Brett dodged skilfully, dancing round and laughing. John lunged as Brett made swift contact with the side of Frank's face – not a hard punch, but a warning strike. John tackled Brett to the ground, the brothers rolling in the dust as Frank roared from the sting he'd felt and lunged down towards Brett. Al watched the grunting and swearing fight, seeing boots and fists fly around a whirling bowl of dust. It was hard to make out anything that was happening, except to know that even both brothers were no real match against Brett's strength. Occasional curses and moans would break the air, punctuated by loud thuds and punches. The three rolled around on the floor, the fight moving several feet away from where Al watched with the horses, who were fractious and upset at the sudden commotion.

Brett could smell the sweat of his brothers, feel their hot bodies pressing against him as they tried to control the fight. They weren't fighting in unison, or working together in any fashion. They were just trying to punch and kick where they could, so Brett was able to deflect many of the blows away from himself and on to one of his opponents. From somewhere, Brett could taste the salty sting of blood and realised it was his own – a cut had appeared on his lower lip, more through clumsiness than accuracy on the part of his brothers.

Frank was suddenly on top of Brett, sprawled over him and raising his fist to hit his face. John was struggling to try to hold down Brett's arms, so that Frank would have a target even he couldn't miss. Brett bucked his thighs and stomach, his bulk enough to throw the lighter Frank off guard and send him flying into the air. He'd had enough now. Brett wanted to show his brothers that he was the boss, he was the one who made his own decisions, and wasn't going to suffer their taunts or sneers any longer. He pulled John's head downwards to his chest, at the same time bringing his knee up far enough and quickly enough to make direct contact. There was a loud crash as the hard bone of Brett's knee hit the front of John's head. John whimpered loudly as he rolled off to one side, holding his wounded head.

Brett stood quickly, turning on Frank, who was rising groggily from his throw. Brett waited for his brother to rise, and then lunged at him forcefully. He let loose a left-hand blow that stung Frank, and then followed through with a mighty punch from the right. It was enough to throw his brother completely off guard, the only thing stopping him from hitting the ground being Brett's hand at his throat. Brett brought his face up close to Frank's weary features. He stared into Frank's bleary eyes, sorry that his brothers had been no match for him – he could have done with some real exercise, this fine day! He grinned broadly and pulled back his right arm. One final punch sent Frank rocketing to the floor to the tune of Brett's mocking laughter. He turned without speaking, the silence a chord of victory, and made his way to his belongings, hitching them on to his sweating back.

It was Al who stopped him from leaving right away. The youngest McKinley ran up and put his hand on his brother's shoulder. Brett turned round swiftly, his arm swinging back in the air, ready to land a blow on the unseen enemy.

'Whoa! I'm not looking for a fight with you, Brett!' Al Grinned. 'I may be younger than the rest of you, but that doesn't mean I'm as stupid. You beat them for sure, and I reckon they deserved every punch they got. I didn't want them to come after you in the first place, but they'd got their minds set on it. You know how they are when they scent blood! Nothing appeals to them as much as the thought of thrashing the life out of you. And with Ma and Pa's "blessing", too.'

'They should have learnt better by now.' Brett's low tones relaxed at his brother's honesty. He grinned at Al, and playfully soft-punched him on the cheek.

'I just wanted to say . . . uh, that is . . . Oh, Brett. I sure am going to miss you around, but I don't want you thinking none of us wishes you well. I hope you find whatever it is you're after. We're the ones who're nuts for not going with you!'

Brett felt touched, as if he had received a blessing for his journey after all. For a moment, he feared for Al, left with the wrath of his older brothers, unwilling to accept the defeat he'd meted out to them. Watching the young boy, the fledgling physique and the wild intelligence that lay behind open and youthful eyes, Brett knew the boy would manage on his own. The boy! Hadn't that been what Brett himself had hated to be called?

'You'll be your own man soon enough, Al. Maybe you'll join me then. There'll always be a space waiting for you, if you do.' Brett held out his hand.

'You bet. Maybe I'll get to join you sooner than you think!' Al cradled his small hand in Brett's, shaking it enthusiastically. The two brothers looked long and hard at each other before Al broke off the moment, looking round at Frank and John. 'Guess I'd better fix these two up so they're in a decent state when we hit home.'

Even so, Al was obviously savouring the beating they'd taken. It would last him for months to come, and might stave off some of their antagonism towards him. He'd be sure enough to remind them of it when the occasion arose!

'Nothing you can do'll make 'em look decent,' Brett joked, slapping his brother on the back. 'Good luck to you, anyhow.'

'And good luck to you, Brett. Not that I reckon you'll need it.'

For the first time, Brett was aware of his brother's admiration for him, and it touched him. All the time he'd been at home, he'd never felt it: but here, just as he was about to leave Al, there was a sense of deep trust and respect. It made him feel proud, but also embarrassed, and humbled him enough for him to lower his gaze. 'I guess we can all do with as much luck as we get, Al. Thanks.'

'Sure, Brett. Take care out there.'

'You too, huh? Don't let them get the better of you!'

Brett turned. He could already hear the muttering and cursing of Frank and John as he made his way back towards the Missouri.

Al was teasing them, playing one off against the other, as if they'd let him and each other down. He heard the horses behind him becoming agitated, then the sound of hooves and the desperate cries of Frank and John. Without even looking back, Brett knew their horses must have bolted, and it was Al's raucous laughter raised above their shouts and cries that he remembered as he carried on trekking.

By the time Brett arrived at the bankside, he'd missed his scheduled boat, which put him behind time for the journey. He cursed his brothers under his breath, irritated that he'd lost time because of their interference. Still, it gave him a break – Brett knew that his original schedule had been gruelling, and perhaps it wasn't such a bad idea to ease up anyhow. His fists were hurting from the fight, and his legs aching a little from the walking he'd done so far. He'd sold his own pony to pay for the trip, with a view to buying one further down the trail. He knew that if he started travelling light, he'd have to shed less of his own precious baggage than if he picked things up as and when he needed them.

The few buildings which had been set up to deal with the steam-boat trade were simple affairs, set up as cheaply as possible and looking like they'd break with the first strong wind. Timber fronts advertised what small offerings they had – simple supplies, some clothing, equipment for a journey undertaken. The arrival of a paddleboat had created some excitement; some men had obviously been reunited with their womenfolk, and the welcomes were as much sexual as endearing. The men fondled their wives, girlfriends and mistresses openly but playfully, taking refuge in their arms and embraces. The small talk of weather, far-away folk and various aches and pains endured on the journey were belied by a lusty hunger for flesh, for the bedroom, the room rented above a bar for a night, the open air in the dark. Anywhere to make the reunions seem real, physical, intimate.

Brett picked up on the atmosphere as he walked along the dirt-track that served as a main thoroughfare. He had his own physical urges to see to, more primary ones even than the desire he suddenly felt for sex. Now, he was hungry for food, his belly aching despite the hearty breakfast he'd made for himself earlier that morning. He had some supplies in his bags, but wanted to reserve them for a time when there was no ready food available. Seeing a saloon at the far end of the track, Brett trudged over, climbed the timber steps and opened the chest-high shutters to enter. He was struck by the smoke, and the smell of bourbon and rye, an appealing and masculine smell, that increased his appetite, and started his thirst. He realised his throat was dry, ordered a finger of rye and asked the buxom girl behind the bar what was good on the menu.

Ruby grinned knowingly, amused by the question. 'Stew's hot,' she flirted. 'Bread's fresh. Satisfy any man's desire.'

'Would it, now? Well, as it comes so well recommended, I'll have a bowl of your stew, and some of that fresh bread to mop up the juices.'

Ruby giggled and took the money Brett offered her. 'You off on the boat?'

Ruby had obviously seen many men pass through, and Brett wondered how many she'd been intimate with. She was a good-looking young woman – Brett judged her to be a couple of years older than himself, with long dark hair that clung to her head in ringlets, and fierce wild dark eyes that blazed against her delicate white skin. Her full dress showed off her ample bosom, and her air was of one who did not make herself readily available, but knew she was attractive, and that this was her main asset in life. Brett guessed she'd already broken a fair few hearts, and would break more before her looks failed her. If he'd have been staying, and had been that way inclined, he might indeed have taken his own chances.

Before Brett could answer Ruby, he was joined by a young man who repeated Brett's order for himself. The youngster had an air of innocence, compared to Ruby's knowingness, a freshness that was apparent in his gushing conversation with Brett.

'I'm off on the boat, too. Thought I'd never get this far. You going to sign up too, sir?'

'Sign up?' Brett threw the question aside, not caring for an answer.

'Cavalry. Ain't that why everyone's going up North? I've been dreaming 'bout it for months, now: bet myself soon as I hit twenty, I'd make my way up there and show 'em my horsemanship. I can handle a gun good as anyone around abouts, and I take care of myself pretty good. Pleased to meet you, sir.'

Brett looked at the eager youth. He had a boyish charm, but his manhood was undeniable. Trim blond hair, recently cropped for the occasion, set off light blue eyes, with a well-defined young face. His lips were full and smiling, and every now and then he licked them in anticipation of the food to come. He was of medium height, with a slim frame only barely useful for a soldier. In the months to come, he would need to build himself up if he would make it into the cavalry. Still, the young man showed no signs of weakness; rather, his lithe frame gave him a grace and charm that was appealing. As the youth fanned himself from the heat, Brett noticed his chest and arms were hairless, and that his skin was soft compared to Brett's own roughness.

'The name's Brett, not sir, though I like your manners, kid. Your intentions are more honourable than mine; I'm off to make myself a fortune in the gold hills of the West.'

The lad's eyes widened. 'California?' He could barely say the word, and Brett guessed he was more impressionable than he should be for his age.

Brett smiled. 'So what's the name of our young soldier?'

'Scott Baker, sir – sorry, Brett.'

'Scott, you care to eat with me?' Brett indicated the steaming bowls of stew Ruby had brought for them both.

'I'd love that. Looks good, don't you think?'

'Anything that's hot would take my fancy now.'

Ruby picked up on Brett's bawdiness, but it passed over Scott, who set about devouring his stew. Thick chunks of root vegetables filled out what little meat the stew contained, though the meal was hearty enough nonetheless.

The two ate in silence, aside from the odd slurp from the stew bowl, or the breaking of bread crust. Although there was only three years' difference between the two men, they could have come from opposite sides of the world. Brett attacked his meal in a functional way, seeking only to satisfy his hunger, whereas young Scott found every mouthful an adventure, eating in awe and reverie. The meal made Brett feel good, and eased some of the tension he had felt since the fight with his brothers. The drink helped, too, and Brett ordered another to supplement the glow that was seeping through him.

Scott carried on gabbling, his vulnerability and openness appealing to Brett. He told Brett of his sisters, growing up with them, and how he always played at being their protector. They seemed proud of his decision to become a cavalryman. He wanted someone to listen to him, to hear his story, maybe to befriend him. For all the boy's conviviality, Brett sensed a deep loneliness in the boy, a longing to please others, to be liked. Strange that he should become a soldier to do so – or perhaps the order and structure, the companionship, the everyday possibility of losing your life for another's, would give the youth his sense of purpose and completion.

The food and drink had made Brett sleepy, and he found himself nodding off as Scott continued talking. In the strangely welcoming world of the semi-sleeping, Brett's mind was filled of images of the young Scott, riding horseback, eyes wide at the adventure of the army, a bright blue uniform sticking close to his body. Scott looked good in a tunic and trousers, black boots, and yellow neckerchief, a cap riding his crown. His lithe frame allowed the uniform to cling to him, and in Brett's half-dream he saw the young man tending the horse. He combed the mane with long, caring strokes, the contact with the beast making the boy seem caring, warm, accommodating. He looked small compared to the great animal, but his tending quietened the strongest beast. The heat of the day forced the hard-working soldier to remove his tunic, slip off his braces, and work bare-chested in the mid-morning heat. Brett's dreaming state allowed him to imagine the young man's hairless form, his sinewy arms and strong back, perfectly formed, broad shoulders from the riding and tending. The work made him perspire: not the heavy sweat that Brett produced, but the sensuous rain of youth that made a young man's form glisten and glow, like the prized gold that Brett was chasing. In the dream, Scott turned round and grinned broadly at Brett as he approached, waving and welcoming him.

The image disappeared as Brett was started by Scott's hand on his shoulder. 'Hey, am I that boring? Didn't mean to put you to sleep, sir. Brett?'

Brett opened his eyes and looked at the boy. He didn't seem any different from the dream, and Brett hoped his arousal wasn't obvious to the boy. He adjusted himself as he sat up and apologised. 'Sorry, guess I must have been more tired than I cared to admit. The food just sent me off. Nothing personal, hey, kid?' He proffered his hand by way as a token of atonement.

Scott took it eagerly, and for the second time the men shook, this time Brett feeling excitement at the soft touch of the young man in front of him. He closed his hand over Scott's, making this connection more intimate than before. He held it for just long enough to let the boy know he thought of him as special, but not long enough to betray anything more. As he slouched on the stool, he allowed his knees to touch Scott's, who didn't move or seem to resent the closeness. Indeed, Scott seemed to encourage it, their boots just connecting under the table.

They spent the next couple of hours at Ruby's, drinking a little more and talking away. Brett was glad of the company, and was becoming increasingly intrigued by the young man and his innocent but sensual presence. Brett regaled the kid with stories of his brothers, their fights, the songs he'd sung, the Borrons, the tales he'd heard of the gold out West. He also talked a little about his plans when he got the gold, the ranch he'd build and the family he planned to raise. It was the first time he'd shared the dreams, having to be careful what he said in front of his family. Now, he could let his imagination run riot, with talk of cowherds the envy of all who saw them, a timber mansion, deep wells with sweet fresh water. Maybe he could even build a store – a town! – named after him.

As he expanded the fantasy, Brett knew that it was all possible, that he could achieve anything now. Confidence flooded through him, ridding him of the unspoken doubts he'd harboured previously, and he became aware of all the possibilities that were opening up in front of him. As he watched the admiration on Scott's face, he knew that there were other possibilities this journey would open up for him, too. This was going to be more than a hunt for gold. This was a hunt for all his desires, for Brett McKinley to experience many excitements and passions.

The time came for them to settle up with Ruby, who winked at Brett as he left. 'See you around, Forty-niner!'

Brett laughed as he made his exit – forty-niners were what the prospectors were being nicknamed these days, and he quite liked the mantle. It made him feel that he'd been recognised, honoured in some way. All of a sudden, his journey was real, and he'd made the leap to a real gold prospector, a real independent man who knew his place in the world.

The two men made their way to the paddle steamer and boarded, piling their few belongings on deck. The evening was drawing to a close, the first full day of Brett's trek. So far so good, he thought to himself. The mid-western sky was becoming darker, the last few rays of light illuminating the broad horizon and setting the river afire. The orange haze shone on Scott's face and coloured his blond hair a glowing corn-gold, his blue eyes squinting in the light. They continued talking as Brett watched the light moving down Scott's body with the setting sun, like a slow seduction. By the time the sun had gone down, the April air had turned chilly; the breeze along the waterfront was enough to make the two men shiver a little.

The lateness of the hour led them to bed down for the rest of the ride. The paddle boat continued on its trek southwards, the water it pushed through offering a babbling lullaby as they took off their boots and overshirts. They placed their boots side by side, not touching, and it made an endearing and almost domestic scene. Brett was conscious of how much larger his boots were in comparison with Scott's, a good size or two larger, yet the men were only three years different in age. They settled to sleep, close but not together, just feeling the warmth of each other's body, not yet intimate in any way. Brett heard the soft purrs of Scott as he slept easily, his snores comfortable as a puppy's. Every now and then a low moan would escape his open mouth, but it sounded contented more than fretful.

Brett lay back and stroked himself in the cool night air. He was having difficulty sleeping, the excitement of the day and his mid-afternoon snooze not allowing his mind to drift away. More out of comfort than serious lust, Brett allowed his right hand to gently rub his coiled penis, the soft movement bringing it to a slowly waking state. He felt the tight scrub of his pubic hair brushing across his wrist, tickling him pleasantly. His fingers explored the growing flesh, tapping lightly up and down the warm shaft. He didn't want to bring himself off, just to experience the slow warmth running through his crotch in the hope it might send him to sleep.

Brett maintained his half-erect state for a while before he removed his hand and felt the light pressure of his undergarments resting on his cock. He lay back and felt it twitch lazily, arrogantly refusing to rise to its full kingly state. Realising that he wouldn't fall asleep immediately, Brett removed the rug that covered him and stood up, making his way over to the railings of the riverboat. He loved the open nights, and often wrapped himself in the darkness at home, watching the stars twinkle and feeling the open air around him, the sounds of coyotes, wolves, occasional bears, birds and activity far away.

Brett became aware of a stirring beside him. Scott's form under his blanket nest began to move, unfurling itself from the warmth and comfort that had kept him asleep. Brett saw Scott raise his head, his eyes blinking up at the man by the railings. For a while they looked at each other; Brett was not quite sure if Scott could see the wry grin he was wearing or, indeed, the dormant bulge that nestled between his thighs, not quite diminished after his earlier fumblings. He broke off the contact and turned his back on the boy, taking the chance to shift his half-erection to a more comfortable position, even though it made his cock more obvious and his arousal more immediate.

All of a sudden, Brett wanted to make his lust apparent. He wanted to show his glorious meat to the boy, to expose his growing manhood, tease Scott with his thick hard shaft. He wanted Scott to know just how horny he was, how well endowed, how hot and male Brett McKinley was. He could feel himself hardening, the familiar twitch from his awesome thick meat bringing his cock upright and gently loosening his foreskin to allow more room for growth. He felt the blood flowing through his thick cock veins, the heat rising in his loins.

He wanted his hard cock serviced, here, now. The thrill of the boat crew or passengers catching him in this state, with young

Scott watching him, gave him an additional thrill, quickening the full erection he now had. Slowly, he turned round to Scott and let his right hand rest gently on his full eight inches, straining against the thin cotton that surrounded his lower half.

Brett watched the younger man looking at him. He took pride in the way that his hard dick stretched the fabric of his clothes, the way it reached out from his torso in an attempt to seek release. Brett knew Scott couldn't mistake what was happening now, and he saw the boy's gaze travel from his cock to his face, and back to his cock. Scott threw off the blanket, exposing his own naked figure in the starlight. Brett saw the shadow of a half-erection between Scott's hairless thighs, a smaller penis than his, but nicely shaped, and balls hanging low between his legs. Brett allowed Scott to move over towards him, stand and face him. He could feel the heat generated between the two of them, the younger man's face reaching up to him, gazing at him, smelling his own masculine scent in the night air.

Scott moved closer, and Brett could hear his heart pounding, the warmth of his chest moving closer to his, his soft skin finally resting against Brett's undershirt. Scott reached up to Brett, his mouth open and panting, hot breath reaching Brett's own open mouth. Brett let Scott move closer, his lips as close as they could be to Brett's without touching, their mouths lined up, hot breath filtering into each other's mouth, Brett deliberately panting into Scott's face. As Scott moved forward to plant his mouth on Brett's, Brett moved his mouth to one side, letting the boy know that he was teasing him, playing with Scott's obvious desire for Brett. Scott whimpered slightly, clearly desperate for the taste of Brett's mouth, to enjoin himself with Brett's hot lips and feel their tongues touch. Brett breathed into Scott's face, into his ear, just touching his lips against Scott's left earlobe. Then Brett lightly flicked his rough hot tongue into Scott's ear, before pulling his face away as Scott moaned with anticipation.

Brett looked into the young man's earnest face, and felt Scott's left hand tentatively against his thigh. Brett didn't pull back or encourage, enjoying the game, not allowing Scott to know how far he would let him go. He didn't touch his admiring partner in return, but stood firm and impassionate, allowing his chest to move slowly up and down. Scott braved further, his hand grazing against the outline of Brett's hard cock. He groaned as he realised its length, the full power that lay between Brett's thighs. Unbelieving, his hand felt for the whole length, slowly moving from the base of the shaft to the tip, where Brett could feel a drop of fluid leaking into the fabric. Scott fingered the tip, felt the small amount of juice, and snaked it down the shaft, before lifting his finger to his mouth. He looked straight at Brett and ran the tip of his finger lightly over his lips, tasting Brett's liquid for the first time. He closed his eyes and moaned, and Brett knew that the young man was now in his power, that he had him completely in his spell, to service and pleasure him right there, on the riverboat, under the fragile cover of the night.

Brett moved slightly, spreading his legs a little for a more comfortable position. Without a word spoken between them, he knew that Scott could tell by his his face what he was expected to do. Scott fumbled slowly for the big dick, using both hands to free it from its prison, his hands running over the solid pole, caressing it and running his hands over the base and hairy balls. Brett groaned slightly, just enough to encourage him to go further, to worship the engorged glans.

Scott's knees buckled, and he knelt before Brett's upright form, still holding the erection in both hands. He looked up at Brett, who sneered at him, and then brought the head of Brett's cock right up to his lips. Brett looked down as Scott planted his lips against the tip of his throbbing dick, covering the exposed head with small kisses and nibbles, before Scott's mouth opened and his lips brushed over the tip. Brett stood there for a moment, savouring the warmth of Scott's mouth, the tongue that gently licked against his sensitive underside, a soft sucking motion on the very head of the cock. Slowly, he pushed forward, inching his way deeper into Scott's mouth, until half of his shaft lay comfortably in Scott's mouth. He loved the subservience of this young soldier-to-be, the willingness with which his mouth enveloped his hard hot shaft.

Brett felt Scott move his mouth forward, over Brett's length, trying to eat more of the tasty meat, and dropped one of his strong arms to Scott's shoulders. His firm hand cupped Scott's blond hair, forcing him deeper into Brett's sweaty crotch, his dick reaching further into Scott's throat. Firmly he pushed the younger man deep down on all eight inches, hearing Scott gag slightly as he fought to accommodate the length. Holding his head there, Brett began a simple fucking motion, his hips moving back and forth as his length disappeared inside the willing wet mouth adoring him. With just a little effort, Brett was able to sink his entire shaft into the pleasure hole, his hairy balls thrust against Scott's youthful but flushed face, as he heard soft suckling sounds at the base of his cock. The lad was good, Brett thought, as he allowed himself to quicken the pace, the thrusts becoming harder and faster.

Brett was aware of Scott pulling on his own cock, their rhythm matching each other's for ease. Brett's cock sank further into the moist mouth as Scott's hand stroked away at his own youthful tool. This feels so good, thought Brett, as Scott's eager tongue and mouth serviced him. He wanted it to last all night, to feel as alive as this all the time. He allowed Scott to take control of the action, letting him work his wet tongue all over the shaft and hairy balls, cupping each testicle into his warm mouth and sucking slowly on them. Brett lowered himself enough to place a hand on Scott's own erection, stroking it slowly. He felt Scott shudder as Brett's larger hand grabbed the excited lad's length, masturbating him with a firm, tight grip. Scott's penis was twitching with the feel of another man playing with him, and he renewed his efforts on Brett's monstrous erection, burying his head into Brett's dark pubic bush and grabbing Brett's muscular buttocks to force it further down his throat.

Although he could have gone on for much longer, Brett felt the need to relieve the boiling surge that was building up in him, to take the moment and let Scott swallow his hot juice, taking it to the back of his throat. Brett grunted and grabbed Scott's head with both hands, starting to fuck his mouth with vigour. He grunted again as Scott looked up at him, eyes pleading for the hot semen in his mouth, for Brett to give him his seed. Brett didn't hold back with his thrusts now, letting his dick sink all the way in, then pulling out and slamming back in. He could feel Scott's tongue working the tip and underside as he pulled out, then move aside as he entered the warm moist cavern of Scott's mouth. Scott's hand alternated between his own cock and Brett's nuts, caressing and squeezing them; occasionally it clawed at Brett's arse and stroked his hairy thighs.

Brett could feel his own juice flowing freely, his pre-come juicing the passage of his rod in and out of the willing youth's sweet mouth. Panting and grunting heavily, he let it be known that his moment of triumph was shortly approaching. One last thrust into Scott's mouth and then he held Scott's head over his cock, allowing Scott to worship the tip in his mouth, his tongue flicking round the sensitive glans. Scott was whimpering with anticipation of Brett's load, pulling faster on his own erection. With a loud roar, which surely others on the boat must have heard, Brett shot his load straight into Scott's throat, a hot milky storm that engulfed Scott's orifice, forcing its way out of the corners of his mouth. Brett carried on pumping as jet after jet of the thick jism poured out of him and was eagerly swallowed. He kept his come-covered prick inside the new home it had found, as the young man licked the head clean, savouring every drop of salty, creamy fluid.

Without warning, Scott stood up, and attempted to kiss Brett, his left hand frantically masturbating himself, nearing his own climax. Brett grinned at the youth's insolence, slowly lowering his own lips to meet the waiting mouth. His tongue slipped inside Scott's open mouth, and then Brett vigorously jerked off the younger man, at the same time sucking the air out of his body. He could taste his own semen in the youth's mouth, a pungent and masculine taste that he enjoyed, his tongue seeking out the last vestiges of his own come, reclaiming it. Scott whimpered, panting heavily, unable to breathe normally with the force of Brett's deep probing, and Brett could feel the lad's cock pumping his seed out into the crisp night air. Even when a jet of sperm shot out and landed at their feet, Brett still pulled harshly on Scott's erection, drawing out more and more juice, milking it dry. The force of Scott's orgasm shook through both of them, Brett initiating him into a forceful and unforgettable act of sex as wild and passionate as the river that coursed round them.

Brett felt the warmth against him, and held Scott for the first time. Still, no words passed between them as they rocked gently against each other, exhausted by the communion they had undergone. After some time, Brett broke the lock, wiping Scott's deposit from his hand on to Scott's chest, as if anointing him in some way. Scott licked Brett's fingers clean, the last intimacy they would perform. As the riverboat chugged along and carried them to their goal, the two men returned to their sleeping territories, closer than before, so that each could feel the heat from the other, the breath on their skin and the soft murmur of contented sleep. Their passion shared and completed, Brett and Scott spent the rest of the night blissfully and peacefully dreaming of the joys of the new day, and their own new lives.

Three

Luke Mitchell was lying on his back, watching the clouds in the sky draw patterns and images for him. The fluffy white paint on the blue canvas became an old man, his father, a teepee, an old woman darning a very long sock, a couple engaged in an impossible sexual position. Luke enjoyed the freedom he felt looking into the sky like this, the way his imagination could play with images, could change their meaning, twist and turn them into something he had invented, created. Sometimes he imagined he could see the faces of dead friends and family, sometimes famous people he had seen in drawings and cartoons. When the clouds moved quickly – before a thunderstorm, for instance – he could see many, angry shapes, like an army gathering to prick the sky and make it bleed. Today, the shapes moved slowly, lazily, as if the clouds, like him, were just waking.

The long grass enclosed him, tall walls of it either side of him. Luke watched them move in the breeze, swaying back and forth. Slowly he stretched himself, lazily holding his arms out towards the sky in front of him, his long fingers reaching up, obscuring the sun for a moment. He let them fall, and run across his chin, rubbing against the stubble there. It was a good week's growth, black and coarse, and he enjoyed stroking it slightly, feeling it stiff to the touch. It was a matter of necessity at the moment, Luke not having any shaving equipment with him, but he liked the way it grew, the contours it took, the way it emphasised his manhood. It was itself the prize for attaining full manhood, a sign of his virility and masculinity. He never let it grow long enough to be untidy, or to grow to a full beard. That would make him feel old, responsible, chained in some way.

Luke ran his hands through his unwashed black hair. It was as dark as his eyes, a coal black that had just grown beyond its original short cut, now unkempt and uncared for. He roughed it up, massaging his scalp as his hands ran through the thick hair. All too soon, he was aware that he was thirsty, not having eaten or drunk properly for the past couple of days. He didn't yet feel weak, his adrenaline still pulling him through the events of the past few days. The long sleep in the high grass had been a welcome luxury, most of the past few nights having been spent fearsomely awake, starting at every movement or sound following the wind. His joints and muscles ached from the miles he had travelled. The thirst wasn't enough to wake him, so Luke lay for a while, feeling the sleep fall out of him, the aches in various parts of his body reminding him of every step, fall, jump and trip he'd made on his way here.

He'd thought he'd been fit before this chase, before he'd had to run for his life. The sports he'd played at the orphanage, and all the work he'd done on farms and homesteads since, had built him stronger than most. He was used to running, too, both short sprints and the longer cross-track races that took so much effort and concentration. That had all been sport, though, and short-lived. Running day after day, never knowing where they were behind you, how close, how much ground you'd lost or gained – it was completely different from the good-humoured sport he'd excelled at.

Luke wasn't sure how it had all started: at what point it had gone wrong and he'd changed from being a lover to a criminal. Of course, his love had always been a crime: he had always known that. But somehow, only weeks ago, everything had seemed much safer, secure. Finally, he'd felt that he was getting somewhere, that the years since those dramatic events of his late childhood were finally behind him. At last he'd found someone who was sharing their home with him, who was acting as if they cared for him. Luke almost laughed at the way in which he'd been fooled, deluded, into believing in a happy ever after. He really should have known better.

He became aware of his own heavy, musky scent. He hadn't been able to change his clothes for nearly a week, and smelt every bit as much Luke as Luke could do. He could feel himself caked in mud from the river bank he'd kept close to, in the hope that anyone tracking him would lose his trail in a mixture of currents, sediment and confusing prints from other men, other animals. Here and there, blood had dried from wounds where he caught himself on gorse, or where a trip had brought him too close to a rock or two, scarring him before he could save himself. He knew that under his clothes he carried a fair few bruises, his skin yellowy-blue in places. He was used to pain: could stand it – even enjoy it, in some circumstances. It was the relentlessness and pointlessness of his current pain that irritated him. He knew all he needed to do was to lie down, to sleep for a day or two, let his body and mind heal. Yet if he did that, he was sure, he would be dead.

Luke rolled over, on to his side. He swore as he managed to lean heavily on a particularly bad bruise on his hip. He could feel a sizeable lump there already, and the bruise was not even a day old. Taking a deep breath, he lifted himself to his knees. The grass around him hissed, caught by another gust of wind. It gave him the impetus to raise himself slowly upright, unravelling himself like a new fern shoot, taking advantage of the moment to reveal himself to the world. The grass was high, reaching his waist, and as he looked over the top of it, he could see that it covered the plain he had come across. The thick carpet of grass crept up over the horizon, and sprawled behind him for as far as he could see. The whole area was flat, and surrounded him for miles. Not a marking point between him and the future or the past – it was all one enormous expanse of high grass, where only the ripples in the wind differentiated one part from another. Occasionally, as clouds followed their own journey in the sky, they might briefly pass over him and their shadow would darken his immediate surroundings, as if the sky itself was blinking.

Where was he? How had he ended up here? Which way

would take him somewhere he could find water to drink? He headed off towards the sun on the horizon, knowing that behind him there was nothing more he wanted to see. There was, in truth, only one way to go, and that was forward. Luke's lazy early morning strides became more earnest as time moved on, and still all he could see was the damned tall grass. He stroked the heads of the grass as he past them, and it reminded him of stroking the horses he'd tended at Matt Wilmott's ranch.

Matt Wilmott! He had met Matt as he was travelling around looking for casual farm work. It had been his life since his parents had died when he was eleven. They had been found murdered by bandits in their own home. The family hadn't had an awful lot to take, and the deaths had seemed pointless – both of them had been elderly when they'd been attacked. Luke hadn't been allowed to see them after the attack, and it preyed on his mind. As a kid, he could only imagine what they must have looked like, and the imaginings were worse than anything humanly possible. Partly out of need to find money in order to live, and partly to escape that horrific legacy, Luke had spent the following fifteen years either in St Mary's Orphanage, or drifting and getting casual work as and when he could.

Which was how he had happened on Matt Wilmott's ranch. Luke had always been good with horses, and Matt needed a farmhand to help him with those he was rearing. The deal had been a good one for Luke – he was given board and food, and a little extra cash in his pocket. Matt had been a good man to work for, too, and concerned for Luke. Although twenty or so years older, he was an attractive, powerfully built man. His wife had been dead a couple of years when Luke started to work there, and Matt still missed having her around. He'd sit and moan to Luke about how the place needed a woman's touch, and how he missed the company. Luke knew that was another reason for being hired – the Wilmotts had been childless when Ma Wilmott died, and Matt saw Luke as a surrogate 'son'.

The first months had been good at Wilmott's. Luke worked hard, and Matt noticed it, and paid him extra. He got on well with the neighbours, and Luke figured that he could stay there a fair few months before moving on again. Then, one evening,

Matt and he had swigged some drink (a lot, he now remembered) and their relationship had suddenly become intimate. Luke couldn't remember much about the evening, but he hadn't been surprised at what had happened.

In the past, working with other men on other ranches, Luke and his fellow workers would play around with each other in the evening. The conversation would turn to wives and girlfriends, real, imagined or left behind, and the talk would become coarser, more explicit. It wouldn't be long before the talk of women's fine shapes, full breasts and soft skin, would arouse them. Luke had always been easily aroused, permanently in the mood for sex. Often, the other men wouldn't be able to keep up, or were so embarrassed the following morning that the act was never mentioned. Occasionally Luke would develop the relationship into something more regular, although the attachments had never become anything deeply emotional.

Until Matt. That drunken evening, Luke remembered Matt's fingers wandering over him, over his shirt, grasping his chest as Matt clumsily seduced him. Normally, Luke would make the first move, but that night he had enjoyed the feeling of an older man fumbling for him, desiring him, enticing him. Matt had been eager, hungry for sex, having only had himself to play with for a number of years. The absence of sex had made him more exciting to be with, the need for sudden release and pleasure, the desperate emptiness that had needed filling.

Luke remembered Matt's face closing over him. Matt's face, lined but not wrinkled, had broken into a picture of ecstasy as his mouth brushed Luke's, and Luke had returned the long, slow kiss, tasting the alcohol on his breath. He had stroked Matt's salt and pepper hair, greying in a respectable manner; he had welcomed the older man's wandering hands exploring his body. When they were both naked, Luke had admired Matt's body, still in excellent shape despite his fifty plus years. How exciting it had been to explore that history of flesh, examining and feeling, licking, fingering, every inch, every mark, every line and stretch. Matt had been an experienced lover, too, learning not only from the years with his wife, but also the dalliances he'd had in his earlier days with other men. Luke had been taught Old Mr

Wilmott's encyclopaedia of sexual pleasure, the first of many lessons Luke was all too keen to learn.

They had made love until the sun came up, Luke ignoring his duties for the first part of the day as he slept in Matt's grand bed, his new lover gently sleeping by his side. The sex had been passionate, needing, but conservative. Neither man had even attempted penetration, so there had been a welcome equality in their passion, and their touchings and fondlings had more than satisfied them both. Luke remembered the first glimpse he had had of Matt's big dick: how large it was, even in comparison with his own, an endowment he hadn't had matched with any of the previous men he'd had sex with. Matt's cock had been a good nine inches long, and impressively wide, providing a welcome handful for Luke as he had stretched his fingers around it. He had enjoyed masturbating Matt, watching the thick rod stiffen; it had pointed completely upright, becoming stronger, thicker and harder as Luke had controlled his own hand-movements, alternating between the painfully slow and suddenly quick. The memory of Matt's groans as he ejaculated, and the sight of streams of hot sperm landing on his hand and the older man's belly still excited Luke, jet after jet of thick white juice showering down.

For several months, the two had been lovers, with Luke beginning to think that he might even stay at Matt's rather than travel on. It had been idyllic, working hard there during the day and by night rampaging through his employer's bed, their flesh bonding in as animal-like a fashion as the horses they were tending. Although the sex had at first been exploratory, Luke having to play the part of a younger man being seduced, within a short time it had become more honest and unreserved. Sometimes, often, they would become so turned on while they were working that they would have to have sex there and then, in the barn, or the kitchen, or out in the open fields. For the first time since his parents had died, Luke had found a place he could call home.

He wasn't to know that Matt was a compulsive gambler, and that the evenings or weekends he was not at the house, he had been spending all his money at a poker game with the neighbours. Luke found out later that the games had been a way for Matt to get some company, to be with other people, but his debts had mounted and mounted. There had always been the promise of The Big One, the one win that would see him all right, and always it had been the next game, the next hand. Of course, it never came: and when Luke had found out about it and challenged Matt, there had been bitter arguments. Their sex life was the first to suffer, and then even their working relationship and friendship had come under strain.

Luke shook his head as he remembered the morning that Matt had accused him of stealing the two horses, and then called in the sheriff. Even now, Luke was angry at the accusation – Luke would never steal, especially from Matt. Matt knew that, and Luke was sure that as his gambling debts had become worse, Matt had sold off the horses secretly, hoping to blame Luke for their 'theft', and not pay Luke for his work. It was a bitter deception, one that only lovers can know or understand. Of course, in denying the accusation, Luke had been forced to take to the road again – he couldn't work for an ex-lover who had branded him a thief and a liar. The sheriff, a long-time friend of Wilmott's, had organised a number of men to round Luke up. They saw him as a lying thief who had taken advantage of one of their own, the stranger in town who was threatening their notions of law and community.

So Luke had been on the run since. His heart still ached from the betrayal, but not as much as his body did from the running. He'd always hated running away. Even the time a couple of years ago when he had got into a brawl with the Tierney brothers, resulting in a long knife wound to the leg, the scar still remaining, he had stood and fought. He had been running now for almost a month, the last week without much of a break, aside from the long sleep that had overwhelmed him last night. He was sick of it. The hiding, the escaping, the fear – he had done nothing wrong! He had to keep telling himself that, or he would go mad. He was an innocent man! It was Matt who had cajoled, lied, cheated: not even man enough to own up to his own crimes! He would never trust again, Luke vowed. He should have known better.

Luke licked his lips, dry and chapped. His tongue allowed

them a little moisture, easing the hateful dryness. With luck, there would be water soon. With luck? Since when had he had any of that? Nothing had seemed to go right after his parents had been killed. In a completely illogical way, he blamed them for everything. If only they hadn't left him, if only they had been able to fight off their attackers, if only they'd gone for help, if only . . . Luke knew that there was really only one 'if only' that preyed on him. If only he'd been there. If only he'd been there, he could have saved them. He could have killed the attackers, he could have stopped them doing whatever they did: he could have, he could have, he could have! An eleven-year-old boy could have beaten off a gang of bandits and saved his parents' lives! Of course he could have. He should have been there! It was all his fault they were dead.

Luke shook his head. The heat was getting to him, the exhaustion driving him out of his mind. He wanted to eat a fine meal, and drink until he could drink no more. He wanted his thirst quenched. His other desires, too, needed fulfilling. He had dreamt of Matt last night, of their long passionate sessions and, much though it had appalled him, he had wanted the physical relationship they'd enjoyed back again. Luke knew he needed sex; it was as natural to him as eating, as drinking. He didn't know why, but he knew it made him feel good, that it was a release for him. Most days he didn't think about it. It was just always *there* – a drive for as much sex as he could get.

Luke paused and looked out. He was sure – it wasn't his imagination – there was a lake out there. He saw trees, large oaks, fat trunks and bright green canopies and, in between them, a beautiful blue of water. He was too tired to whoop with joy, but he nevertheless quickened his pace and grinned broadly. Finally, he could drink fresh water, quench his overriding thirst. Maybe there would be some fruit, or wildlife, and he could get himself a nice little meal. With any luck, he'd be able to stock up on food and water, not knowing where the next chance to eat might be. Bliss! He could smell the water in the air, hearing the bright chirping of birds playing across the water's surface. It was a large lake, surrounded by broad and welcoming expanses of protective trees – excellent cover, and a welcome break from the grasslands he'd been travelling, the past few days.

Arriving at the water's edge, Luke threw down his few belongings and knelt by the water, pausing for a moment as if in contemplation of the great gift he had come across. He cupped his hands and scooped up some of the cool fresh water, pouring it into his open mouth, letting the excess splash across his face and fall down his chest. He drank the water longingly, scooping more in his hands and drinking deep. It was a long time before he'd had his fill, savouring the fresh clean taste of the liquid he had so craved. Having drank as much water as he could, Luke filled his water bottles, making sure he had as much water stored as possible. He returned the heavy bottles to his sack, content that he wouldn't run out of water again for a number of days.

Luke stripped off his clothes, caked with mud and blood. They stuck to his flesh as he attempted to prise them off, his shirt and pants soaked with sweat. He watched the dirt fall off the clothes as he soaked them in the water. The dried mud swirled round them in a watery mist, clouding the area with the dirt of days. Luke enjoyed the feel of the cool water on his hands as he scrubbed his clothes against some of the rocks in the water, loosening much of the muck and blood, cleaning them as best he could. When he'd finished washing them, he wrung them out tightly, squeezing until he could get no more water from the garments. There was something reassuring about the pressure he exerted on his clothes, as if the action of wringing them dry exorcised the demons of his life, the simple physical act relieving him of all the pain. The water falling on to the ground was all the hurt he'd suffered, the clothes washed clean of anguish. If only it was so easy to undo all that had gone before!

Luke lay the clothes out against a couple of large rocks, allowing them to dry in the heat of the day. He found some shade and lay himself out, too, his wet skin glistening in the sunlight. He stretched his long legs, his feet sprawling out, and rested his head in the cradle his hands provided behind his head. The clouds he had played with earlier when he woke were obscured now by the leafy roof above him, the blue white and green a natural canopy that lulled him towards sleep. His back flat against the ground, Luke closed his eyes and savoured the few moments of peace he had been able to steal for himself. He'd allow himself a couple of hours here, maybe even spend the night. Surely he could afford the time. How far would they be behind him now? Would they even have come this far for the sake of a pony? Luke wasn't sure – he remembered the sheriff's snarl when he had protested his innocence, knowing that he had never liked him anyway. Maybe he resented Luke's relationship with Matt, Luke fantasised maliciously.

The warm air soon dried him, but still Luke savoured the sun on his skin, letting it wash him in a balmy comfort. Having worked his whole adult life, he was unaccustomed to lazing around in the sun, but enjoyed it nonetheless. It was as if he was making up for lost time now. He turned over lazily, resting on his front, his soft penis intimate against the ground, his arms sprawled out at his sides, his left cheek resting on the ground. Luke's naked hairy arse pointed to the sun, arrogant and enticing. He longed for something other than the sun to ravish his fresh, clean body now. The thought sent a warm tingle through him, resulting in a lazy twitch of his cock. How he wished it was firm flesh underneath him now rather than the dusty ground. A long, lazy fuck was just what he wanted!

Luke sensed something, a flash in the corner of his eye as he felt his arousal. Just beyond where he was sheltered by the trees and rocks, another figure had approached the waterside. Luke slowly got himself up, and pulled his clothes towards him off the rock. He hid them in one of the bushes to his left, not wanting to put them on and cause more movement. He crouched behind another bush, taking care that he didn't scratch and graze his naked flesh. From his hiding point, Luke was able to look right at the new arrival without being seen himself.

The visitor to Luke's lake was a Sioux Indian. Luke recognised the clothing and apparel of the brave tribe, men he had often seen hunting and dancing, proud warriors he personally respected. The Indian's clothes were carefully fashioned from buffalo hide, cured and cut to fit this young man's athletic physique perfectly. Luke decided to call him Lone Buck, a name that seemed to fit the handsome stranger perfectly. Not only did he appear to be three or four years younger than Luke, but he had the grace and strength of an elegant animal, smooth sleek skin, dark and perfect. Lone Buck's long black hair was braided into a ponytail, his face unadorned by any colourings or jewels. Set against the dark tan of his skin, Buck's eyes glistened like coal, dark bright eyes that were now scanning the outline of the lake. Luke froze, hoping that he would not be seen. The young man's eyes seemed to bore into him, but nothing dangerous had been noticed behind the bush, and the man's attention followed the curve of the water.

Buck had the results of a successful hunting expedition with him, a small deer carcass, and he set about pulling his arrow from the animal's body and preparing the animal. Luke imagined the hunter after his prey, the hours that Lone Buck must have watched and waited. He could imagine the Indian following a herd of deer for a long time, or waiting quietly for them to arrive in his favourite hunting spot. He almost felt the quiet power of Buck, aware of every breath and noise he made. All the time, feeling powerful and waiting to make a strike, to assert his mastery of nature. Luke wondered what it would be like to hunt with him, to communicate with him only by nods and signs, to feel the quiet intimacy of hunters after their prey. They would be driven by a mutual hunger, a need to succeed while keeping their movements unnoticed, their path covered and hidden. And, after the chase and the exertion, they would take their meal together, their appetites to be satisfied.

As Luke watched and imagined, he felt his cock beginning to swell, its form slowly unfurling as it nestled between his legs. Watching the hunter before him, he became excited at the thought of intimacy with this complete stranger, whose world was so very different from his, whose language he did not understand. Yet he was attractive to Luke, a strong and handsome newcomer in his life, so different from the other white men and farmhands he had played with. There was a quiet sensuality to him, a knowing passion that he enjoyed. His features were well defined, a strong nose and broad chin, high cheek-bones, almost feminine, but also giving his face a handsome masculinity. His movements were natural, necessary, and performed without haste or waste of movement. The hands that worked over the deer were strong yet sensitive enough to caress the hide of the animal he had killed, and to perform what Luke assumed must be a short meditation or prayer over the food he had gathered.

As Luke saw the young man, he dropped his left hand between his legs and started to stroke the growing erection. Luke was horny now, and was watching the movements of Lone Buck, imagining how he made love, how he masturbated, how he looked beneath the clothes he wore. In the tight seat of his hide trousers, Luke could see the line of his crotch, obviously not aroused, but a detectable line all the same, and one that was tempting. Yes, very tempting. Luke stroked his cock in long lazy movements, enjoying the fantasy and the fact that he could not be seen. His masturbatory jerks became bolder and stronger, responding to the urges he was feeling and becoming more passionate. Luke could feel his breath quicken, his heart beating faster and stronger than before, as he imagined ravaging the Indian's body with his tongue, lips, mouth, hands, cock. He wanted them to roll among the dirt and rocks and water, uncaring about the differences between them and their tribes, lost in the passion of intimate sexuality.

The man washed his hands, splashing water to his face. As Luke closed his eyes, he could imagine the two of them naked, splashing in the water, the drips from their hairy genitals falling into the lake. He imagined them horsing around, battling each other to gain dominance, assert their athleticism over each other. Luke imagined his wet body coming into contact with the other man's, their lips searching for each other, hands quickly feeling each other's hot flesh, cooled only by the water around them. He imagined the water like a bed, supporting them as they frantically made love to each other, rubbing and kissing each other to orgasm, cocks spurting come over each other, intimate in each other's arms.

Lone Buck stiffened as Luke fantasised. The increasing power of his imagination had forced Luke to wank harder and faster, and his movements had attracted the attention of the Indian. *Shit!* He was going to get caught. Yet even the danger of the situation didn't stop Luke's lustful imagination; in fact, it increased the excitement of the situation. He felt his cock large and heavy in his hand, a sex weapon at his every whim. As he saw the Indian begin to reach for his belongings, Luke realised he was about to take a chance, a risk, he had never done before, but which seemed right at that moment. The heat of the situation meant he had to go further with this.

Slowly, naked and erect, Luke stood up from where he had been crouching. Calmly, with his eyes strictly on Lone Buck, he stood up fully, taking one step away from the bush, standing with his feet wide apart. He didn't stop massaging his throbbing cock all the time he exposed himself, taking pleasure in his nine inches of hot throbbing flesh. Lone Buck looked at him, obviously confused by what was going on. They should be natural enemies, but Luke made it clear that his intentions were much more intimate, more sharing than threatening. Luke's brashness astounded him, but it made him so horny, standing there pulling on his big cock while watching the reactions of Lone Buck.

The quiet distance between them was only punctuated by the rhythm Luke was using in his jerks, a slow and constant back-wards and forwards motion that took in the very tip of his cock, now leaking juice, and the very base of his hairy balls, hanging low between his thighs. He watched as Lone Buck took in what was happening, as his eyes followed a trail from Luke's flashing grin, down the thick patch of his chest hair, to his groin, where his hand pulled his cock out in front of him, a thick arrow pointing in the direction of Buck. The Indian brave looked at Luke's grinning, cocksure face, his broad chest, his hard cock. Finally understanding, Lone Buck nodded and grinned back, flashing his perfect white teeth at Luke. Hand holding his own crotch, he slowly approached Luke.

The men faced each other, Luke a little taller than Lone Buck, and the Indian gently put his hand out towards Luke's lurching dick. The Indian's touch was firm, sensitive, and Luke closed his eyes and moaned. When he opened them again, Lone Buck had revealed his own cock, smaller than Luke's but now fully erect and touching Luke's own throbbing monster. The Indian's mouth was raised towards Luke's and he could feel the warm breath on his lips, their mouths opening and Buck longing to make contact.

Luke teased him, lowering his mouth, then pulling away, finally letting his tongue gently flick at the young Indian's willing mouth. All of a sudden, they fell on each other, their mouths one hot cavern, their tongues clashing and battling for supremacy. Luke could feel himself sucking the breath from the Indian, his mouth tasting sweet and full of desire.

With their mouths locked, the two men ran their hands frantically over each other's bodies, their cocks humping against each other, engorged with blood and hot lust, waiting to be released. It was pure sex, two strangers with no language but raw desire, passion, lust. Lone Buck was whimpering with desire as Luke's hands found his cock, pulling the long member and gripping his balls tight. Luke could smell the Indian's sweat, hot after the hunt; his mouth found its way down Buck's neck, nestling itself in his long hair, and Luke bit him softly, leaving small purple love-marks in a trail down the side of his neck. It spurned the Indian on; Buck moaned and pulled faster and faster on Luke's prick, lowering it between his thighs.

Luke couldn't stop himself from following the motions of the younger man. He felt his cock bury itself between the thighs of the other man, the hot flesh welcoming his pole and enveloping it. With gently fucking motions, Luke let his cock slip backward and forward between Buck's thighs, feeling the hairy balls nestling above his own hard dick, and Buck's erect dick bouncing against their bellies, twitching and straining for release. Luke kissed his partner more urgently, having no words to express himself, no coarse phrases to heighten the scene he found himself in. It wasn't comfortable, thigh-fucking like this: standing upright, with Luke naked and the Indian partner only half naked. Every now and then, Luke's hard cock would scrape against the hide clothing, a coarse and painful feeling that only heightened the pleasure of the soft flesh he was reunited with.

Luke was beginning to grunt now, his lustful thrusts becoming harder and quicker. Lone Buck whimpered against Luke's dominance, allowing himself to be used as a fuck toy for the older, taller, stronger white man. Yet Luke knew there was an equality in their thrusting, man to man, standing and driven sex-wild by each other. He could feel his cock slipping in and out of the younger man's thighs, and developed the movements so that he could thrust upwards into the curving cheeks of his smooth arse, resting the tip of his cock at in the warm ridge of flesh that he found. He sensed that Lone Buck was jerking faster on his own cock; their bodies were now entwined together, their sweat mixing, Luke's chest damp with desire.

They quickened their pace, Luke thrusting longer, deeper, harder, between the firm muscles of the Indian's legs, his cock reaching further into the fleshy cheeks of his backside. Lone Buck's hands wandered through the forest of Luke's chest hair, under his armpits and bringing him closer, deeper, to him. Lone Buck had started to make slight sounds, his voice high pitched and urgent. Luke matched this with his own low grunts, a hard rhythm against the Indian's birdsong. Now, their bellies slapped against each other with Luke's thrusts, lubricated by pre-come from Lone Buck's twitching cock, Luke's own juice running down Buck's cheeks.

Luke pulled right back for one last hard thrust and looked at his hard cock just meeting, touching Buck's. For a short time their juices mixed, glistening in the daylight, and their eyes met, knowing this was the moment of release and union. Luke forced his mouth down on to Buck's; their tongues entwined as if moulded together with the heat of their passion. Luke grunted aloud, and thrust his arrow between Buck's thighs for the last time, the action bringing on the unmistakable throes of an orgasm, his cock stretching up behind Lone Buck and nestling its way between his buttocks. He was coming, all too suddenly and forcefully, jet after jet of hot jism splattering against the dark skin of Lone Buck's back and arse-cheeks. He heard the other man scream aloud at the same time, and saw the white come jetting from Buck's cock and on to his chest. They drew themselves closer together, the last twitches of orgasm running through them both, come covering their bodies and sticking them together.

They stood in each other's embrace, stroking themselves on, Luke rubbing his own spunk into Lone Buck's skin, as if signing some blood contract between them. They had become lovers with no language: no words spoken between them, just an understanding of mutual pleasure. The spontaneity and danger of it thrilled Luke and the surprise encounter obviously delighted Lone Buck, who now set about offering some of his food to his new lover. Later that day, at the lakeside, they dined on roasted deer meat, a venison more tender than any Luke had tasted, with fruit that the young brave had picked that morning. It was all as fresh as they were, as sweet as their moment of joy. Luke Mitchell and Lone Buck lay in each other's arms after the meal had finished, savouring their illicit encounter.

Four

As the boat pulled into Fort Leavenworth, Brett McKinley realised he had lost sight of Scott Baker. After their session that night, Brett had been aware of the boy sleeping close to him. Tired and elated after their ecstasy, Brett had fallen into a deep sleep, dreaming of Scott charging on a horse, meeting him on McKinley's own ranch, bought and built with the richest seam of gold the West had ever seen. The dream had been as exciting and passionate as their lovemaking, leaving Brett in an excited state on waking, excited by the start of his own journey and also the possibility of reliving the intimacy he had found the night before with Scott. Instead, the joy had disappeared and he could hear the crowds shouting on the bankside drawing his attention.

The crowd was made up largely of women and soldiers from the fort. The women were joyously greeting relatives, and gasping at the luxuries that the boat had brought to the area, food necessities and special gifts from further away – lace, clothes, perfumes. Amid the whoops of delight, earnest faces looked out for friends and family, anxiety breaking into delight as another loved one was spotted. The morning was bright, the air sharp and the atmosphere excitable.

Brett searched the crowd of people now leaving the boat, intent on their new destinations. They flowed much like the river, and their progress seemed inevitable, their numbers dwindling like a short gush of water. Among the number of young men, Brett caught a glimpse of one he recognised as Scott. Once on the riverside, Scott turned and looked in Brett's direction. McKinley saw the young face break into a smile, and the young man waved at him. Brett returned the salute, a strong farewell wishing Scott on to his destiny. The boy was as full of promise and excitement as he had been when he first met Brett at Ruby's, the day before.

Brett took a deep breath of the new morning air, and made his way to the landing point. It felt strange knowing that, of the many people who were there, not one would be looking for him. The solitariness of his quest suddenly hit him after the intimacy he had shared the night before with Scott and, for a moment, Brett considered following the lad to arrange a further meeting. He decided against it, however. Instead, Brett resolved to enjoy the solitariness, to take pleasure in his own company. Back home, he was constantly surrounded by people – it would make a nice change to have time to himself, to be able to think his own thoughts, do things that amused him and not have to think of his brothers or parents. He was no longer constrained by what other people thought or did, free and independent to do as he pleased.

When he'd woken, Brett had discovered Scott had left him a bread roll, some cheese and an apple. No doubt, his folks had packed him off with plenty to eat, and Brett appreciated the generous gesture. He found a railing to support him, leant against it and chewed on the roll. The home-baked bread tasted good if plain, and it was soon eaten. The cheese he savoured, a slightly nutty taste and crumbly texture that livened his mouth after the blandness of the roll. He followed it with a swig from his water bottle, the cool liquid refreshing his palate. He rubbed a little of the water against his brow and ran his wet fingers through his hair. He realised that this was probably for vanity, and laughed at himself.

Biting into the apple, Brett walked on, away from his leaning post and in the direction of the fort. If possible, he wanted to make up some of the time he had lost. He was aware that he was not the only forty-niner out to seek his fortune. Ever since reports had come in of gold way out west, men had been passing through on their way to fortune and glory. It was only January the year before, 1848, that the famous pioneer James Wilson Marshall had discovered gold at Sutter's Mill in California. The news had spread like wildfire: the only thing people talked about for months. Brett knew that many of the local inhabitants had already staked their claims. McKinley was also aware of President Polk's US Congress address that December. Mr James Polk had claimed there was untold wealth in California, and it was the idea that the President himself had mentioned the gold that had decided Brett's mind. He felt that the President was making him a personal promise of wealth and fame.

Brett had heard that some of the Old Worlders and even South Americans were making their way over, Europeans and others who had heard of the promise of riches. He wondered if his own family, the McKinleys back in Ireland, would think of coming all this way to claim. He hoped not, knowing of both the journey to his own continent, and the following journey to the far side of California's Mother Lode region. Brett didn't trust the Old Worlders coming over and staking land that should belong to people like him, people who had promised themselves a future in their own fair land. He doubted there could be enough land to satisfy everyone, and that many of the Old Worlders had bided their time to see how the Americans had survived in this new land, while wanting to retain control over them with their foreign laws and ways.

The Forty-niners – or the Argonauts of 49, as they had also been dubbed – were about discovering and taming their country, making their homes in the home of the brave. New laws, New ways, not the shackles of the past. It was all new and bright, a shower of opportunity. Brett was part of that group of men who would change forever the face of the Americas – he was making history. That bold thought was what had started him off on this epic voyage, and what would see him through to the bitter end. He was leaving behind all the old securities that Scott was clinging to, the law and order and traditions of the past. Brett's future was in the new and unknown.

Brett stopped as a troop of cavalrymen drew up in the small town. They dismounted and tethered their horses up, before entering one of the bars further down. Their excitement was catching, their voices and laughter reaching him and drawing him into their circle. There were five of them, all seeming to know each other closely, friends in the way that only soldiers ever can be. Theirs was an intimacy born from danger and fear, where all acted as one, a fighting machine. Months and years of training had drilled them into how to fight, to sleep, to work, to laugh together. They walked with the rhythm of a group, parts of a body rather than individuals.

As they turned into the bar, one of the soldiers, a tall man about the same age as Brett, turned and saw him. He was a lithe man, leaner than Brett, with short red hair and blue eyes, a Celtic complexion that marked him out from his comrades. The flame-red hair made his eyes sparkle with fire, and Brett was immediately attracted to him. The soldier saw him, noticed him, and tipped his hat at him. With the tipping came a the breaking of a broad smile on his handsome, tanned face, producing two small dimples at each corner of his mouth. The hat came off and revealed more of the fire-red hair, locks tousling round the side of his face. As Brett acknowledged the welcome smile, the soldier saluted him jokingly. He wondered if he thought McKinley was a new recruit, as easily impressionable as Scott. Yet there was something attractive about the soldier's cockiness.

'C'mon, Taylor, you're buying. Stop horsing around.' One of the soldiers draped his arm over the red-haired Taylor and drew him towards the bar. As he did so, he turned and saw McKinley. He, too, grinned. 'What's the matter, Taylor? A new man in town?'

'Leave be, and maybe I'll get you that drink. Though, with your stomach, it'll be back up in no time!' Taylor playfully raised his fist against his comrade's cheek. It made contact enough for Brett to hear the slap, and to guess that this was part of a routine between the two men.

Brett felt a longing for their intimacy, a jealousy at the shared games they created for themselves. It wasn't that he wanted their uniforms, their belonging to a unit, their regime. But their intimacy he liked, their ability to read each other's thoughts. As they disappeared into the bar, it crossed his mind that they might be lovers, that they shared physical intimacy in the way he and Scott had. The thought turned him on, and he wondered how exclusive that intimacy might be. The idea of the two of the soldiers making love was appealing, and Brett found himself dwelling on it.

For the rest of the day, however, Brett concerned himself with the realities of his journey. He stocked up with provisions and tools for the journey, pleasing himself that he was able to bargain to his considerable advantage. His out-of-town manner gave him the advantage of storeowners assuming his gullibility, whereas he played an elaborate game with all of them. Brett had never liked being made a fool of, and he noticed how the shopkeepers played other customers along, to their advantage. He hadn't come this far to be cheated out of what little he'd managed to save! He grinned and told himself one day he'd be able to come back and buy all the shops up, even become mayor of the town. That thought, and his successful buying, gave him a warm glow as his day finished.

By the close of day, Brett had managed to get all his provisions, certainly enough to see him well on his way. He hadn't yet managed to find a horse, or to find out if there was a convoy for the west leaving from the township in the near future. Although the whole point of the trek was to strike out on his own, Brett knew that it would be much safer to travel with others for as much of the way as possible. There were so many different dangers – Indians, bandits, the wild beasts, the unpredictable weather, to name but a few – that he would prefer to take his chances in the safety of one of the many nomadic tribes that were now making their way westward. He knew that in all probability some sort of convoy would be leaving in the next couple of days, and was happy to wait for the right opportunity. He'd keep his ears open and watch the new arrivals as they came in. It wouldn't take him long to figure the ground out.

In the meantime, Brett took the opportunity to acquaint himself with Fort Leavenworth. It was bigger than St Joseph, and Brett preferred it. Its more northern position made it seem more secure, and its proximity to the Oregon-California road made its outlook more cosmopolitan than the inward-looking St Joseph.

The variety of people who passed through it, and who had set up various stalls, thrilled him. Around him, he heard a variety of accents, mostly from the Mid-West, but occasionally further South, and he noticed the dark tan of Mexican men as he looked around. Occasionally, he caught a European accent – the rich musical lilt of the Irish, the hard clipped accents from the German states, the effusive Scandinavian chatter. Brett enjoyed the music that came from far away places, and associated them with characters in the songs and stories he'd heard as a child.

He ate a meat pie as the sun started to sink in the horizon, savouring the well-seasoned flavouring and warm crust as he ate. Occasionally, he licked the meat juices from his fingers, gulping the food down in long and hungry snatches. After he had finished the meat, he treated himself to a slice of apple pie, as delicious as that he had back at St Joseph. The pie was tart and sharp, enlivening his senses and softening his breath from the mustiness of the meat. His hunger satiated once more, he continued his prowl around the town, basking in the lights which were now being lit as he wandered the trails between low, timber built buildings, and out towards the main body of the fort itself.

Fort Leavenworth hung out on the horizon, a little away from the purely civilian area: enough to secure the settlement's safety, but also at a distance to separate the soldiers in fulfilling their military duties without distraction. It was a broad, imposing building and, as he looked up at its walls, Brett could see shadowy movements along the fort's upper structure, and the occasional flicker of torches. There was much laughter up above him; he sensed that, certainly for the moment, all was at peace, and the threat of outlaws and Indian tribes was not a worrying one.

The fort had many visitors entering and leaving, and acted as an oasis for those on duty elsewhere. It was out in the Wilder West that the troubles were occurring, he knew, and that here the wounded, tired, and the untrained were whiling their time away until the next foray into danger. Occasionally, he would hear the soldiers boasting about their escapades, and the derisive laughter of mates who guessed the true nature of some of the tall stories being related. Occasionally, he would hear a wild shot, the excited chatter of voices and then a waiting silence. It was mostly the high-spiritedness of men about to lose their freedom to the cavalry, or the battle to be the local top-dog or gang leader.

Brett walked on and followed the perimeter of the fort. It excited him to think of what was happening inside: the card games, the watch, the swapping of tales. He also knew there would be the hope and anxiety of young recruits like Scott, which he could understand. He had felt it in Scott's embrace, the need for excitement and danger, but also the trembling that came with taking chances, the ache of unknowing and the vulnerability that was only heard in silence and never expressed. He leant against the timber frame of the wall, snug and protected by its existence, allowing its energy and vibrancy to pass through him. Strangely, he began to feel part of the life and energy of the building, as if he too was part of the defence of the settlement, this new territory that was full of hope and promise.

A voice startled him from his reverie. 'Hi there.'

Brett opened his eyes, not having heard anyone approach, and suddenly realised that, although he'd felt so safe, he'd let himself be taken by surprise. 'Hi.'

His eyes could make out a form approaching him, but still to far away for him to make out who. Instinctively, he allowed his hand to slowly reach to his pistol holster.

'Nice night, don't you reckon?' The voice wasn't threatening, but low and sultry. A slight drawl accompanied the words, seductive and soft.

'Guess it is. The end of a great day.'

From the shadows, the figure entered the light that half shone on Brett's face. Brett recognised the man as the soldier he had seen earlier that day, the one who had been referred to as 'Taylor'. He smiled at Brett as he approached him, the same broad smile McKinley had noticed earlier. He came closer to the new acquaintance, and a moment passed between them. Without moving his eyes from Brett's gaze, he spoke again.

'Got a light?'

'Sure.' Brett pulled out a match and struck it against the timber behind him. The match flared, and the smell of burning flared Brett's nose. In the flickering light the match gave off, Brett saw the young soldier move his head forward slightly, holding a hand-rolled cigarette to his warm lips, and dipping it into the flame. Brett watched as he drew on the small stick of tobacco, and again their eyes met. The soldier continued drawing on the flame and the heat, while looking into Brett's eyes. The light flickered against the red hair of the flame's recipient, a golden halo surrounding the red hair, making it glow incandescently.

Slowly, calmly, and almost reluctantly, Taylor withdrew his head and leaned beside Brett against the fort wall. 'Thanks.' He snaked a hand out to Brett and opened it palm first. 'The name's Taylor.'

'Taylor?' Brett questioned, expecting more.

'That's the only name I use. Taylor.'

'OK.'

'And you?'

Brett took the hand offered to him and shook it. The shake was firm but intimate and warm. They maintained eye contact and grinned at each other as they shook. They held each other's hands for just a moment longer than was usual or customary, aware of a mutual attraction. 'Brett McKinley. Brett'll do.'

'Brett. I like it.'

Brett grinned, pleased that his name had found approval.

'So, you joining?'

'Nah. I'm striking out.'

'West?'

'I reckon so.'

'Thought about that, myself. It's tempting. Even for a soldier.'

'Guess you got it made here.'

'Yeah, but at some point a man's got to go after what he wants.'

'This not what you want?'

'I need more. A man has his own desires, and sometimes they go beyond the military.'

Brett instinctly knew where the conversation was going, and could feel the excitement mount in him.

'You want one?'

Brett turned his head to Taylor.

'A smoke? You want one?'

'Sure.'

Taylor dug out another of the small tight cigarettes he'd fashioned earlier that evening. He brought it up to Brett's face; Brett opened his mouth slightly to receive the gift. Taylor placed the cigarette loosely between Brett's lips and lowered his head towards Brett's, indicating that he should take the light for his own cigarette. Brett breathed in and felt the heat from Taylor's smoke, also aware of the heat of another man's face so close to him. So close, but not yet intimately so.

Brett felt the smoke in his lungs, but there was also something more, something that penetrated him much deeper and with much more effect. He could feel Taylor's hot breath around him, the heat of the soldier's body pressing towards him. He still wore his uniform, and Brett could smell that it had been fresh on that morning, the lines on it perfectly fashioned. They were not touching, but reaching out to each other and teasing each other. The cigarette lit, Brett waited for Taylor to pull away, which he did slowly.

'There,' he said at last.

'Tastes good,' Brett responded. He held the little cigarette tightly between his first finger and his thumb, pointing it downwards to the ground when he wasn't raising it to his lips for short, deep drags.

'You get to like the taste, huh?'

'I guess.'

Without seeming forward, Taylor draped his arm round Brett. It was comradely, in the way he had seen him with his friends earlier that day. Taylor finished his cigarette and threw it to the ground. Brett watched him as he finished drawing on his own smoke, taking one last long draw on it before throwing it on to the ground next to Taylor's spent stick.

Without speaking, they were kissing under the faint light, their mouths brushing against each other. Brett heard and felt his own day's worth of stubble against Taylor's soft clean skin, then felt a slight moan escape from him as Taylor's mouth found his, pressing against it passionately. Taylor was assertive, masculine, a fine match for Brett, and they fought to find entry into each other's mouths. As their kissing became more frenzied and intense, each opened their mouth slightly, until Brett was able to slide his tongue along Taylor's lips, wetting them with his own desire. His tongue found Taylor's, and moved around it, pressing further into his new lover's mouth. He forced Taylor's uniformed body against the wall, pressing his frame into him and pinning him down.

Now, more forcefully, Brett drove his tongue inside Taylor's mouth; their tongues were entwined and hot. Brett began to tease Taylor, kissing the soldier and then moving away as Taylor attempted to kiss him back. Again, he kissed him deep and long and then pulled away as Taylor tried to reciprocate. He could feel Taylor panting with passion, and let his hands grab the throbbing cock that lay straining behind Taylor's uniform. He watched Taylor's face as he grabbed its girth and pulled on the length. It was a fine-sized cock, thicker than his but not as long.

'You like it, huh? You want more of my hard cock?'

'It feels good, yeah.'

'Listen, me and some of the guys got something going back there. How 'bout you join us?'

'You reckon it's my kind of thing?'

'Sure. You'll fit in fine. They'll love you.'

'Show me.'

Taylor motioned for Brett to follow him, and led him further round the perimeter. He came to a back door, knocking on it twice in a well-rehearsed rhythm. The door opened a little, and there was an exchange between Taylor and another man which Brett didn't quite catch. The door opened, and Taylor beckoned him inside.

The light was dim in the soldiers' quarters, but Brett could make out a couple of figures. He presumed that they were the same ones he had seen with Taylor earlier that day and, as his eyes got accustomed to the darkness, he saw that they were. They were both broad and well-built, with short dark hair. One had a slight moustache, and the other was clean-shaven but had obviously not shaved that day. Brett could smell the scent of men in the room, and realised that both men were semi-naked – one had his neckerchief and boots on, while the other was topless. Both men were playing with enormous erections.

Taylor led Brett over to the centre of the room, and continued to kiss him as passionately as he had outside. The two other men sat watching and masturbating as Brett and Taylor allowed their hands to wander over each other, fumbling over each other's hard dick. Brett felt Taylor squeezing his hard cock, and became overwhelmingly turned on at the thought of sex here with three soldiers, the four of them in an orgy of sex and desire. His hand grabbed on to Taylor's firm backside, and he squeezed the cheeks with his large hands.

Without speaking to each other, the two other men moved over to the centre of the room. For a moment, Brett was just conscious of three pairs of hands all over his body: three mouths hungrily kissing him on the lips, the neck, the top of his head, his arms, his chest, his back, and further and further down. As he continued to tongue-kiss Taylor, the other two men crouched down before the pair, kissing their backsides, legs and thighs, arms wrapped round their thighs.

Engulfed in the warmth of Taylor's lustful panting kisses, Brett hardly noticed a hand searching inside his pants for his thick hard cock, massaging it up and down, rubbing it closer into Taylor's hard flesh. The fourth soldier was already working on unbuttoning Taylor, and pulling his monster flesh out into the open. The soldier boys played with the cocks, rubbing them together so they became one hot mass of hard dick meat, sizzling with pre-come, slapping against four pairs of hands, and four sets of moans and groans.

Brett could feel the hard length of Taylor, a good seven and a half inches of firm flesh, thick at the base and tapering slightly towards the end. He let his fingers run up and down the shaft, playing with the gooey hole at the tip, covered in Taylor's fluid. He brought his fingers to his lips and savoured the sweet salty taste of Taylor's promise, running his fingers over the other man's lips so that he too could taste. It became a game, then, with Taylor reciprocating the movement, his fingers playing with Brett's cock and then slipping over his lips, before being offered to Brett for him to sample his own pre-come. The sweat from Taylor's fingers mixed with his own fluid, and it tasted good.

The other two soldiers were now playing their game, softly kissing their chests and thighs. Taylor and Brett masturbated each other into their faces, rubbing against them with their full cocks, and letting them taste the pre-come off their fingers before allowing them to softly kiss the tips of their dicks. The man kneeling before Brett was the soldier with the moustache, and Brett twitched a little as he felt the bristle of hair rubbing on the underside of his shaft. He looked down to see the two men playing with his cock and Taylor's, semi-naked, while the two standing men remained clothed, only their big dicks protruding out.

Brett began to undo Taylor's tunic, playing with his smooth chest, while the other man began in turn to undress him. He began to kiss and nibble Taylor's neck and lowered his mouth on to the soldier's chest, so that Brett could lick and then lightly bite his nipples. He squeezed them, eliciting a gasp of desire from Taylor. Below, the other two soldiers were now using their tongues over the two exposed dicks and over each other, their mouths enveloping both cocks so that their tongues could meet over the firm flesh and pleasure all four men at the one time.

Brett and Taylor moved their hands down, urging the men to suck on their cocks more urgently, deeper, to take them more fully. The soldiers on their knees did exactly as they were told, jerking themselves off while deep throating the men's cocks they were kissing and sucking on. Brett and Taylor stopped their kissing and concentrated on a rhythm for the men to suck their cocks in unison, pumping their willing, eager mouths with the hot inches of cock before them. They held on to each other's shoulders as they fucked the men's faces, their cocks going in and out, deeper and deeper. They would occasionally throw their heads back and grunt, taking in the wild scene they were part of, and maybe stroke one of the guys' cocks as a reward for good sucking.

Brett wanted to go on all night, his cock sucked by a complete stranger while he played with Taylor, who in turn was having his prick gobbled down. All four men were sweating now, highly aroused, four large knobs needing release. Taylor was beginning to moan audibly, short grunts that matched the willing mouth falling up and down his erection. Brett matched it with short, fast sighs, slight compliments to the hot mouth working his own tool.

In return, the two men sucking moaned in pleasure at the taste of the engorged meat they were servicing.

All of a sudden, Taylor broke away from having his cock sucked, pulling Brett with him. He pulled him to the floor, where a few blankets lay, and started frantically pulling the rest of their clothes off as they began to reach the floor.

'C'mon, let's do each other. I'm so hot for you: have been all day, since I saw you get off the boat.'

It was the first time Taylor had spoken since they'd entered the room, and his low voice spurred Brett on, as he reached to feel the hardness of Taylor's manhood.

'Oh, yeah, I want that. The two of us, together, here, now.'

They fell on each other, their mouths and tongues exploring each other. Hot passionate kisses led them both searching downward, clothes strewn aside in lust. Tongues and mouths started to explore hot sweating chest hair, kissing and licking muscled stomachs that moved up and down in breathless desire. Both were groaning now in ecstasy, the sound of lips on flesh matching their masculine grunts of passion.

Beside Taylor and Brett, the other two soldiers turned their desires to each other. Their mouths smothered each other's cock-heads, tonguing each other's uncircumcised helmets, drops of pre-come lapped up by another's willing tongue. Their mouths moved as if they were blowing harmonicas, each other's hard shaft an instrument of meat they could play on. Their mouths ached as they tried to reach round the thick shafts, gently nibbling the hardened flesh, as their tongues traced a wet journey over every bump and vein. Their mutual pleasure was evident, low moans filling the air, and their pumping became one rhythmic motion, cocks entering warm willing mouths.

Brett caught himself watching the two men out of the corner of his eye. He could see their short-haired heads bobbing into each other's groins, their full buttocks clenching and humping each other's faces. He thought of penetrating them, his hard cock sliding into their tight sweaty man-holes, man upon man. He imagined fucking each of them in turn, moving from one to the other, each time using his own tool to plunge into their depths.

He suddenly became aware of Taylor gently biting his cock,

soft bites that made him stiffen and groan loudly. Fucking the other two soldiers would have to wait, Brett decided, as he was being given too much pleasure from Taylor's willing mouth. Brett returned the favour by sucking on Taylor's hairy balls, taking one then the other full into his mouth, rolling them around the inside of his warm mouth. Taylor pushed his warm hairy groin deeper towards Brett, so that Brett almost suffocated on his partner's hairy mound, Taylor's dark pubic hair pressing into his face. It was beginning to drive Brett beyond control, and he pushed his muscular thighs either side of Taylor's handsome face, gripping tight and thrusting backwards and forwards into his mouth. Taylor responded to the increased urgency in Brett's movements by sucking deeper and harder, allowing Brett's thrusts to dictate the action, his own cock now firmly embedded between Brett's lips.

Beside them, the two other men were close to the end of their journey of desire. Their movements were much faster and more urgent, the slapping of cock into mouth producing an audible sucking noise that continued to fire their passion. The musky smell of men's sweat was pungent in the room now, mixing with the faint aroma of pre-come as all four men leaked their juices.

The two soldiers knew that their moment was nearly upon them, and they encouraged each other to drive themselves over the edge. Their moans became very close, and it was clear to Brett that they knew each other long enough and intimately enough to time their motions so that their climaxes came at the same moment. There was a slight pause in their lovemaking, a lull as the cock-sucking slowed to the point where only the very cock tips were being suckled and tongue-teased, the heads gently flicked inside the mouths. Brett knew that they were giving each other a sign for climaxing, and he watched as the two cocks were sucked deep into the two men's mouths once more, loud groans filling the air, both men growling that they were coming.

With only the intimacy that soldiers can know, the two men next to Brett began to reach their climax together. Both men howled with pleasure, feeling each other's cocks reach their fulfilment, gagged by their mate's meat. The men continued humping each other's mouths, and Brett saw the faint dribbles of white hot juice trickling out of their mouths. The grunts became soft satiated moans as the stinging scent of come hit the air.

The soldiers lay back and watched as Brett and Taylor increased their own pace, very near to their own orgasms. Brett became lost in the pleasure Taylor was giving him with his tongue, flicking and rolling it over his hard shaft, his saliva mixing with Brett's own pre-come as a generous lubricant, making the hard rod slip further and deeper into Taylor's willing mouth. In return, Brett pulled on Taylor's cock in long hard jerks, taking only the tip of the glans into his mouth, where he could smother it with his warm tongue. Every now and then, Taylor would swallow hard, sucking Brett into his throat for a deeper penetration. Brett reciprocated with faster and longer pulls on Taylor's cock, thickened now with lust and ready for release.

Brett wanted his own orgasm, and started to grind his heavy hips powerfully into Taylor's face, a renewed urgency in his movements. He literally began to fuck Taylor's mouth, feeling the warmth and wetness as his cock slipped in and out, balls slapping against Taylor's chin. In return, Taylor began to fuck Brett's fist, reaching into the warm opening of Brett's lips, oozing pre-come which gathered round Brett's lips. Knowing their time was arriving, the movements and jerks became faster and harder, until both men were fucking each other without penetrating their arses, using hands and mouths as willing orifices for hard meat. They began to moan louder and louder, riding hands and mouths, deeply entwined in flesh, sweat and pre-come.

'Oh, fuck, I'm gonna come.' Brett shouted out, the coarseness of his words turning him and Taylor on.

'Feel my cock pumping – get ready for my load,' Taylor responded. 'Taste my soldier juice.'

Taylor's thick cock swelled in Brett's hands; the tip thrust into Brett's mouth and a sharp pungent stream of white come hit the back of his throat. He swallowed it down as Taylor groaned and pumped four more shots of hot juice into Brett's mouth; Brett fought to swallow it all. The fourth jet triggered Brett's own orgasm, his mouth opening in a gasp so Taylor's final gush of ejaculation hit him full in the face as he himself pumped his seed into Taylor's mouth. A loud howl accompanied Brett's first orgasmic shot, the thrill of release causing him to close his eyes and pump deeper as the second and third jets of come forced their way out of his cock.

The men swallowed each other's come, the exchange of intimacy signing their contract as lovers and equals, the mix of sweat and semen providing a pungent taste that hung on their breath, as they regained themselves after spending so much energy. Brett and Taylor drew themselves up to each other, their mouths touching, fastening on to each other. Without speaking, they kissed deep and long, their mouths opening and sharing each other's secret treasure. Brett tasted his own spunk on Taylor's tongue and gratefully received it into his own mouth, allowing Taylor's tongue to find those small reserves of semen he retained in his own mouth. Their juices, saliva and semen, mixed and passed between the two men.

The other two soldiers joined the couple, claiming a partner each. Mouths upon mouths, tongues entwined, the men's juices were passed from one another in an orgy of come-eating. Four men's intimate juices were savoured by them all, lingering kisses passing semen from mouth to mouth until all four had tasted each other's passion intimately, and one tasted of them all.

They fell asleep in a huddle, the four men wrapped round each other, legs arms and bodies entwined. Brett could feel the gentle beat of Taylor's chest as he slept, a comforting steady clock that lulled him into the sleepy world of dreams, the warmth of the three soldiers guarding and comforting him in the deep black of the night.

Five

The night passed quickly for Brett, filled with dreams of glory in war. He dreamt of fighting hordes of anonymous soldiers, whose faces he couldn't see. Beside him was an army of handsome men, naked and muscular, armed with desire and passion. His army moved in unison, one large masculine entity, thinking the same thoughts. There was no fear: only a sense of purpose and togetherness. His fellow soldier's muscles were his; he could feel their taut sinews, their strong legs as they moved towards the faceless enemy. It became a fight without weapons, without daggers, guns or even hunting knives, but a fight in which courage and his own sense of power were stronger than blades or bullets.

In the dream, Taylor was grinning broadly at Brett's side, his powerful physique sweating with the heat of an early afternoon sun. With arms draped over each other's shoulders, they defiantly approached the unknown enemy, leading their masculine force into an incomprehensible battle of spirits. As they came upon the mass of otherly warriors, they seemed to simply stride through them, breaking the very flanks of their opponents with a raucous laughter. Knowing that their sense of power and determination had broken the challenge before them, Taylor and Brett abandoned themselves in playful wrestling, grappling the spirit shapes blocking their way, crushing them out of existence.

Brett dreamt that he caught Taylor's face looking at him, their steely eyes locked in a knowing stare. They could see beyond each other's gritty play-fighting, stripped of fear and pretence, conquering their enemies together. Around him, his soldiers gathered and he felt the warmth of their bodies, swamped by the power of their collective masculinity. Just as during the night before, when they had lustfully shared each other's passionate orgasms, Brett could feel his fellows' innate life force. He felt a surge through his own body, watching it happen to them all, melting together as his lips forcefully found their way to Taylor's, meeting and embracing, driving into each other . . .

Brett started, suddenly awake, a sense of loss pouring over him. Even lying next to Taylor, the soldier's soft breathing blowing like a summer breeze over his own sweat-soaked skin, Brett knew that the dream was gone. The feelings of togetherness were even now passing, a sense of distance yawning before him, as if Taylor and the other soldiers were falling down a chasm in front of him. Suddenly he felt isolated again, as lonely as he had ever felt at the family homestead, as different from them as he felt from his brothers. He had enjoyed their company the night before. They had brought out a side to himself that he had only fantasised about, a side that he had wanted to experience for so long. It had been about release, about the communion of men, the animal within. And, having enjoyed it for that moment in time, he knew he could never experience it with them again. Even should Taylor wake now, as rampant with desire as Brett himself felt, they could never experience that moment again.

He watched Taylor's sleeping form, his eyes lighting on the handsome face. It was peaceful, calm: not animated, the way it had been the previous night, during the throes of passion. Brett liked the serene look on Taylor's face, and wondered how much serenity Taylor would have in his life as a soldier. Whether that face would pass into old age, or if it would be mutilated in war or conflict. Brett silently brought his right hand to his own mouth, lightly kissed his fingers, and used them to baptise Taylor's own lips with his kiss. Taylor moved slightly in his sleep, sensing the leaving perhaps, or responding to Brett's silent prayers for him. This wasn't love, Brett knew. It wasn't a romance, but a strange friendship borne out of desire and lifted by an intimate bond between the two young men.

A chill hit the air. Brett woke from his reverie and felt a renewed sense of purpose and mission. There were new adventures to be found now, new passions to be discovered. He silently wished Taylor and his soldiers well, slowly lifting himself up. He began to dress cautiously, pulling on his clothes in such a way as to become a small ritual of parting. Careful not to make any noise, Brett picked up his belongings and crept out of the barracks. Every noise seemed magnified, and he briefly wondered what he would say should the soldiers wake before he had left. 'Thank you and goodbye?' Better this. Better the wordless parting of friends than the embarrassed stutterings of lovers clinging to lost pleasures. He allowed himself one last smile and let the new dawn hit his face as he stepped outside.

Outside, Brett soon lost the familiar musky masculine scent of his sleeping lover. The air was crisp and clear again, a soft morning drizzle wetting his face as he lifted it to the sky. The delicate spots of rain hit his skin in a gentle tapping rhythm, beating the sound of the new day. He could feel the droplets of water fresh on his face and hands; his hair wetted enough to fall over his eyes, causing him to wipe his forehead with the back of his wrist. The light of the rising sun was dazed, misted by the faint rain.

Under his feet, the dirt was wet enough to cling to his boots, little brown souvenirs of the barracks and the grounds that he would carry with him for many more miles. Wiping some of the rain from his eyes, Brett took a few steps forward, away from the scene of last night's orgy, and shook out the aches from his body. He could feel some of his muscles – his legs, thighs, lower back – still singing from the exertions of the four men. It was a fine pain.

Brett reminded himself of his proposed itinerary. How would he find out if there was a group of travellers, forty-niners even, who were making their way to Sutters Mill or California on the trail? He guessed he'd have to keep his ear to the ground, hang around some of the bars and eating places round and about the fort. That would mean heading back into the main part of the town, away from the fort and the barracks. He had caught occasional snatches of conversation when he had arrived, mentions of dreams and gold, but hadn't paid enough attention to the people talking to be able to place conversations with individual faces, or even remember where he had heard such snatches. Brett silently cursed himself for his lack of strategy. There were times like these that he felt like a real hick, a child with no real idea of life on the road. Did he really think he would make it all that way? On his own? It was laughable!

He dwelt on the challenges ahead of him. Had he thought this through? Perhaps his brothers, his father, his loving mother, were right in warning him off this course of action. Perhaps they had seen something of him that he had been ignoring, that they could see beyond his own arrogance and pig-headedness. They must have seen a child on the homestead, part of the family, the natural successor to all they had worked for. And now he had walked out on it all, had left them and all that they had worked for. A dark depression was looming over him already. How could he move from such bright hope to such lack of confidence in a matter of minutes?

Brett sat on a boulder by the mud track to take stock. He couldn't go back. He had to go forward. Everything was in front of him for, even if he wanted to return home now, his own pride would stop him. Besides, he had so much of his money tied up in tools, instruments, clothes and stock for his journey that any change in his plans now was unrealistic. He couldn't let himself give in to this, and his mind returned to the moment when he had first left, those feelings of freedom and release. Opportunity. Daft moments like this were just proof that he had to go on, if only to prove to himself that he could do it! Maybe it was weariness, the excitement and physical challenge of the last few days just catching up on him.

'Morning.'

A voice beside him pulled Brett back to his senses. He shook his head briefly, and looked up to see Taylor standing beside him. The red-haired soldier was looking at him quizzically. 'You pushing off?'

Brett felt himself flushing with embarrassment, aware that he had been caught sneaking out. For a moment, he felt like he had as a child when his Ma had caught him sneaking out of the kitchen, having dipped his fingers in some batter or dough or cake mix. Taylor had caught him off guard. 'I . . . I guess, yeah, I was figurin' to make headway again.'

'You in a hurry to leave us all?'

'I . . . No, not a hurry . . . I just figured . . .'

'Figured to hit the road early?'

'Yeah, somethin' like that, I guess. I don't know, I reckoned there weren't no point in waking you and the others . . .'

Brett's excuses trailed off as he sat and watched Taylor take out his smokes, and tip one into his mouth. There was something angry about it, and Brett realised that Taylor was hurt. He became aware that he had betrayed the man who had befriended him, and in doing so had broken some unwritten contract. Soldiers didn't just sneak out away from each other. Taylor had invited him in to be one of the family, and he was expected to have some form of loyalty in return. Taylor let out a long low breath of smoke, almost as if he was exhaling his own pain at the betrayal.

'I thought you might be staying in town for a couple of days,' Taylor finally offered. 'Me and the boys been lookin' for some new company to hang around with us. I mean, they're good company and all, but, well, you can get tired of each other if you're hanging around each other all the time, you know?'

'I hadn't realised you were thinking that way.'

'Hey, don't get me wrong . . . You gotta go, then you gotta go. We just ain't had us no strangers joining us for a while. There's always people coming through, of course, that's the nature of the place: but when me and the boys saw you, we thought you were kind of holding back for a while. You didn't seem to be like most of the forty-niners.'

Brett let out a snort: part guffaw, part incomprehension. 'In what way? How'd you figure that one?'

'Hey, I wasn't meaning anything . . .' Taylor flashed his grin. Brett could see the soldier was sleepy-eyed, and thought maybe he was grouchy in the mornings anyhow. Perhaps morning rows were his way of finding the morning. Taylor took another drag of his smoke, and blew a long straight trail of smoke into the air. 'The thing with soldiers is . . . well, they're soldiers.'

Brett laughed. 'I guess I can't argue with that.'

'It's too early.' Taylor also laughed. 'Sometimes, it's just good to hear a man talk about stuff that's not fighting talk. Sometimes a man needs to know there's more to the world. That make sense?'

Brett looked hard at Taylor. Here was an older Scott, someone who had seen years of fighting, had seen injury, death, the realities of it all. That's what Taylor had been responding to the night before, what all three soldiers had recognised – the significance of the moment. That tomorrow – well, who knows what tomorrow might bring. A call to arms? For a moment Brett thought again of his dream, of how wrong it had been – that the glory of fighting fearsome foes together was more likely to be replaced by a dreadful fear that this might be the last morning, the last fight, the last time you and your battalions were together. Brett wondered how long it would take Scott to feel that way.

'All I got on my mind is all the gold that's waiting for me way out West.'

'You reckon? Well, send us some over when you get there.'

'Happen I might, Taylor. I reckon I'm gonna have plenty to go round anyhow. Besides, I might have a better offer. I might need myself a private army to help protect my mountains of gold for me.'

Taylor laughed, and Brett felt some of the tension between them slipping away. 'Now, happen I might take you up on that. Gold can make for some pretty good soldiers. You could have yourself a deal there, partner!'

'Deal?' Brett joked, spitting into his hand and mockingly offering it to Taylor.

Taylor laughed back, and took his hand firmly. 'Sure.'

Taylor's hand clung on to Brett's. He could feel the heat resting in his hand, Taylor's masculine grip keeping them connected. Then he felt Taylor pulling his hand down, closer into the soldier's body, taking him to the prize between his thighs. Taylor held Brett's hand against his crotch, resting it on Taylor's covered cock, nestling in his britches. Brett could feel its limpness warm against his hand, its soft form stirring beneath his touch. He could trace its form with his fingers, sloping downwards between Taylor's legs, and then Brett could feel the soft tip buried between Taylor's balls. The soft sack felt tender, treasured, under his hand.

'It's sounding good to me,' said Taylor.

'Yeah. I'm liking it, too.'

'Bet you could sure do with a hand over there.'

'Could do. Some things a man needs help with.'

'You got that right. When you got a thing that's worth something, you gotta take real good care of it.'

'I'm sure I got myself something good, right enough.'

Brett felt Taylor urge his hand over his cock, rubbing him against it. There was a slight swell to the form now, the feeling of life stirring in Taylor's manhood. Brett could feel them both getting turned on by talking, Taylor's low tones blending with his as they continued talking about nothing much in particular, content to remain physically connected.

' 'Course, there's plenty of gold hunters . . .'

'And there's plenty of soldiers . . .'

'You know we're the best you gonna get.'

'That's maybe right. Except I ain't really seen you in action . . .'

'You want some action?'

The question assaulted Brett. He could feel his hand trapped against Taylor's engorging form. The heat from his groin was exciting Brett, Taylor deliberately teasing him with his cock, gentling moving his hips into Brett's hand. He began to slightly thrust his crotch forward, then back, softly mimicking the movements of the night before, as they had come together. Now Taylor lowered his other hand on to Brett's, letting the movement become more obvious, running Brett's hand between his thighs, feeling his nuts through their cotton casing. He let Brett's hand wander over his right thigh, under his legs, on to his arse-cheeks. Then Taylor moved Brett's hand back over his cock, making him grab it in his hand and finger it. Brett began thinking of the previous night again, how he had tongued and kissed and sucked Taylor's throbbing erection, and taken his juice inside him.

'I liked the action I've had. You're good in action.'

'Yeah, I'm real good, Brett. I'm a regular man of action.'

Brett could feel the monster awakening in his hand. 'Maybe I'm looking for some action this morning.' As he said it, Taylor's face was opposite Brett's now, his eyes daring him on. Although still reasonably distant, Brett became aware of Taylor's hot breath on him, could almost taste the man in front of him.

'You seem like you're good in action, too,' continued Taylor. 'You were keen on the action last night, huh?'

Brett let out a low whistle. 'For sure. Though now I know I didn't get my fill last night.'

'I really liked the way you tongued my dick. You are one hell of a soldier's cock-sucker.'

The coarseness in Taylor's tone struck Brett heavily, and it surprised him. He hadn't been aware of how turned on he was himself until he heard Taylor turning obscene. He could feel the effect on Taylor, too, who was now almost fully erect. His hand was still being directed against Taylor's thick shaft. Taylor's hands pushed his own into the mountain of flesh rising up. Brett pushed his forefinger into Taylor's erection, finding the tip of his cock, and exerting pressure just under his cock-hole. It had the desired effect, and Taylor's dick jumped against his touch. Brett kept his pressure just under the crown, feeling the clear pattern of Taylor's cock underneath his britches now. Taylor's hands urged him to repeat the manoeuvre, and Taylor shifted his stance somewhat to allow greater access to his excitement. Brett felt him spread his legs a little more, shifting in the dirt, his boots planting themselves firmly on the ground.

'You liked that, soldier? You liked my gold-hunting tongue over your hard dick?'

Brett was enjoying it now, understanding the rules of the game, the power of what he was saying. He could see and feel the effects of his words on Taylor, a firm bloated hard-on under his touch now. Brett was himself stiffening, the familiar stirrings of a morning erection. It was almost as if the dawning sun was itself warming his sugarstick. He added his free hand to the church of warmth against Taylor, then moved the scaffolding of fingers over his own crotch, letting Taylor know that he was in on the game, too. Taylor's fingers found his hardening knob, clenching it lightly in his fingers, tracing its length. He enjoyed the sensation of this spectacle of clothed masturbation in public, grateful that no one was around, but also excited by the prospect of an unwitting interruption.

'You liked to feel a farm boy's hands stroking your hard cock? My rough hands over your hairy balls?'

'Yeah, cowboy, it felt nice.'

'How about it? Can you feel my hard shaft now? Rub your hands against it. Feel my big dick.'

'Yeah, I can feel your hard shaft, feel it throbbing in my hand. I like the way you were playing with my tool, too. I could strip you and fuck you right here. You'd like that wouldn't you? Getting fucked by my soldier dick?'

'Yeah.'

'You're like my missus back home. She can't get enough of me when I get going with her.'

'Your wife likes you to give her a good fuck, huh?'

'Oh, yeah. She loved it right from the very first time I let her have my hard dick. She gets so hot and juiced up, you wouldn't believe it.'

Brett could feel Taylor's fingers tighten over his erect penis, both of them becoming increasingly excited. All of a sudden, Brett imagined Taylor intimately with his wife, secure in their warm bed together, Taylor's sexual appetite directed towards making love to his young spouse. The idea of Taylor enjoying a woman's flesh, his lips, fingers, exploring her, penetrating her, filled him with a new desire for Taylor. He wanted to explore this man's marriage bed, to feel his lust, his desire for the opposite sex, while giving him the pleasure of his own sex.

Taylor felt the change in the dynamic, too. He realised that Brett was becoming excited by the idea of him with his wife, with their intimate couplings, the different positions he had taken her in. Although she had been timid at first, Taylor had unleashed in her a wild passion that even he had trouble keeping up with! In truth, he had had a few women before he met his Betsy, but she had taken to their days and nights of passion with a real delight.

She had told him that she had never been with a man before, and he believed her, and it excited him that he had been the first to bring out such strong emotions in her.

Taylor had first seen Betsy when she came as a new teacher for their small school. Until recently, the teachers in St Louis had been gentlemanly masters or elderly widows, husbands lost to the glories of war. Taylor had never been one for learning himself. He had been amazed at Betsy's knowledge, her love of history, art, literature, and the way she was able to talk about such things. But he also knew from very early on that he was able to offer her something much more elemental, something she had tried hard to resist until she had met him.

He remembered her that first day when he had seen her entering the wooden school house. She had a corn-yellow bonnet on, golden ribbon tied in a bright bow under her small, slightly pointed chin. He could see her deep black hair brushed under the bonnet, and later he would discover with joy that it fell halfway down her back when loose. He remembered still the way in which the bonnet framed her pale milky skin, and the way her coal black eyes pierced him when she saw him looking over. She had looked away, bringing her delicate small hand to her button nose, covering her full red lips from his gaze, although he had noticed the beginnings of an embarrassed smile as she started to turn away. He'd taken his time in watching the long dark eyelashes flutter nervously and he had noticed with eagerness the way her hand had reached to scratch her blushing cheeks, then dropped away again to her side.

And, of course, Taylor had not been able to stop his own gaze from drifting down over her young feminine form. He had noticed the elegance with which she had manoeuvred the rickety wooden school house steps in her long powder-blue cotton dress. Her poise had been perfect, as had her figure. The lacy trim at the front of her dress didn't quite hide the pert mound of her breasts, fulsome and shapely. Her generous curves continued downward, hips hidden behind the light blue material of her dress, but her shape unmistakable nevertheless. Even at that moment, Taylor had imagined her long shapely thighs, the roundness of her hips and buttocks, the arching of her back. He had felt the physical sensations in him, his heart pounding with desire for her, wanting to feel himself mount and ride her, to strip away all the frivolities and pretence around her.

He had managed to steal some time with her every now and then, setting himself up as a carpenter to repair bits and pieces around the school house. Of course, Taylor had never been all that good a carpenter and he suspected that she knew that, but he was young, and there weren't many other men of his age around at the time. Everyone was joining the army these days, and he knew that he would, too. It wasn't that he wanted to, it was just what was set out for him. He had no other real skills, and felt embarrassed when Betsy would point out that something he had mended for her had broken apart only a day or two later! But she had been good-natured about it, and she also flirted with him. OK, so it might only have been showing him some of her leg once in a while as she walked up the school steps, but it gave him a thrill, and he would end up jacking off later that night, imagining his hard cock between her legs or breasts. As he cleared up his own come, he wondered what it would feel like to spend his seed deep inside her, lying between her thighs as his ejaculate mixed with her woman's wetness. He could imagine offering her his limp penis to lick clean after they had both come, and letting her taste their shared juices on his manhood.

They had dated a few months and then married, before he went off to become a soldier. Their days and nights had been spent together: passionate, torrid, lustful times. Every time he returned to St Louis, they would engage in carnal rediscovery of each other. Of course, he had never told her about the sex he had had with soldiers and strangers – it wasn't something she needed to know. That spur-of-the-minute sex was very different from what he enjoyed with his Betsy, and it was only because he missed her company that he sought out the company of men to share sex with. As she was his wife, so he was a man with strong sexual needs, and sometimes those had to be met with the men around him. The other soldiers also knew and understood this, often being in the same position. There was always sex of some form available.

And so it was now. As he felt Brett's hardening cock, Taylor realised he needed release now. It was too open at the minute, though both men were hot for each other, and the talk of fucking his Betsy was giving him even more of a hard-on. He leant close to Brett. 'You're getting me real worked up here, and I can see that you're ready for it, too,' he whispered, squeezing Brett's cock to prove his point. 'Let's go down where no one will disturb us for a while. I'll show you what makes my Betsy so horny when I'm home with her.'

Brett took a breath. He couldn't resist now, and he'd tarried too long to get away as he had originally planned. He nodded in agreement, and felt Taylor squeeze his cock in teasing pleasure. Taylor looked over his shoulder, and took his hand away from Brett's groin. 'Don't worry, I'll be coming back to mine that field again, pretty soon,' he grinned.

Taylor moved down the dirt track, the mist cooling their ardour slightly, as Brett was led away from the barracks. There were a number of outhouses further down the track, and it became clear that this was where Taylor was leading him. Brett enjoyed watching Taylor move ahead of him, watching his young soldier's arse as it made its way to an outhouse to the right of the wet dirt track. Brett could see the shape of Taylor's thighs, and the occasional glimpse of his half erection, betrayed by the contours of Taylor's britches. There was also the telltale dampening of the material at the knob end, indicating Taylor's own excitement.

Taylor opened a door to what appeared to be a shed. His head disappeared through the doorway. Brett heard him call something softly, but there was no reply. Taylor turned to him, grinning. 'We're on,' he promised, and disappeared inside, holding the door slightly ajar for his playmate. As Brett stepped inside, he saw that he was entering what must be some sort of store room for the barracks. Or had been, for there were only empty sacks scattered around on shelves devoid of anything other than scattered dried seeds and grain. Taylor was already spreading some of the sacks on the floor, and taking off his boots as Brett made his way inside.

Taylor gestured to a space by him, patting it as an indication for Brett to join him. Brett pulled off his boots, set down his luggage, and joined Taylor on the floor.

As he sat, he turned to face the young red-haired man and laid a hand on his thigh. 'So you got yourself a wife back home. You must kinda miss her, out here.'

'Yeah, she's way back in St Louis, and here's me and my old man looking for it over in Fort Leavenworth. I could do with feeling her round me, now, feeling her pull me inside her. She's pretty, too. I'm a lucky man when I'm with her.'

'It sounds it,' encouraged Brett. He wanted to hear more, and was letting Taylor know by stroking around his cock.

'For sure. She loves me mauling her breasts. She's got the best nipples I ever laid my mouth on. I love getting them tasty peas between my lips. Makes her moan. She loves me to take them between my teeth, just nibble them slightly. She'll cradle me there like a baby, letting me take my fill of those nice young titties.'

Brett moved his hand over Taylor's cock. He rubbed the slight damp patch, feeling the sticky liquid between his fingers, before licking them as Taylor continued.

'She likes me to play with them, cup them in my hands and cover them with kisses. I move down on her soft skin, then, kissing down her belly, till I get to that soft button of hers, that bellybutton, and tickle it with my tongue. She's usually squirming by then, and I like slipping my hand between her legs, feeling the heat between her thighs, that dampness that lets me know she wants her Taylor. She likes me calling her name as I let my finger enter her. "Oh, Betsy", I tell her, "you're wonderful, my little Betsy."'

Brett fished for Taylor's hot cock, feeling it fill with blood. He felt Taylor relax back, spreading himself comfortably, as he allowed Brett to pull out his erection, and gently stroke it. Brett rubbed the pre-come down the shaft, rubbing the liquid into Taylor's hairy balls, before gripping the hard shaft in his fist.

'By this time, my Betsy needs two fingers inside her, maybe three. And I'm still kissing those beautiful bosoms, smelling how sweet she is and how much she wants to love me. And then I take her beautiful little hand, and I let her know how much I want to love her. I let her stroke my love dagger just like you're stroking it. She's got smaller hands than you, gold-hunter. She has to stretch those hands just to fit round that monster.'

'You sure got a big cock, soldier. A big thick hard cock. I bet Betsy loves feeling your hard cock, too, just as much as I do.'

'You're right, there. But she likes it better when she feels the tip of it pushing against her. I like to just tease her, too, to rub the end against her sweet pussy-hole, as she kisses me and fingers the shaft for me. When I kiss her, she holds open those wet lips for me to get inside her. She's so excited, it's easy to enter her then. I follow where my fingers and tongue have been, letting my knob fuck her. It's so good when she's on top, too; I can feel her sink down on my shaft.'

Brett imagined Taylor's cock at work, sunk deep within Betsy's hole. He slowly wanked Taylor, spitting into his hand to add some lubrication to Taylor's natural juices. He was so turned on himself, through sharing Taylor's intimate revelations, that he had to take his own erection in hand and masturbate both of them at the same time. He heard Taylor groaning loudly, knowing that his manual dexterity matched Betsy's, and the swelling in his hand told him how much Taylor was enjoying his attention.

'I get so deep in her, she calls my name, and starts squirming around me, getting my shaft deeper inside her. She keeps kissing and loving me, and I'm plunging into her, working up a real nice rhythm. We've got to know each other real well. We can set up a real good thing between us, my hard knob slapping into her, getting faster and harder. I like giving her real pleasure, too. That's why she loves being on top: she can lead the action. I play with her bosom, stroking her thighs as she rides me, feel her fingers digging into my nuts, pulling at my balls.'

Brett took the cue, and massaged Taylor's bollocks, while still stroking his cock tight and hard from tip to bottom. There was a copious amount of liquid coming from his cock-hole now, making a soft rhythmic sound that accompanied his ministrations. Taylor began to hump Brett's hands, pushing himself in and out of the cupped palm. Their breathing was quickening and Brett began to move his hands faster up and down the thick rod he was holding. He took his left hand, and gently spat on his index finger. Watching Taylor's eyes close with pleasure, Brett fingered round the man's anus. His wet finger gently probed round the sweaty asshole, feeling the muscles relax even as the muscles in Taylor's knob strained in his grip.

'Ohhhhhhh, yeah, that's real good! Oh, yeah. I sink deep in her, and she just makes this little noise, there's this soft whimper that I love, 'cos I know she's going over the edge. That's when she rides me like a cowboy. She bucks up and down, but I keep on inside her, until I can feel her muscle spasms. She starts screaming and tightens her pussy hold on me, and I can feel her pulling my spunk into her . . .'

Brett slipped the tip of his finger into Taylor's relaxed backside, letting it find its way through the sensitive sphincter and inside his tight arse. He felt the man bucking now, slamming his manhood in and out of Brett's clenched fist. The thick meat was hardening, ready to explode in his hand.

'I let her have her moment, then I follow her. I can feel her juice pour over me inside her, then I thrust my husbandry into Betsy and howl like the wolves at the moon before my whole body explodes inside her . . .'

Taylor groaned for real. Brett slipped his finger deeper into the soldier's rear as the cock in his hand plunged one final time into his fist. He felt the splatter of hot spunk at the same time that Taylor roared loudly, then jet after jet of hot milky white jism spat out of Taylor's pumping staff. It was too much for Brett himself and, when he was sure that the torrent of Taylor's sperm had finished, he straddled the soldier's chest. Using Taylor's fluid as lubricant, Brett frantically wanked his own cock hard, pushing it into Taylor's bloodshot face. A few final hard strokes took Brett to the point of climax, and he grunted as he watched his ejaculate hit Taylor's face and chest, spewing into the soldier's red hair. He looked down to see Taylor, with his eyes closed, smiling and rubbing Brett's hot juice into his skin. They had both shot a copious amount; Taylor's come was still hot on Brett's hand and forearm. Brett gently massaged his hands into Taylor's heaving chest, letting them both cool down from their heated orgasms.

Brett lay back on the sack-covered ground, wiping himself off.

He was glad that Taylor had caught him just before he was about to slink off, and that they'd had one more shared orgasm. He could imagine Taylor when he got home to Betsy in St Louis, imagine their impassioned lovemaking.

'I'm gonna have to make a move, soldier boy. Be sure to give my regards to the boys back at the barracks.'

'Sure, gold-hunter. They'll be glad to hear it!' boomed back Taylor.

'And maybe you'll say hello to your wife from me, too. To Betsy.'

'Ah, yes,' said Taylor. 'Betsy, my sweet Betsy . . .'

Brett looked over at Taylor silently grinning to himself, his softening cock lying on his right thigh. The red-haired soldier was gently singing the name of his wife to himself, and Brett wondered how long it would before the two were reunited. Shutting the door of the outhouse behind him, Brett made his way back towards the heart of Fort Leavenworth, leaving Taylor whispering the name of his beloved Betsy over and over.

Six

――――――

'C'mon, boy. Morning's up.'

Luke heard the clang of metal and realised what passed for breakfast in this brutal place had been delivered. A mug of treacle-black coffee, as hot as pitch, sent wafts of bitter-smelling steam towards him. At least it was hot, the only way Luke liked it. He'd never understood Matt, who would brew a coffee and then leave it for a good half-hour to cool down. It was another sign that he was better off out of Wilmott's life. How could anyone drink the cold bitter liquid Matt had called coffee? The thought of it made his stomach turn, even as he broke up the two doorstep slices of day-old bread served with his own beverage.

'You enjoying that? I makes a good brew, I reckon. Even if I do say so myself.' Sheriff Williams combed back his greying hair, and peered through the bars of the jail. 'Drink it down. It'll do you good. Reckon you may find yourself having some visitors, later on. Word is that we got ourselves a couple of old rogues coming in, so don't get too precious about your room here.'

If only you knew, Luke thought. The years he had shared rooms with other boys at the orphanage had left Luke with very little sense of privacy or ownership. He remembered when he was much younger, how he heard the crying at night as someone new joined the dormitory where all the youngsters were forced to sleep in narrow uncomfortable wooden cots. Sometimes, when they woke in the morning the acrid smell of urine would still be in the air, as bed-wetting was common for the anxious children the orphanage of St Mary's had adopted.

He had never suffered that way himself, and was glad of it – it was the subject of much taunting and bullying, and Luke had always tried to keep his head down so as not to be singled out for such attention. That wasn't to say he hadn't meted out a beating or two, but that had been more to do with survival than malice. Occasionally, he had taken it on himself to administer what he saw as justice, when one of the older lads chanced his arm and beat the younger ones. Even if he had never received the benefit of such 'justice', Luke felt better adopting his codes of conduct, and seeing that the others lived by them – or knew the consequences.

The orphanage had never allowed much privacy, and Luke couldn't stop himself from laughing aloud at the suggestion the sheriff had made.

'What's that? I say something funny?'

'No, sir, Sheriff Williams, I was just thinking to myself, hey, I could do with the company in here, anyhow!' He grinned broadly at the sheriff, who returned a quick smile.

'Hey, now, I don't want you getting too comfortable in there, you know. I won't be having the pleasure of your company for much longer, I reckon!'

'How's that?'

'We'll need to be moving you on. You can't face justice here. You'll be going back east for that. Besides, I don't like no one spending too long in my jail. I get used to the company, and that ain't good for a hard-assed critter like myself.'

Williams was being ironic, of course. Jail was never easy, and sheriffs would never be friends of his, but Luke knew that Williams was at least fair. He was a man who looked on his custodians with a fatherly wisdom. In his forties, Williams was a tall and sinewy man, not unattractive. His hair was greased, more grey than what little chestnut brown remained from his youth. His skin had a clear complexion, though it was wrinkled by the sun, and the laughter lines round Williams's grey eyes bestowed a

sense of gravitas on the man. In their odd moments of conversational intimacy, Williams would occasionally confide in the
younger Mitchell, telling him how the law had been his life, even
as a young man. Luke believed him: not in the sense that it was a
mission for the sheriff, but that it was all he had ever known or
understood.

'You're getting old, Sheriff, that's what it is.'

'Now, don't give me that lip, son,' chuckled Williams, 'or I'll
be spitting in that coffee before I give it you next time. Or maybe
worse!'

'You'd have to get the old equipment working first, Sheriff!'

'Don't you be worrying 'bout that, son. There ain't nothing
wrong with my equipment. And you needn't take my word for
it either, boy: there's plenty who could testify to that for me!'

'I wouldn't want to be taking anything off you, Sheriff, except
them keys you got that would let me outta here.'

'Oh, yeah? You want these? Well, you just come and get them
off me!' The sheriff teasingly wiggled his ass in Luke's direction,
the cell's key on a chain attached to his back pocket. Luke
fleetingly noticed that, for a man of his age, Sheriff Williams's ass
looked cute. Joining in the joke, he blew a kiss in the direction
of the extended posterior.

'Yeah, well, if you keep kissing my rear like that, we might
just make you into an honest man.'

'You reckon, Sheriff? You know, I don't think there's anything that could make me an honest man. I was born bad, and
I'll be bad till the day I die.'

Sheriff Williams stopped a moment, a look of seriousness
descending on his weather-beaten face. 'You believe that, boy?
That you'll go to your grave a wrong 'un?'

Luke could see that he had offended the man, that he had
betrayed the values that Williams lived by. For some reason, the
older man really believed there was hope for Luke, that he could
change. In his heart, Luke couldn't believe it. There was something about him which caused trouble, attracted it to him and to
those in his life. In his heart, he couldn't see anything happening
to change that, and it had now become his reality – Luke Mitchell
was, and always would be, an outlaw.

However, to appease the sheriff, Luke simply lied. 'Sheriff, with folks like you looking out for us, there's hope even for me.'

Williams grunted in acknowledgement that he'd been proved right, and moved away to his large wooden desk in the corner of the prison building. As he disappeared out of sight, Luke lay back on the bunk and cradled his head in his upturned hands, arms stretched out behind him. His mind turned back to being surprised by Williams and his posse only two days ago. Exhausted, he had fallen asleep in a barn, thinking that it was disused and he was unlikely to be found. Unfortunately for him, an over-amorous courting couple had been using the barn as a secret rendezvous point, and on seeing him sleeping there had assumed he must be nothing other than a dangerous criminal. Sheriff Williams had been contacted immediately, and arrived before dawn with several of his men. Luke's reputation had gone before him, as a favour to Matt Wilmott, and he had been locked up within a matter of hours.

Williams had been good-natured about it, but his side-kick Rogers had been a right pain in the proverbial ass. Toothy, gawky and with lank, greasy, dirty-blond hair, Rogers had taken an immediate dislike to Luke, and taken every opportunity to heap scorn on him. Luke guessed that Rogers took a dislike to everyone he ever met, except for some of the maidens he took opportunities to leer at, and who would turn from him in embarrassed discomfort. Luke hoped that they hadn't seen what he had – Rogers uncomfortably adjusting himself in his pants as his excitement became the better of him. It was an ugly sight, even to Luke, and he guessed such young women would have found it repugnant. The very idea of Rogers involved in any form of lovemaking unnerved Mitchell.

Even on the journey back to the cell on the makeshift wagon the sheriff and his men had brought with him, Rogers had 'accidentally' kicked or thumped Luke more times than he could count. Most times, Luke had been able to dodge the tobacco-laden spit that Rogers ejaculated in his direction, although at odd moments Rogers scored a hit in his hair or on his clothes. The constant chewing of Rogers on his tobacco, and the disconcerting clicking noise he made while chewing the cud, caused Luke to close his eyes for most of the journey, and attempt to sleep. Such peace did not come, but at least closing his eyes had spared him the spectacle of Rogers scratching himself, and the bug-eyed stare he had developed.

Williams knew what Rogers was up to, and no doubt had seen him in operation with countless other prisoners, too. Luke had noticed the senior man making sure when he could that Rogers was only left with him for short periods. He had a feeling that something may have happened previously, that perhaps Rogers had overstepped the mark with some poor unfortunate prisoner. Even without the sheriff's vigilance, Luke would take care of himself and wouldn't have Rogers getting the better of him. As much as he might trust Williams, he distrusted Rogers to the same degree.

Luke cursed his luck for being found. There were advantages in the short term, however – he had been allowed to bath, to shave his growing beard, and he had been fed better than at any other time since leaving Lone Buck at the lakeside. Yet he knew that he needed to start forming a plan of escape. He had already risked too much to go back now, to watch Matt Wilmott's triumphal gloating. Somehow he would find a way out of here. It would mean waiting, watching for opportunities to present themselves to him: and if he could get one over on Rogers, then so much the better.

He had been watching and noting the routine of the day, as best as he could see that there was one. The sheriff would always be in first, at the crack of dawn, and then potter around in what passed for a kitchen beyond Luke's view. He could hear the clatter of breakfast duty, heavy iron pans, the roar of fire as Williams set about the morning's first tasks. Rogers would drag his churlish self in around half past eight, barely managing to be civil to the sheriff at that time in the morning, let alone the prisoners. There must be a regular morning meeting between them to discuss whatever would happen during the day, because he would hear their hushed tones, and sometimes a door closing muffling their discussions. Lunch was at noon, and anything between and after would depend on how unlawful the townsfolk had been. He assumed that Rogers and the sheriff must share the night shift between them, but so far only the sheriff had taken up the duty.

There had been no obvious breaks when Luke might be able to make a bolt for freedom, but Mitchell knew that Rogers was generally sloppy and didn't pay attention to detail. He also took a wry nap in the middle of the day if the sheriff wasn't around. This didn't help Mitchell directly, as long as he was on this side of the bars, but it was worth noting. If Luke had an ally, a conspirator, he was sure they would be able to formulate a cunning plan and he would be free once more. If Luke had someone who cared enough for him to help him, to liberate him, to save him from the infernal law enforcers who penned him in. If only . . .

For the moment, he was here, locked in a cell, and in danger of being returned to the lying, drunken Matt Wilmott. There was precious little time for his daydreaming now. Luke needed to sharpen his mind, look for every possible opportunity for escape, every slip made by Sheriff Williams and the sluggard Rogers.

All of a sudden, there was a commotion in the jail, and Luke could hear a number of raucous voices shouting over each other.

'OK, in here, you two. Careful, now! I don't want nothing damaged!' Without doubt, that was the nasal whine of Rogers, a sneer in his voice.

'Watch it! I ain't no cattle.' This was lower, accented, a thick masculine voice.

'You're worse than that. You ain't even worth being an animal.' Rogers laughed at his own feeble joke.

'What's going on here?' The sheriff attempted to gain control of the situation.

'We got ourselves two more criminals, Sheriff. Any more room at the inn?'

Luke moved off his berth, and peered round the bars. Just inside the door, he could see Rogers with his back to him, sweat stains marking his back and under his arms. Two large men were with him, shackled at the feet and wrists with large cumbersome iron cuffs. One of the men, the one Luke thought he had heard, was black, over six feet tall, his head completely shorn of hair.

He looked sullen, his big broad shoulders slumped forward, his eyes downcast. He wore old clothes, dark and dusty, his boots caked in mud.

Next to the tall black man, a slimmer man was standing. He looked Mexican to Luke, although Luke had only seen a young Mexican in the orphanage, a child whose mother had left town and a drunken husband, her only child taken into the care of St Mary's. This man was smaller than the black man by three or four inches, with a swarthy olive complexion, dark black eyes, and a slim, long moustache that stretched over his lips and sank down the corners of his mouth. His shirt was short sleeved, and Luke could see a long scar along his right forearm, from wrist to elbow, snaking its way along his skin. It must have healed a long time ago, leaving a pink welt in the tissue. Occasionally, almost self-consciously, the man would scratch it, rubbing his fingers along its length.

'Josh and Rodriguez here are looking for a cell for the night,' Rogers joked. 'A little company for Wilmott's boy over there.'

As Rogers turned to sneer at him, Luke blew him a kiss. Rogers, infuriated, scurried over and kicked at the cell bars. 'You little . . .' he cried, before stopping himself from losing control. 'You'll get yours soon enough, Mitchell,' he warned.

'I hear you don't get any, Rogers. Rumour is, you can't get it up when you have to.'

Luke's taunts were followed by sniggers from the two new convicts. Flashing grins were shared between them.

'That's enough! Mitchell, go sit yourself down on the bunk over there and leave us to get on with things.' The sheriff brought an end to the brief contretemps, and dragged Rogers over to the table to finish off the paperwork that went along with the new inmates. Before turning back, Rogers couldn't resist spitting his tobacco-filled phlegm at Luke, a gob of it landing on the floor at Luke's feet.

'We ain't finished, Mitchell,' he hissed as he returned his attention to the newcomers by the desk.

Luke sloped back to his bed, amid the background hum of voices. The two prisoners used low, subdued tones, which were interspersed with attacks of Rogers's staccato whine. Williams, heavy and even, controlled the conversation, asking mundane questions about age, birth, status, crime. Mitchell hardly heard any of the replies, concentrating as he was on a large dark cockroach in the corner of his cell, which was making its way from one side of the room to another. Every so often, it would scuttle forward, then stop and check the air for movement or sound. When it detected none, it would continue on its merry way, before reaching the other side and disappearing behind a tiny crack in the plastered walls. Damn, Luke thought to himself, even a cockroach has more freedom than me!

The shuffle of chains alerted Luke to the fact that his new companions were about to join him. The sheriff had the big bunch of keys in his hand and was unlocking the cell door. Could he rush the sheriff now, Luke wondered, make out of the jail and be gone? He dismissed the ludicrous idea as soon as it had come to him, knowing that such action was unfeasible. Still, he was planning, waiting, hoping . . .

'This here's Josh and Rodriguez, Luke. I hope you're going to treat 'em mighty fine while they're staying with us, and I reckon you three'll be having quite a bit of time to get to know each other a little more.' The sheriff held the door open a little as he handed the keys over to Rogers. Rogers knelt down to unshackle the leg irons from Josh. The tall black man gazed down at the deputy.

'You like it down on your knees, there?' Josh flashed a grin at the deputy.

Rogers quickly straightened up and cussed under his breath. He pushed Josh into the cell with Luke before turning to Rodriguez. 'Don't you give me no lip, either,' he warned the Mexican, before unshackling him and pushing him in along with Luke and Josh. 'Don't get too cosy in there, now.'

'All right Rogers, leave be,' the sheriff commanded, and clanged shut the heavy door. The three men listened as he turned the key, locking them safely inside. Safely, that is, for the god-fearing, law-abiding citizens of the town. Three more dangerous criminals put away, he could hear Rogers boasting at the bar to his gullible mates. No doubt there would be stories embellished with gun fights, heroism on the part of the deputy, inhuman crimes on the part of his quarry. The story would no doubt become embellished again at the end of the drunken evening as Rogers tried to catch himself a woman. And, predictably, be rejected by all but the most desperate of females.

At first, the two newcomers sat in silence with Luke in their new cell. He watched them taking in the surroundings, cautiously refusing to make eye contact with him. Instead, their eyes darted over the poky cell, over the plastered walls, the thick bars of iron, the dirt-covered floor. Josh's eyes were wide and dark, and Rodriguez had his half closed in concentration. They steadfastly continued to make sense of the jail, not making any effort to communicate with Luke. Luke knew that this was a game they were all playing – they were checking out how territorial he was over the cell, and whether he was going to assert himself as the leader, the king of this domain. He would let them sweat a little longer before making a move.

In the uncomfortable silence, Josh and Rodriquez rubbed their ankles and wrists, where the cuffs had made painful indentations. Rogers was known for over-tightening the restraints, one of his perverse pleasures. As they shook their feet, letting their wrists drop limp, then flexing them upward and downward, the blood began to pump back into the desensitised areas again. The shuffling of feet as sensations returned to bound toes and ankles indicated that the men hadn't been bound for long before getting to the jail: certainly not as long as Luke had been. Every now and then, one of the newcomers would issue a sigh, a deep breath of relief or boredom. There would be silence then for a minute or two, another breathy sigh and a prolonged silence. Luke began to softly tap his finger against the wall, expressing a rhythm that was going round in his head.

'You been here long?' Rodriguez eventually offered a conversational opener.

Luke slowly turned to face the man, looking him squarely in the eye. 'No, not long. Couple of days, maybe. I lose track of time.'

'Ain't that the truth,' joined in Josh. 'There ain't no such thing as time in jail. No time doing time.'

The tension had eased slightly, the three men having made

initial contact. Luke didn't feel threatened by either of them; in fact, he felt at home with them, and the company was agreeable after spending so much time with Rogers and Williams. These men were much more of his ilk, and he could communicate with them in a way that an outlaw never could with a man of law.

Again, a silence. This time, though, Luke caught the men slyly eyeing him up, assessing him. If he caught them looking, they would quickly look away, pretending to be inordinately interested in a pattern of cracks on the wall, or a shape they were drawing in the dirt floor.

'You get any trouble from Rogers?' Luke initiated a sharing of their experience, and they took him up on it.

'Nothing too hard. He ain't as tough as he likes to think he is.' Josh's judgement was sound on Rogers, at any rate.

'He's a kid. No match for men like us,' Rodriguez boasted. He subconsciously traced the line of his scar as he spoke, as if reminded of a time when he had proved his own manhood. He had about him the weariness of a man who had been through hard times, and expected there to be many more ahead. He spoke only with a slight Mexican accent, and it seemed to Luke that he must have left his home many years ago to sound so nearly neutral. His eyes twinkled as if he was enjoying his own private party, and Luke's attention was drawn to the tight black curls of hair on his forearms and poking out of his undershirt.

'So what you here for?' Luke knew that his line seemed almost as feeble as one that Rogers might use on the girls in town, but it was necessary nevertheless. He wasn't sure, however, how he would accept the reply. Were they murderers, rapists? Or just men like him, trying to get by in a world where the rules weren't their own?

Rodriquez lifted his hands in the air and grinned widely at Luke. 'Guilty. We were rustling, just like the man said!'

'We'd just had our own cattle stolen. It's not as if we weren't desperate. And I sure as hell believe that Sonny Lawkins had something to do with ours going missing. It's hard enough for a black man in these parts, without hassle from the likes of him. I was just trying to keep my head down and my nose clean.'

His buddy slapped him on the back. 'Sure, Josh, you never

been trouble to anyone. And Lawkins probably did have something to do with those cattle going missing. He's sly. But he's got the money; we ain't. Money talks, you know what I'm saying?'

Their predicament hit home for Luke. He could understand how difficult it might be for them, particularly with a rich but tight-fisted and insecure neighbour. Looking at the two men, he didn't doubt that they worked hard and long to make a living. These days, it was a thin line between being on the right and the wrong side of the law. And those men that were the right side of the law were often there only because the law suited him. Like Matt Wilmott. The pain wasn't lessening, nor the anger.

'What can you do?' The Mexican lifted his hands in a gesture of despair. 'What can you do?'

'Hey, I didn't even steal the damned cattle and I'm still in here!' Luke flashed a grin at the two other men.

'I'm prepared to believe that. You got an honest look about you, brother,' Josh commented sincerely.

'I don't know about that,' Luke confessed, 'but I sure as hell weren't guilty, this time round!'

Luke felt an affinity with the two cowboys, even if they were cattle rustlers. He felt that if he told them about Matt Wilmott, about their relationship, about the gambling and drinking, the jealousy, the hatred and even the passion, maybe they would understand him. They could relate to the harsh realities of life out here; they'd also been on the receiving end of injustices. He felt it prudent not to share too much, though. After all, he had only known these men all of half an hour.

Instead, Luke acknowledged that they trusted his honesty. 'It's good to hear you say so. I'm a man of my word. The name's Luke Mitchell.' He offered his hand to Josh. 'I take it you are Josh —' and after shaking the black man's big hand '— and you are Rodriguez.'

Rodriguez chuckled. 'There ain't no dammed secrets in these places.'

'You got that right!' Luke laughed.

'You been finding it OK here?' Josh asked.

Luke looked over to him, and ran his eyes over the strong, tall physique. Looking more closely at him, Luke could see the muscular definition of his body, the man's large thighs bursting the seams of the frail pants he was wearing. Luke was pretty sure that the pants weren't his own, that they'd been picked up – maybe stolen – from someone else along the way. A much smaller man, obviously. Josh's features were clearly defined; he had a large flat nose, strong eyebrows, high cheekbones. There was a regal quality about him, a strength of purpose and presence that Luke found attractive. Sweat glistened on his shaven black head, slowly running over his forehead; he swept it out of his eyes by big, rough dark-skinned hands.

Josh's legs were spread apart and, as the large man relaxed back into the wall, Luke imagined what secret treasures nestled between the man's thighs. He had never seen a black cock, and imagined what it would look like: softly limp at the moment, but urged into rampant turgidity by Luke's wet tongue. He thought about licking the man's dark balls, up over a shaft to a pinky black tip, beads of juice glistening at the crown. It seemed all too long a time since Luke's cavortings with the young Indian brave at the lakeside, and he was getting a hunger for meat again.

Breaking off the lustful fantasy, Luke replied to Josh's question. 'Well, you seem to have pretty much sussed out Rogers. The sheriff's a fair man, but he takes his role pretty seriously.'

'You got family, Luke?' Rodriguez chewed a fingernail as he asked the question, his hands dirty and work-worn.

'No. No family.'

'Same here. It can be a lonely world out there, without family. Josh here, he's my only family. I left my folks back in Mexico a long time ago, and haven't looked back since.'

Josh and Rodriguez exchanged looks, and once more Rodriguez slapped Josh's broad back. They grinned warmly at each other, and Luke suspected that they were more than co-workers. He could imagine that their physical endeavours and exertions did not end when the sun set on their homestead, but adopted a more carnal nature in the dark of night. The thought excited him, and he imagined them coupling up, their differently coloured skin becoming a two-toned animal of passion.

'Yeah, you seem pretty close. Guess you've seen some times together.'

'I owe this man my life, and that's the truth.' Rodriguez held up his scarred arm for Luke to see. 'See that? Got that fending off a bandit attack, came right at me out west. A whole pack of them – the Clements brothers, they were called. Hadn't been for Josh here, those critters would have had more than a pound of Mexican flesh off me.'

'He tells a tall tale, my friend. Rumour is, he got that fighting off a whore he wouldn't pay!'

The two men laughed, and it was obviously a routine between them. On the one hand, Rodriguez was acknowledging he owed his life to his friend, and on the other Josh refused to let it dominate their partnership. The Mexican lay his hand on Josh's right flank, naturally, but Luke felt a *frisson* of sexual power between them. Josh lightly clapped Rodriguez's hand, and looked over at Luke. He knew that Luke had seen beyond it, that Luke recognised the nature of the relationship, and looked away.

'What say we try passing the time, fellas? We're not gonna be able to sit jawing with each other, the whole time we're locked up here.' Rodriguez reached inside his breast pocket, half torn away from his dirty blue shirt. He pulled out a battered pack of playing cards, the corners dog-eared and split. Taking the cards out of the pack, and gently palming the container to his side, Rodriguez professionally shuffled the cards in his hands.

'Poker?' he offered Luke and Josh.

Luke laughed. 'I ain't got no money, if you're looking to fleece me!'

'Nothing to lose then, my friend.' Rodriguez started dealing three hands.

They passed a good few hours playing game after game. The two newcomers were well practised, and had obviously played each other many times, seeming to know without looking when one was holding something back. Luke won a few games, but mostly lost – Rodriguez was a skilled player, with a sharp and severe poker face, revealing little about what hand he was playing. The only time his face broke to show his true emotions was when he joyfully announced he had the winning hand, and watched his opponents shrink in defeat.

The game was disrupted at noon as they were brought the

day's main meal, a heavy soup filled with vegetables and a little meat. It was brought to them by Rogers, who looked with disdain on the card game they were involved in. As they played, they continued the chatter, and Luke learnt more about the two men, how they lived and worked together, how Josh had indeed saved Rodriguez's life, but against three bandits rather than a whole gang. The day passed quickly; Luke relished the company after his solitary confinement over the past few days. Even Rogers annoyed him less.

As night came, Luke felt happy with his new 'guests'. Sheriff Williams made his customary check on the cell, wishing them all a good night, as he had done every night since Luke had been here. The only light came from the paraffin lamp at the sheriff's desk, and Luke knew that would be out around midnight. Two more bunks had been left in the cell for Josh and Rodriguez, who had settled down quickly after the day's activity. It had taken Luke a long while before he could settle on his first night here, but Rodriguez and Josh didn't seem to have the same problem at all.

Luke curled up on his wooden bed, and prepared for sleep. Another day without an escape bid, but it was possible that he might make allies with his new friends and attempt something, with their help. After all, they seemed to know more about the system than he did, would be more prepared to spot and seize an opportunity. And they were both strong and active men: something which could only be to their advantage, should a fight develop.

Nodding asleep, Luke became aware of movement in the corner of the room, where Josh and Rodriguez were lying. Luke ignored the shuffling sound, which he presumed was one or other of the men trying to get comfortable in the wooden beds they slept in. Closing his eyes, Luke pulled the moth-eaten blanket the sheriff had left him over his shoulders. Outside, the silence was broken only by the occasional howling of a wolf in the distance, or a drunken passer-by. He was only half-conscious of Sheriff Williams saying his night-time prayers, and then the whole jail being plunged into darkness as he turned out his office lamp.

Luke heard another shuffling. He thought little of it, but it was followed by another. The men must be stirring, he told himself. Perhaps their sleep wasn't as peaceful as he had first thought. He turned his head to the wall, and pulled the blanket up over his ears, shutting out the activity close to him.

It continued, however, and Luke heard a soft moan issue from muscular black Josh. Luke opened his eyes with a start. Lying there in the dark, with Rodriguez and Josh so close in the same cell, he became aware of movements between them, the soft creak of their separate beds. Luke didn't dare turn to see what was going on, but again in his mind he could see the erotic image of the two men rutting with each other. He lay back and rested his head on the wall. He lay still, becoming aware of every soft movement around him. There were only tiny movements from the corner where the men lay, occasional twitches, but he was aware of their heavy breathing. Their breathing was close together, not quite one pant after another, but a rhythm forming between them, echoed by the creaking of their beds.

Luke rolled over on to his back, his eyes fixed on the ceiling. He was becoming accustomed to the dark, beginning to make out shapes, contours; objects came into focus for him. The dark filter of the night obscured the details, but his imagination was colouring in the grey shadows to give him colour vision. He looked over at the two men, trying to make out what was happening.

The difference between the two forms was noticeable, so that at least Luke could make out who was who. Josh, his large form spread out so that both legs cascaded to the floor, was on the inside bunk, while the lither form of Rodriguez was next to the cell bars, his back to them. Josh was lying on his back, his head turned up towards the ceiling and, as far as Luke could make out, his eyes were closed. Rodriguez was bobbing his head up and down over Josh's groin, hands massaging the black man's trousered thighs. Josh's trousers were pushed down over his buttocks, revealing a monstrous black shadow covered by the Mexican's open mouth. Rodriguez slipped his hand further up the crotch, massaging what Luke presumed were Josh's exposed balls.

As Luke watched, he saw Josh's eyes open and flicker, a short grunt issuing from his half-closed mouth. He watched as Josh's hand snaked its way down the Mexican's body. The large black hand grabbed what Luke assumed must be Rodriguez's cock, also released and in the open. Mitchell watched as Josh began to slowly pull on the Mexican's meat. Rodriguez responded by burying his head in Josh's crotch, guzzling down on his large black cock. Josh's other hand moved down and rested on the dark hair of the Mexican sucking his knob, softly stroking his lover's head. He moaned again, and Luke also heard the intensified slurping of Rodriguez as he greedily filled his mouth with Josh's lustful erection.

Their secret lovemaking was also having an effect on Luke. He slid his right hand beneath the blanket, and felt the shape of his growing shaft, as the blood began to pump it to size. He was careful not to make too much movement, not wanting to disturb the intimacy between the lovers, content to see black and white flesh lusting together. Afraid that anything too sudden might break the lovers apart, Luke contented himself with fingering his semi-erect penis, stroking his balls, and running his fingers under his buttocks and over the insides of his thighs.

Luke watched as the two men continued with their clandestine intimacies, a voyeuristic thrill coursing through him. He could tell that the men had been lovers for a number of years, such was their skill in pleasuring each other in the dark of the night. They were hitting the mark for each other, hands and fingers skilled at teasing each other to orgasm and beyond. Their relationship was historic, learned, an intimacy borne out of extensive knowledge and experimentation. The way their bodies moved into each other, the encouraging murmurs, told Luke that he was witnessing a nightly ritual, that the men only rarely lay together without also enjoying each other sexually.

Their action was quickening. Josh was pumping on Rodriguez's turgid tool more strongly, the lighter rod of flesh filling his dark hand. The Mexican was firmly burying his head into Josh's dark crotch, swallowing the black sword of desire that reared up from between the outstretched thighs. Then, his head retreated away from the base, mouth still tight around its width, until just the purple crown was cradled between his lips.

Luke longed for those lips to be wrapped around his own manhood, and for him to be tasting and loving Josh's hard snake. He closed his eyes, rubbing his own hard cock, as he imagined lowering his lips over the engorged tip, planting a kiss on the black man's pulsating arrowhead, and taking it deeper into his warm, willing mouth. Luke could see his face buried between Josh's thighs, sucking on the hard thick shaft, looking up into Josh's dark eyes as he felt Rodriguez's moustache rubbing softly against his balls and cock. He imagined the three men sucking and wanking each other until all three exploded in unison, watching each other's juice fly.

Luke heard a low moan from Rodriguez. The Mexican lifted his head off Josh's hard member, and kissed his way up the broad black chest, nuzzling into Josh's thickset neck. His lips moved upwards, nibbling his lover's ear, finding his thick warm lips before settling. Josh kissed him back, full on the mouth, lips joined together. The men kissed long and hard, extending the action into a long open-mouthed kiss, tongues snaking into each other's mouths, flicking over teeth and lips, wrapping round each other. Luke gazed in awe at the two lovers, jerking each other's twitching pricks as they necked in the dark, sharing hot passionate kisses to set the night on fire.

Rodriguez broke away slightly. He put his mouth over Josh's right ear as Josh leant his head back against the wall in ecstasy. Luke heard him moan in a hoarse whisper, 'Josh, I want you.'

Josh grunted shortly in response.

'I want it. I want you to fuck me, feel your hard dick inside me.'

'It's risky, here,' Josh said weakly. 'The kid . . .'

Josh opened his eyes and looked over, his gaze followed by Rodriguez. Luke froze, his eyes shut, his body tense.

'Fuck the kid. Let's do it. I really want you to ride me. Fuck me, Josh: fuck me now.'

'Oh, yeah. I want to feel your tight hole over my shaft, your hairy man-hole taking my meat.'

Luke risked opening an eye, and saw the men moving positions. Now they were on the floor, Rodriguez on his hands and knees, his face buried against the bars of the cell. Josh crouched behind him, spitting on to his fingers. Luke watched slowly as Josh fingered around the Mexican's hairy cheeks, gently slapping them before letting his finger rest on the button-hole. Josh spat again, then Luke strained to see as Josh's black forefinger inched its way into Rodriguez's hole, sliding inside him, accompanied by a low sigh from Rodriguez. The finger came out, went in again, came out again, a gentle rhythm forming. When it was accompanied by a second finger, Luke felt his cock twitch, and rubbed it inside his trousers. Two fingers were slipping in and out of Rodrguez's horny rear, preparing the way for the erection Josh was slowly stroking.

Luke was hard and excited by what he was watching. He had never seen two men fucking before, and he was reminded of the intimacies he had shared with Matt Wilmott. Now, watching such two different lovers secretly sharing their lust, he was aware that he could disturb them at any moment. Too excited to stop himself, too nervous to join in or masturbate openly, Luke continued to rub himself through his pants, feeling the sticky wet patch under his fingers spread and follow the line of his erect penis.

Josh shuffled over to rest his throbbing manhood against Rodriguez's buttocks, slapping them occasionally with his hard shaft. Rodriguez grabbed the bars with his hands, parting his legs for Josh's love gift.

'You want it, lover?' Josh hissed in the dark. 'You want to feel old Josh taking you and making your sweet ass all mine?'

'Oh, yes,' Rodriguez begged. 'Bring me home!'

'Mm, I like to hear you call for your daddy . . .' Josh spat loudly into his hand, then rubbed the spittle all over his shaft, before spitting again and buttering Rodriguez's open ass with it. Luke could see the head of Josh's spear shining with pre-come, gently nudging the crack of Rodriguez's backside. The Mexican breathed in hard, preparing himself for the assault on his love tunnel. Slowly, Josh forced his tip between the warm mountains of flesh, throwing back his head in victory. The two men stayed like that for a while, Rodriguez relaxing his sphincter muscles around the hot crown inside him. Then another inch was slipped in, before Josh slowly pulled back, then delivered another inch of his fleshy pole inside Rodriguez.

'Oh, yes, you feel so good, so hard and ready.'

'C'mon, tighten your ass against me. Get ready for the whole damn thing.'

'Yeah, bury your balls inside me.'

There was a stirring over by the sheriff's desk, a quick movement, which stopped the two men. Josh was bolt upright, his cock still inside Rodriguez, who gripped the cell bars in fear. Luke looked over, and saw that someone had walked past, tapping the door slightly. He presumed it would be Rogers returning from a drunken night out, and relaxed as the two horny lovers quickened their movement.

'C'mon, let's do it, man. Fuck my hole.'

Josh grabbed his partner's shoulders, and started bucking his hips, forcing himself deeper inside the willing arsehole. Fast deliberate thrusts made Rodriguez whimper with delight, as Luke heard Josh's heavy balls slapping against the sweating cheeks. The movements were deliberate and dominating, ramming inches of hot black meat into the tight lubricated channel. Both men were breathing heavily now, the moment of their union close upon them.

Luke frantically rubbed himself, and Rodriguez took one hand off the bars to deliver long fast strokes on his own tool. He thrust his head forward and upward, resting against the iron bars, clenching them with his left hand as Josh started to buck wildly, pulling his partner back on to his cock.

'Yes, Josh, I'm gonna start shooting!

'I'm gonna fist off on your ass! I'm ready to go!'

Josh pulled out of Rodriguez deliberately, and jerked frenetically on his cock, pulling himself off over his partner's cheeks. Rodriguez did the same with his own length, as Luke quickened his own movements while watching them. Suddenly Josh looked round, and caught Luke watching him. He grinned broadly as he finally jacked himself off in order to jettison his load over Rodriguez.

'Yeahhhhhhhhhhh!'

The sound of his voice broke the silence, causing Rodriguez

to shudder and orgasm, his jism spurting between the cell bars, covering a few of them with his hot sticky come. Josh continued to shoot milky white jets over Rodriguez's backside as Luke felt his own orgasm approaching. Unable to release himself in time, he allowed his body to shake with the throes of pleasure, and his cock to start pumping his thick liquid into his pants, feeling the warm spunk line his trousers. The restraint of the material made his orgasm more intense, and he shuddered with each exciting quake.

'Hey, boys, everything OK out there? Thought I heard one of you cussing in your sleep.' The sheriff's bark broke the afterglow.

'Oh, everything's fine back here, Sheriff. Don't you worry about nothin'. Everything's just fine!' boomed back Josh, chuckling as he wiped his cock on Rodriguez's skin. 'It just takes a while for us to settle down somewhere new. But we's settled now.'

Luke grinned in agreement in the dark, his own warm juice cooling and caking into his groin. Sure, he thought, everything was just fine back here. Just fine!

Seven

Brett watched two men taken from a wagon as he arrived in Independence. With them was a gaunt man who barked orders at the shackled couple, one black and one who looked as if he might be Mexican. McKinley took an instant dislike to the sheriff's deputy as he led them inside the ramshackle jailhouse. Brett wondered what caused such losers to become lawmen, and remembered the empty boasting of his brothers, who had reckoned on becoming sheriffs and judges. The thought was ridiculous now, and he wondered what was happening back at St Joseph, how his parents were coping with their surly sons.

Having left Taylor, he had wandered around Leavenworth before making the decision to come here to Independence. He had seen Taylor in town, a while later, and they had exchanged glances, Taylor rubbing his crotch and grinning at Brett from across the street. Brett had blushed momentarily, then shouted over to the soldier, 'How's the missus?' It had then been Taylor's turn to redden, before replying that she was in good hands. They had parted again, waving each other on to the rest of their lives.

Brett stopped and watched a trickster on the street corner down from the jailhouse. The man was roughly dressed, elderly, with grey hair that was caked with sweat and grease to his head. The man flashed a toothy grin at a couple of children passing by, before showing them a coin, which disappeared underneath a cup. He added two more cups to his makeshift stage, an upturned crate with a red silk scarf over the top. Challenging the children to watch carefully where the coin was, he moved the three upturned cups round and about, swapping his hands over to confuse the enraptured youngsters.

'Now,' he said looking earnestly at them, 'if you can pick out the magic coin, why then, I'll let you have it!'

First one, then another pointed to the cups on the table. The third beamed triumphantly, assured of the fabled magic coin. Confidently, he pointed to the third and final cup, in the middle of the other two beakers.

'You sure, now?' the trickster checked.

'Of course,' the kid said confidently. 'I been watching!'

When the final cup was turned over, to reveal nothing underneath, it was met with a gasp of disbelief from the assembled watchers. The old man then called the last child over, who was still staring at the empty space which he was sure had contained the magic coin.

'Now what have we here?' said the old man, his gnarled and bony right hand reaching behind the youngster's ear. Brett watched the kid's face break into an excited look of awe as the magician produced his coin.

'Wow,' he said, and then the inevitable, 'How'd you do that?'

'Ah,' came the reply, 'it's magic!'

Brett had lost count of the number of times he had seen similar tricks performed, and had come to the conclusion that it must indeed be magic, for he could not fathom how such things happened. He'd figured that it would be a good thing if there was magic in the world, although he was more likely to depend on his own endeavour rather than some mysterious spirit for his good fortune. In his heart, he knew that the magic was something to do with the old man's hands, although for the life of him he couldn't figure it out. The man caught him watching and grinned, the gaps in his teeth showing. Brett saluted him, and walked on.

Independence was the real start of the Oregon–Santa Fe trail, which so many were now taking to the west. It wasn't entirely secure, and it would certainly be a number of months before making the gold hills of the west, but it was a well-understood route. There were traders and settlements along the way, including the famous Dodge City, although many dangers also.

Independence was a buzzing town and, as at Fort Leavenworth, Brett felt the tremors of excitement at being in a large town. There was something different about Independence, though; even the name appealed to Brett. It reminded him of his mission, his life's desire. He knew only a little of the place's history, things he had picked up since arriving here. People were often pleased to talk about their home, and his short questions had been met with interest, and long detailed explanations, only some of which he could remember.

Founded in 1827, and only incorporated as recently as 1849, it had been popular with travellers to the west since 1833. It was close to the first US outpost in the Louisiana territory, Fort Osage, which had been built in 1808. Not too long ago, in 1831, a religious man called Joseph Smith had set up a colony at Independence of a religion still new and strange to Brett, called Mormonism. The influence of their strict rules still had an impact on the town, and Brett was aware of their reverence for law and order, even for fools such as the sheriff's deputy that he had seen with the two prisoners.

The folks here had talked about how they had laboured to build up the town, sweating under the hot sun. The timber dwellings and dirt tracks hadn't just come from nowhere; many men had sweated and toiled to bring the town into existence. Each of them had believed in the dream of Independence, had invested the word with their own meaning. They referred to it as the place of dreams, where men became who they really were. It was even said that the town had been named after the spirit of independence, shown so strongly by President Andrew Jackson himself.

Brett savoured the atmosphere of the place, thinking of where to go and what to do next. He was feeling thirsty now, and also wanted to become a little groggy, woozy with alcohol. The events of the past few days had been exciting and new, and he wanted to feel relaxed. Just a drink or two at a bar, to wind him down, was all he wanted. He continued to walk along the main street, past the many stores and hardware shops, looking for somewhere suitable to sit and drink for a while. Knowing that Independence was such a busy town, he was pretty sure it wouldn't be long before he came across somewhere suitable.

He was proved right when he came across a saloon just down from the jail, a small cosy snug. The excited and lively chatter inside appealed to Brett and he walked in, heading for the bar. It was busy with talk of hunters and trappers, exchanging stories of hunting expeditions. Many of the men seemed to have drifted in from – or were on their way to – Westpoint. They spoke about the pelts that they had got, how many they had and how much they could sell them for. Listening to the boasting in the air, Brett was pretty sure much of the talk was idle chatter, unrealistic or unfulfilled hopes. There was talk also of settlements such as Bent's Fort, Fort Laramie, South Park, and many other places where the trappers and hunters were hoping to make a profit from selling the beaver skins and assorted pelts.

Brett asked for a beer, which he was politely served by a tender in his forties. Spying a table in a corner, Brett went over with his drink and sat down, quietly mulling over the past few days, his family, Scott and Taylor. So much had happened since he left home, and he was more confident than ever that he had done the right thing. As the alcohol began to have its desired effect, Brett sat back in his chair and surveyed the bar room.

There were about twenty people drinking in there, a large table of trappers, whose conversation he had overheard on his entry, to his right by the door. A couple of them now looked to be greenhorns, inexperienced trappers who had come west in the hope of learning a trade. Elsewhere in the bar were blacksmiths, saddlemakers, trackers, traders: all the skills of Independence in one room. To his left, he heard a man who he presumed to be the town doctor promising a worried man to look in on a child who might be developing measles.

For the young and infirm, such simple infections often proved to be fatal. Every parent worried on the first sign of a red rash, even though as often as not it might prove to be heat rash. Brett pitied the doctor, never quite able to escape his solemn oath and ignore the pleas of the sick. Brett knew too that the stresses of medicinal work often led physicians to drink more than was good for them, and for themselves to become infirm patients.

Here and there in the bar were also native Indians, many dressed in the usual westerner apparel, some in their own colourful traditional hides and clothes. Wary of them, but also intrigued, Brett sat and listened to their language.

There were few women in the bar, mostly serving drinks. No lady would be seen in the establishment, although occasionally an irate wife would break in and demand the return of a slovenly, drunken husband. Desperate to appease her, and prove he ruled the house, he would bawl her out and demand she returned home, before sheepishly making an excuse to leave and go home. Brett smiled at such domestics; that wasn't a situation he was ever planning on getting involved in. No woman would be tying him to her apron strings.

One of the women, a vivacious red-haired Irish girl, drew Brett's attention. She had the gift of a soft lilting Irish accent, and couldn't have been away from her homeland many years, such was the distinctiveness of her speech. She was talking about 'the grand crack', and playfully teasing her customers. She moved with grace and vibrancy, and Brett could see many of the men paying her a lot of attention. More than once, too, he had seen her fiery spirit as she slapped the face of a man who would overstep the mark, taking his attentions too far. Invariably, this would be followed by a chorus of cheers and applause from the other men, as if it were a game which was played out nightly. Brett wondered too if her charms were attractive to other women, or whether she was attracted only to the opposite sex.

She came over to Brett and cheerfully greeted him. 'Hello, young fella! Can I be getting you anything more?'

Brett grinned 'Ah, go on, then, as you offered so nicely. I'll have myself another.'

'There's a lad, and such a smile on him, too! If I wasn't taken, myself, I'd be after looking to get myself a husband now.'

'You're married?' It was small talk, although Brett was genuinely interested in who the young woman was partnered to.

'If you can call it that!' She cocked her head over to a man in his early thirties in the corner, laughing and joking with some friends. The man she indicated was also Irish, his rich accent rising above the chatter of the other men, punctuated by howls of laughter. 'That's my man Colm, there, the good-for-nothing! Sits, drinks, gambles: like most of them in here. You've got a look of something different about yourself. If I were ten years younger, Siobhan here would be chasing after you, for sure!'

'Colm is your husband? Seems a reasonable enough fella. I don't know a man who doesn't drink or gamble — a man has to have something to occupy him, every once in a while. Here's to Colm and Siobhan,' he said raising the dregs of beer in his glass and drinking them down with relish. 'I'll be having that other beer now, Siobhan.'

'It's coming right up. And what name would you be going under, now, I wonder? I wouldn't be surprised if there was some Irish in you, with your dark looks. A bit of the gypsy in you, perhaps?'

Brett was stumped, for he wasn't entirely sure of his own ancestry, but certainly he had the look of a Romany about him, although he had never acknowledged it until now. 'Happen I could be, now you mention it, Siobhan. For all I know, we could be related.'

Siobhan laughed, a short and lively sound that came from a full heart. 'Wouldn't that be the crack!' she giggled, and went off to the bar to get Brett's drink.

While she was away, Brett took the chance to look again at Colm. He could see why she would have been taken with him. He had a distinctive Irish charm about him, and a stout heavy frame. His glance danced out across the room, and Brett could imagine him ten years younger, charming the girls he met, and wooing the young Siobhan. He understood then that it was Colm who had wanted to come to America, and that Siobhan would happily have followed her man to the ends of the earth. He could understand also the tall promises Colm would have made to entice her over, how they would make their fortune in the land of promise. And also how Siobhan saw those promises disappear as quickly as the cents and dimes into booze and cards.

Yet, he was sure, Siobhan still loved Colm. Even as she was fetching his beer, Brett caught the two looking over and exchanging glances. Colm grinned and playfully blew a kiss over to his beloved, which Siobhan ignored. She teased him, turning her back, but then turning her head over her shoulder, she returned his kiss. Colm mimed being shot in the chest, his heart pierced. Brett wondered what Colm was like in his lovemaking: whether he was fierce, powerful, or tender and loving, attentive to his wife. Brett believed the lustful Colm could be both, but also wondered if more often than not, he was boozy, clumsy and incapable. He imagined Colm snoring next to the frustrated Siobhan.

'There you go, love.' Siobhan set the drink down before Brett, and gave him a bright wink. 'Slàinte' she added, wishing him well.

Brett took a swig of his beer and then laid the tankard down. It was sharp, bitter, and refreshed his palate. He gulped the dark liquid down, savouring its flavour. Siobhan watched him as he drank, smiling.

'Good?' she enquired.

'Mighty fine indeed! Just the thing for a young man's thirst.'

'Oh, now, a young man must be thirsting for something more than a drink, I believe. What's your name, young fella?'

'Brett. Brett McKinley,' he said, with a reluctance that surprised him. He almost felt as if he wanted to be someone different: another man, with another name.

'And do you have a young lady? I'm guessing not – no wedding band, and you have the look of a man alone,' deduced the Irish woman.

'Well, you've guessed correctly,' Brett confessed.

'I guess you're on the road West, looking to settle down there. Colm promised me a similar thing, some years ago.' She looked blankly at nowhere in particular, which was just the place she was thinking of.

Through the door came the same thin man Brett had seen earlier near the jailhouse. He nodded at several of the men, giving some of them a cursory 'morning', as he strode to the bar. The greeting was returned by a few of the men, a low muttering being the most common reply.

Ignoring his subdued welcome, Rogers strode to the bar,

thirsty and pent-up. Although the bar wasn't all that busy, there didn't seem to be anyone there to serve him immediately. As a man of law in the town, he clearly wanted respect, and this was just one more occasion on which he saw himself being undermined.

'Bar!' he barked to everyone and no one in particular.

The talk in the bar continued as Rogers stood waiting for his drink. Siobhan sat herself down next to Brett for a while. 'Are you staying in town long, Mr McKinley?'

'Don't suppose so,' he replied. 'I'll be looking to make a move pretty soon, try and get west before the winter sets in.'

'The weather is no man's friend, that's for sure,' Siobhan commented sagely. 'If you're serious about the trip, maybe you should be talking to Colm awhile. He's not much good himself, bless him, but some of the folks he's with know a good deal about the trail. They might be offering some advice to a friend of Siobhan's.'

Brett knew that, at some stage, he would take her up on the offer. Colm seemed to have the gift of drawing around him men who had experienced life, who had simple wisdom and knowledge. Such tips would be useful to Brett; the terrain west was so alien to him.

'Drink!' Rogers riled again from the bar, this time turning around to find a focus for his demand.

The men in the bar turned briefly to look at him, aware that this was a daily ritual for the deputy who thought so highly of himself. More highly, certainly, than any other Independence townsfolk would.

At Brett's table, Siobhan ignored the bleating Rogers. She'd heard his tirades many times before. When drunk, he was ridiculous, and Siobhan had physically thrown him out into the streets after closing time on more occasions than she could remember. Colm had never got on with the deputy, but knew the value of keeping the right side of him, and had warned her not to offend him too greatly. Colm had also been aware of the leering glances Rogers gave his wife, and had managed so far to stop himself brawling with him. There was something about

Rogers which rubbed people up the wrong way. No one in the town could claim to be his close friend.

'There's a couple of them fellas have known people gone out west, and many of them know the trail a fair way out there. I'll introduce you to our Colm – though he's a bit far gone to be doing anything worthwhile, just at the moment!' She flashed a treacherous grin at Brett, aware that she was being disloyal to her beloved.

It happened so quickly, Brett wasn't quite sure of what was going on. Rogers, becoming increasingly irate at the bar and making louder and louder demands, had spied Siobhan talking to him, and made an assault on the table.

'So you're lounging with the greenhorns rather than serving your customers now, Siobhan? You useless bitch!'

'I won't have you talking to me like that, Rogers. I don't care who you are. Showing a little politeness to strangers in town is part of my job. It's called doing good business.'

'Well, while you've been lavishing your "politeness" on this one,' Rogers sneered, 'I'm dying of thirst over by the bar.'

'I can't see you dying of thirst now, deputy. I'm sure there's more than enough beer still swilling around in your system from last night's drinking.' Siobhan's tone was light and dismissive, seeking to avoid a confrontation, but her words had the opposite effect on the roused Rogers.

'I won't have you talking to me like that – not in front of your customers. Not in front of anyone! You should be showing me some respect, woman. You'll need a man like me around, with your useless lackey of a husband!'

'Colm's more of a man that you'll ever be, Rogers. There's more of a man in his little finger than all your sorry self.'

It was beginning to turn nasty, and heads were turning from the other tables. Colm had caught the mood of what was going on, and indicated for Siobhan to calm things down. Brett stood up slowly, careful not to inflame the situation further.

'Siobhan, erm, Mr Rogers, we can keep things easy here, right?'

'What business is it of yours, stranger?'

'I'm just saying, you'll get your drink, there's no argument here.'

Rogers looked at Brett and McKinley knew he was jealous of the attention Siobhan had been paying him. Even though it had just been friendly bartalk, he knew that Rogers probably only got the time of day from Siobhan normally.

'I suppose you'll be between her thighs, too, like the other strangers she rides in town!'

He had gone too far, and the room went quiet. Colm covered his face in his hands, and a loud slap stung the air, as Siobhan's hand caught Rogers's pocked face. Never before had she struck with such force, and never before had she hit the sheriff's deputy. There was no cheering or applause at this slap, though. There was nothing good-natured about the exchange.

At the same time as Colm stood up on the other side of the room, Brett placed himself between the Irish tigress and the red-faced Rogers. Brett stood facing Rogers, seeing the white imprint of Siobhan's force against the flushed red of the deputy's embarrassment and rage.

'What say I get you that drink, deputy? A treat from a stranger.' Brett's voice was light in tone, but commanding in nature. He stood taller than the deputy, and was obviously more muscular. He looked powerful in comparison to the smaller man, and anyone who wasn't as enraged as Rogers would have seen the opportunity to end the stand-off.

'I won't be accepting a drink from a stranger, and I'll thank you to keep out of my business.'

'I'm trying not to make it my business, but you're not making that easy for me . . .'

Without warning, Rogers attempted a blow at Brett, who dodged it and put his arms up to defend himself. From another table, Rogers picked up a bottle, and came towards McKinley. The bar was in uproar: the men shouted for a fight, secretly hoping that Rogers would get what was coming to him. Colm rushed over to take Siobhan away from the fight, but she was incensed at the deputy's actions.

'Rogers, you ass! Leave the boy alone!'

Colm held her back from the deputy, away from the raised bottle aimed at Brett.

His forearm broke the blow as Rogers struck with the bottle, but the glass smashed against his flesh, and Brett felt the ripping of his skin. Blood oozed out of the wound, a red sticky mess that trailed down Brett's arm. He lunged at Rogers, grabbing the arm with the broken half-bottle and forcing him to the ground. They struggled as Brett tried to disarm the senseless deputy. Twice he slammed the man's arm against the floor, the third time managing to loosen his grip on the dangerous weapon.

The circle of figures around them were shouting things incomprehensible to Brett, whose mind was focused on the sharp, jagged edges of the bottle, uncomfortably close to his face as he grappled with Rogers. He was conscious of his physical superiority, but also of the weakness he was beginning to feel from the wound, and the red river along his arm. With a mighty heave, he brought his knee into his opponent's chest, winding him enough to force the bottle out of his grasp, and to kick it away from them.

Now it was just man against man. Brett landed a hard blow against the deputy's chest.

As Rogers groaned, Brett aimed another blow to the man's right cheek, landing with a crash. Using his greater strength, Brett was able to straddle Rogers's chest, sitting on him and pinning him down. A cheer went round as Brett grinned down at his defeated foe. Rogers looked up at him, fear in his eyes as he wondered if Brett would decide that he wanted to show him a lesson.

'What's going on here?' Sheriff Williams broke the atmosphere with his demand, and the crowd parted to allow the man in to see what was happening.

'Rogers? What the hell . . .?' It was unusual for the sheriff to swear, but the sight of his deputy involved in a bar-room brawl was uncomfortable viewing for him. It wasn't the first time, but the injury – just judging by the amount of blood – was far more serious than similar previous knockabouts.

'Well?' the lawman enquired, looking towards Siobhan, clearly expecting a truthful account of what had just passed.

Siobhan knelt down by Brett, looking at the cut to his forearm.

Stealing Colm's neckerchief, she wiped away the blood to see the extent of the wound. Dr Mason, who Brett had previously heard promising to look after the child with suspected measles, came over to check the wound more thoroughly.

'It's deep, but not too serious,' Mason pronounced. 'The lad will live,' he added, using the neckerchief to produce a makeshift tourniquet and stem the flow of blood.

'Your deputy,' Siobhan said, casting a disapproving stare at the groaning Rogers, 'took it upon himself to slander my good name, and then attack one of my customers with a bottle.'

'Is this true, Rogers?' Williams accused his aide, receiving nothing more of an answer than a guilty puppy-dog expression. 'Get him out of here,' Williams ordered, and a couple of men lifted Rogers to his feet.

'But my drink . . .!' he started, before realising that he might be getting off lightly as it was.

'Now, son, you'd best get yourself cleaned up. You can take him to my personal quarters. At least I might be able to convince him that not all hospitality in Independence is as sour as my deputy's. Siobhan, will you go with him and get that wound cleaned up? Boy looks like he might benefit from a stiff drink himself, too. I'm paying.'

'Right you are, sheriff,' Siobhan said, leading Brett out of the door. Brett was now feeling weak from the wound, and allowed his new friend to lead him away. He was accompanied by slaps on the back and raucous applause as the men in the bar congratulated him for giving Rogers 'what he had coming to him'. Brett was too woozy to enjoy the attention given him, or appreciate the adoration heaped upon him.

The sheriff remained in the bar, talking and listening as he built up a picture for himself of what had just occurred. He knew that he wouldn't be charging Rogers, but it was all good ammunition for him in reprimanding the sly deputy. Besides, he would have mileage out of it – for the next few weeks, Rogers would be on his best behaviour. All those unsavoury jobs – the cleaning, the washing, the slopping out, would be undertaken without comment. Williams spent time making amends with the bar owner, a swarthy man named Temple, although Temple and he went back years. The sheriff was aware that it was empty talk – Rogers would be back in the bar, and would probably be causing someone else some trouble soon enough.

'I guess that's the show over, folks. You can get back to your drinks now, and I'm sorry my deputy has such a habit of getting a bad name for my office! I'll be dealing with the matter myself.' It was taken for granted that this was code for Rogers being given nothing more than a dressing down. Not that anyone cared – the real punishment would be the number of times Rogers was reminded of being knocked down by the kid. The thought of that warmed the chatter and smiles of the men as they ordered more drink from the bar. Whatever else might happen, a brawl was always good business for the bar!

The sheriff dropped in on his quarters before returning to the jail, not wanting to leave his three inmates unsupervised for too long. He had only happened to pop out when he had heard the commotion in the bar and gone over to investigate. He hadn't meant to spend more than a few minutes collecting supplies, and was conscious of leaving Luke with the two new prisoners, although they seemed to be getting on all right. His quarters, opposite the jail so he was never too far away, were clean and simple, a modest man's dwelling.

Siobhan was still fussing as Williams entered his spare room. The young stranger was sprawled shirtless over the mattress, and Williams was struck by his hairy and muscular physique. Siobhan was finishing cleaning the wound, a savage rip: although, now the blood was cleared, the wound wasn't so frightening. Siobhan looked up at the sheriff as he entered, and Williams thought he detected a slight blush as her hand drew back from the young man's chest. She had been cleaning his torso, too, and the wet hair on his front was matted with water, stroked downwards by the wetness. The sheriff knew that Siobhan was faithful to Colm, though he never could understand why. But, surely, this half-naked man would have tempted any woman!

'I was just checking things are fine. I'll be back late tonight or early tomorrow morning. Will you see the boy is fed, and gets some rest, Siobhan? I can trust you to shut the door and see to things?'

'Of course you can, sheriff. I was just listening to the young man sing. He sure has a voice on him.'

The sheriff shook Brett by his good hand, introducing himself: 'The name's Williams, I'm sheriff round here. I'm sorry you met my deputy before you met me.'

Brett smiled at the sheriff. He would much rather have met the sheriff first, too. Although much older, the man had a good body for his age, not too weighty, and the silver in his hair highlighted a handsome and well-worn face. The grey eyes were bright and sharp.

'I'm Brett McKinley of St Joseph. I appreciate what you're doing for me, sheriff. You're a good man.'

'I'll be looking in, later. Rest up now, young McKinley.' The sheriff let go of Brett's hand and winked at him. 'You'll be safe with Siobhan, here. And I hope she's gonna be safe enough, with a young buck like you!'

'Oh, she's safe enough with me, sheriff. You never said a truer word!' Neither had Brett himself uttered a truer word!

The sheriff left, and Siobhan finished attending to him. She lent him an old shirt of Colm's, and Brett could smell the man's musky scent faintly on the linen as she dressed him. After feeding him and making sure he had plenty of fresh water by his bedside, Siobhan left Brett to his own devices. The fight had unnerved him slightly; he suddenly realised how vulnerable a stranger in a town the size of Independence could be. He'd done nothing wrong, but he had been the man Rogers attacked. Siobhan had told him how pitiful the man was, but it didn't make Brett feel any better. The wound stung, but was now well wrapped up. Once the bleeding had been stemmed, he began to live with the discomfort. It was his right forearm, an automatic defence, but it made most other things difficult to do. It flashed through his mind that he could practise masturbating left-handed. He was curious, but left the idea. Just for the moment, anyhow.

The sheriff returned late in the night with a bottle of bourbon for the two to share. He knocked on Brett's door, and entered with a couple of glasses for them both. He offered a glass to the invalid, and Brett savoured the taste as the dark gold nectar slipped down his throat.

'Looks like you did me a favour there tonight. Rogers came creeping in late to offer taking over my early morning shift, so I get to go home early! Varmit ain't done that sort of stuff for weeks.' He chinked his glass against that of the new hero of Independence.

'Glad it was all worthwhile,' joked Brett.

'How's the wound?'

'Oh, it got fixed up pretty good, though I'll be a bit cack-handed for a while.'

'Oh, yeah? Anything you need doing?'

There was a trace of suggestion in the sheriff's last remark, and Brett wasn't sure how to follow it up. 'Oh, well, there's some things a man's got to do for himself, I reckon!' He grinned at Williams.

'That so? I've always thought there's not much point in a man doing something himself when he can get someone else to do it for him.' The sheriff sipped more of his bourbon, not looking at Brett.

'I've gotten used to scratching my own itches.'

The sheriff laughed slightly, getting up from his chair next to the bed and stretching himself. 'Now, I've found there's some itches a man just can't reach by himself. And I think of myself as a versatile man, Brett, I sure do! I can reach most places to sort myself out.'

'Yeah, well, so can a dog, sheriff. I've seen how versatile they can be!'

The two men laughed together, understanding what Brett was talking about. Their conversation had turned and, despite the innocence of its subject matter, both men were aware of the innuendo and sexual tension arising.

'I reckon if a man could look after himself, the way a dog does with his tongue,' continued Brett, 'he'd be a real happy man.'

The sheriff paused slightly before responding, his tone conspiratorial. 'Well, there's some folks have that privilege. Maybe not in St Joseph, but out here you gotta take good care of yourself.'

Brett looked at the older man, his toned physique. The sheriff looked like he could take care of himself, all right, and had done for years. Now Brett wanted him to take care of him, too. To take care of the growing erection he was stroking underneath the blanket. He could feel the blood coursing through him, away from his wound and down towards his groin.

'I'm getting pretty used to being taken care of here. First Siobhan; now you. Of course, there's some things you can't expect a married woman to take care of. Things only a man can be doing.'

'Siobhan's unlucky not to be married to a man like you. A man who could do things for her. Now, it's all well for her. She's got a husband, she answers to him. Me, I'm a lawman. I take an oath to serve and protect. So it's my duty to serve a good law-abiding citizen like you.'

Brett looked again at the sheriff, who was now standing over the bed. As Brett slowly rubbed his growing erection, he watched the sheriff drop his hands to his hips, watched too the lump that was forming in his crotch. His eyes followed the squareness of his hips, the muscled buttocks, the strong thighs. Resting at the top of them Brett spied a pair of handcuffs and grinned up at the sheriff. 'You get to use them things? Or are they just business?'

'Been known to,' grinned the sheriff, 'but I reckon I don't need 'em on someone with a wound like yours.'

'I wasn't thinking of them on me. I was wondering what a sheriff looks like cuffed up, and how willing to serve his law-abiding citizens he'd be, then.'

'Now, there's a thought. And seeing you in that bar, I reckon I can trust you, too.'

'Believe it.' Brett looked straight at the sheriff, making it clear that there was an agreement, a contract between them. In return for the sheriff's service, Brett would be responsible for him. Both of them felt the power of the situation, the sheriff relinquishing his authority to this young stranger. The sheriff unhooked the cuffs from the belt and offered them to Brett, who sat up in the bed.

'Get on your back. On the bed.'

Brett moved off to allow room for the sheriff, who lay himself prostrate on the mattress. Brett grinned down on him as he drew the man's hands together, cuffing one to the other, raising them above his head, and then attaching them to the bedstead. Williams lay at Brett's mercy.

Brett straddled the man's face, rubbing his groin against the lawman. He slowly ground his man mountain against the moaning mouth, teasing him with his growing inches. 'Lick it. Get your tongue out and lick me.'

He felt the tongue warm on the front of his underpants, darting back and forth across the shaft. He moaned with pleasure as Williams worked his way up and down the imprisoned flesh. With his left arm, he grabbed the back of the older man's head, forcing him deeper into his crotch. He held the man's head there, humping the servicing tongue. Looking down, he saw the sheriff rolling his eyes in ecstasy. The man wasn't even tasting his cock, yet he was obviously enjoying it. It must have been the first time he had been dominated like this, had someone else controlling him. For a man who normally controlled, the pleasure was evident.

Brett pulled away from the sheriff. 'I want to see you take care of yourself. I want to see you licking your own, getting your tongue round your own meat. Reckon you can do that for me?'

The sheriff grinned up at Brett. 'I been practising for ya. I told you we could take care of ourselves in these parts.'

Brett pulled the sheriff's underpants off, to unleash a stiff, thin and long monster. He stroked the shaft, bringing it to full life; the sheriff struggled slightly against the cuffs. Brett released the man from the brass railings of the bed, but kept the man's hands cuffed as he sat back in a chair at the end of the bed. He watched the sheriff, still agile for his maturity, sit himself up, legs crossed, and his hard-on standing tall between his legs.

'Suck that cock. Get your head down on yourself,' he ordered. The role of master, new to Brett, nevertheless fitted him like a glove.

The sheriff lowered his head towards his groin, his face still a few inches from the thin tip of his cock. Beads of juice rested on the head, and he flicked out his tongue. Flesh met flesh; his own juice caught on the tongue. Positioning himself closer, more crouched, Williams could get his tongue to the tip of the glans, the tongue inside his cock-hole, to savour his own excitement.

Brett stroked himself lazily as he watched Williams licking and tonguing his own cock. It turned Brett on to watch a man do this to himself, and he was fascinated with the skilful agility with which the man could pleasure himself. Straining a little more, the sheriff managed to get the tip of his cock in his mouth, looking over to Brett for approval. Brett used his lazy left hand to pull on his dick as he watched the self-sucking, envious of such ability.

'Go on, suck it. Taste your cock.'

Urged on by Brett's crude instruction, Sheriff Williams continued to take his glans between his lips, his tongue snaking over the wet tip. Noisily, he sucked himself in front of the rapt Brett, attempting to take his pole deeper and deeper into his mouth. He looked over at Brett again when he knew he had taken as much of himself as he could into his throat, and started concentrating on sucking himself to orgasm.

As the sheriff's movements became more urgent, so did Brett's. He used his left hand so that it felt like someone else, a sensation new to him. The sight of the sheriff, handcuffed and sucking himself, was exciting for Brett to watch – both incidents were novel to him. Brett watched as the sheriff's moves became more frantic and deliberate. He watched as the sheriff's long erection slipped in and out of his mouth, the glistening tip covered in spit and pre-come. He heard the sheriff moaning and gobbling as he enjoyed his own taste.

They looked at each other as Williams groaned aloud and started pumping his cock deeper into his mouth. The first jet of fluid shot straight into his open mouth, the next few alternating between his mouth and the cheeks of his face.

Brett jumped over and placed his own cock at the tip of the man's lips. 'Finish me off. I'm so close,' he ordered.

The sheriff willingly obliged. Looking up at Brett with his face still stained with splashes of his own juice, the sheriff finished what Brett had started. He was experienced, and hungry for the taste of another man's meat. His tongue eagerly flicked over

Brett's hard length. Having watched him bring himself off, Brett was now ready for his own sweet release.

It wasn't long in coming. The sheriff had built up a pace, working on himself and, with a loud moan, Brett allowed that pace to overtake him. One final tonguing, stretching right up from his tight balls, brought Brett over the edge, and he shuddered with delight. His body shook with the throes of a perfect orgasm. Hot white fluid rushed out of his knob and into the sheriff's mouth, who swallowed it in delight. The spurts continued until the sheriff was suckling on Brett's softening penis.

Brett slowly withdrew and bent down to take some of their mixed juice on his tongue. He lapped at the sheriff's face as the older man cooed with satisfaction. Then he lay back on the bed and let the sheriff rest against him, careful to keep his wounded arm safe. Brett felt the exertions of the day take their toll on him, and was soon falling asleep in the comfort of the warm bed.

It was only later that he became aware of the sheriff shaking him, red in the face with laughter. Williams was pushing at Brett with his feet, kicking him playfully in the side. 'Wake up, you li'l varmit! Uncuff me! Uncuff me, so's I can get me some sleep, you snoring son of a bitch!'

Brett pretended to sleep a few moments longer, before pouncing on the sheriff and pinning him down with his good arm. He grinned at the sheriff, his broad handsome grin, and they laughed. Brett hadn't meant to fall asleep and leave the sheriff cuffed, and the image of Colm snoring next to his awakened wife Siobhan flashed through his head.

'Give me your hands.'

The sheriff obediently offered his wrists to his youthful lover, allowing Brett to rest them in his hand.

'You sure you want freedom?'

'It's what this country's about!' laughed the sheriff.

'Means you got to take up all them responsibilities again, sheriff. Being a lawman instead of shackled so everyone else has to do things for you.'

The sheriff paused for a moment. He had always been the responsible one, had always looked after his charges. He'd got too used to freedom to give it up long-term.

'Unchain me boy. If only so's my arms can get hold of you.'

And, after Brett had released him, he allowed the sheriff to hold him in his arms as they passed the night in the lawman's bed, opposite the jail cell where the handsome young outlaw Luke Mitchell lay.

Eight

Over a hearty meal of eggs, fried but the yolk still runny inside, the sheriff and Brett talked at length. Brett was enthralled with the stories that the sheriff shared: stories of adventure and outlaws, heroism and desperation. The sheriff seemed to relish the chance to chatter and entertain the handsome young man. Brett knew Williams was making himself out to be more of a hero than he could possibly be, but also recognised the veracity behind all the stories: Williams was certainly a dedicated and professional lawman with a strong sense of justice and fairness.

The sheriff also talked of the young man in the cell at the moment, an outlaw by the name of Luke Mitchell. The story going round was that he'd stolen from his boss. Williams had his own take on the situation. Conspiratorially, he winked at Brett as he confided that he had a suspicion that young Luke had been much more than just a stablehand to Matt Wilmott.

'A good-looking lad like that. Hell, I'd have been tempted,' he said. Brett surprised himself at feeling hurt that the sheriff might have desires for anyone other than himself. Then, in a quieter voice, Williams continued, 'Of course, that boy shouldn't be in there. Seems pretty obvious to me, he just shouldn't be there. If I could turn him loose, I would. Might even turn my head, should the boy escape.'

They had sex again after finishing eating, although this time it

116

was brief and hurried, as Brett tried to distract Williams from his work at the jail. It was a hasty climax. Eventually, they had both agreed that the idea of Rogers running the show for more than was necessary was too frightening a thought to bear.

The morning sex, brief but releasing, put a spring in the sheriff's step as he left for the jailhouse.

'Pop on over later,' he offered Brett. 'I'll show you around.'

'Thought I'd seen all the sights you have to offer. Twice,' Brett joked.

'Oh, no. You'd better believe, I got plenty more sights to show a youngster like you!' The sheriff grabbed his crotch and licked his lips suggestively. Brett whooped as he walked out. Once outside, he became respectable lawman Sheriff Williams and left the steamy night and morning of lust hidden behind him.

Brett mooched around the house, after finishing the strong coffee and breakfast he'd been made. He dunked his plate in a bucket of rain water outside in the small yard. The sheriff kept a few hens for his own supply of fresh eggs, and Brett spent some time watching them strut and listening to their clucking in the yard. He watched them peck at specks of grain left over from their early-morning feeding. He had heard the cock crowing as he lay sleeping with Williams and, with a start, he had woken up, thinking he was back home at St Joseph. It had been a relief to feel the man lying next to him, to wallow in his scent and warmth.

Brett meandered over to the tub in the back, took off his over shirt, and splashed the cold water against his face. He washed his upper torso, under his arms, his face and hands. The water was icy cold and wakened him to the day, before he was startled by a woman's call from the house.

'Oh, I am sorry.' Siobhan blushed and looked away. She had come carrying goodies and some more of Colm's old clothes for Brett to wear. 'I didn't realise. The sheriff gone off, then?'

'Yes, he's just set off, replied Brett, not bothering to cover himself up.

'I'll catch him over the way, then. Good morning to you!' Siobhan grinned and dashed out of the house, as Brett dried himself off and picked up one of Colm's linen shirts. It fitted him all right, not tailored, but loose, except round the shoulders where it emphasised his own broadness. He changed his trousers into a pair of dark breeches, and shaved quickly in the cold water. He felt good, fresh, ready for the day.

Brett left the sheriff's house, and walked down to the bar. He was stopped by several of the hunters and trappers who had seen him the day before, many of them congratulating him, or tipping their hats to him. He caught the mood with a broad grin of his own and, when he spied Colm sitting at the entrance to a hardware store, he walked over and greeted him.

'Hello, there. I wanted to thank you for the clothes!' he said, slapping the man on the shoulders.

'Well, if it isn't himself! Say, they fit you pretty well!' Colm stood and welcomed his new friend, enjoying the infamy of being addressed familiarly by Brett. 'How's the arm?'

It was a little stiff, bruised, although the wound had remained clean and uninfected. He showed it to Colm, who whistled.

'And there was I thinking you'd be losing an arm.'

Brett shrugged 'Takes more than a quick wrestle to do me harm.'

'Well, I wouldn't want to be trying anything like that now. Not with a fellow like yourself. Siobhan was after telling me that the deputy had been trying to start something up with her.'

'Oh, no, I don't think it had much to do with Siobhan. She's a good woman.'

Colm looked at him for a moment, assessing the competition. There was a frisson between them. 'She is that, all right. I count myself a lucky man.'

Brett let the moment go, hoping it would reassure Colm.

'You have no one yourself, then?' the Irishman asked.

'No. Like I told Siobhan, I'm travelling through, on my way out west. In fact, I was hoping maybe you could help me.'

'Is that right, now? Well, I'll see what I can do for you, friend. I'll be wanting to keep the right side of a man who can pack a punch like yourself!' Colm laughed, and seemed relieved when Brett joined in. 'Well, what Colm knows, now Brett knows. I got myself a couple of hours to spare, if you want to chew over some ideas.'

They spent the next couple of hours chatting away together. Or, rather, Brett spent the next few hours listening to whatever Colm had to say, which wasn't necessarily what he had asked to hear. He might start off telling Brett to go one route rather than another, follow this direction rather than that. Inevitably though, he would come round to talking about himself, about Siobhan, about his homeland, about stories he had heard or – Brett suspected – invented. Often, midway through a sentence, he would come back to the point he was making and continue to offer Brett a surer route or a better companion to ask. Yet Brett found the company acceptable, and found him looking at the man's handsome face, and warmed by the man's charm.

Colm liked the attention, Brett could tell. He seemed lonely, despite his outward persona. Colm certainly enjoyed the company of another man, and was exciting to be with, albeit in a non-sexual way. He seemed to enjoy the camaraderie, a gentle masculinity full of charisma. Every now and then, to emphasise a point he was making, or to show his attachment to the young man, Colm would slap Brett's leg, or gently rest his hand on it and squeeze it. He would often take Brett's hand in his and draw a map for him, using his fingers to trace tickling lines along his palm. He was naturally tactile, not seeing anything other than congeniality in the physical closeness.

Often, Colm would break away from Brett, and bid a good day to a passer-by, who would in turn approach Colm and greet him heartily. In this way, Brett found himself introduced to numerous trackers and hunters, Indian scouts and merchants. Colm was generous with his friends, sharing acquaintances easily with Brett, and building on his reputation as The Man Who Beat Rogers. If he'd planned it, Brett couldn't have hoped for a better introduction to the people of Independence.

It was Siobhan who broke their bonding conversation, as she called Colm back to the house to mend some fencing.

'Can't it wait?' he protested.

'No. The animals are escaping! You were supposed to have fixed it days ago. Nothing more than a couple of nails went in! Now get back there and sort it for me.'

Colm grinned guiltily at his new friend. 'I'd best see to it. Hell, if I see to her fence, she might see to me later tonight. Not a bad trade-in, huh?' Colm gave Brett a hearty pat on the shoulder. 'May you have luck in your travels, my friend.'

'And thanks for your help.'

'Just mention Independence Colm along the way and someone will see you right, you can be sure.'

Brett believed it, too, what with the number of people going to and from Independence who seemed to know the man. His head was still swimming with the bits and pieces of factual knowledge and hearsay that Colm had told him. The information would have to distil for a while. Brett watched as Colm put an arm round his wife as she continued to scold him. All of a sudden, the conversation was broken by playful laughter as Colm grabbed his wife and tickled her ribs. Colm turned and winked at Brett, letting him know that things were looking good for tonight, at any rate. Brett grinned acknowledging the pair's secret, and waved the high spirited couple off as he made his own way back into town and towards the jail.

As he was entering the building, Rogers ran out on some errand or another. He barely stopped to look at McKinley, but grimaced and turned away, pretending not to notice the man who had caused his downfall. Brett smiled and watched the man disappear down the street, still wincing from their duel the afternoon before. The farmhand rubbed his own scarred forearm in triumph. Turning and shaking his head in disbelief, Brett stepped into the jailhouse.

The sheriff's large desk sat immediately opposite him as he entered. The large tall-backed wooden chair that sat behind it was empty. Brett hollered a 'howdy' as he took further steps inside. He looked over to his left, where the walls fell aside to become the jail cells themselves. A wall of bars rising vertically, from floor to ceiling, separated the standing Williams from the three men inside. Brett glanced over and looked at the men. One was a tall black man, another a lithe moustachioed Mexican. These two men were standing talking to the sheriff, whose back was turned to Brett. McKinley recognised them as the two men he had seen entering the jail, the previous day.

Lying on a wooden bench in the corner of the cell was the

third man. This must be the one the sheriff had talked to him about over breakfast. Hadn't he referred to him as Luke or something similar? Yes, Luke Mitchell, and Brett could see why Williams was taken with the handsome young man. Even lying down, Brett was aware of the outlaw's strong presence, his handsome features, his toned physique. There was a nonchalance about him, almost an arrogance, which was undeniably appealing. As Brett approached, the man looked at him and caught his eye. They acknowledged each other, sizing each other up.

'Sheriff, looks like you got a visitor!' The man on the bed interrupted the sheriff's conversation with his cellmates.

The sheriff looked round and grinned at Brett.

'Well, good mornin' to you!' he said, planting a hand firmly on Brett's shoulder. 'I was wondering when you might be turning up. Glad you could make it.' He turned Brett away from the cell, back to the office.

'So, hey, Sheriff, you was just telling us we was about to be moved on!' The enquiry came from the tall black man.

'All in good time, Josh. Rogers has gone to get the carriage to take you off.'

'Suppose it won't be for a few days then,' joked Josh, to the merriment of his friends inside.

Brett looked over and grinned his approval. The man on the bed caught it, too and grinned back.

'Looks like your young friend has made his acquaintance, too,' Luke said from the bed.

'Don't know if you'd say that,' Brett replied. 'We didn't see eye to eye, exactly.'

'He's the one!' the Mexican sprang up holding out his hand. 'I told you there was talk about Rogers being bettered last night. You're welcome here, mister!'

'Enough of that, Rodriguez. Stop your gloating. Brett here don't want to spend time chattering with the likes of you.'

The three men in the cell started laughing between themselves and goading the sheriff.

'Looks like Williams wants the new boy to himself,' Josh said.

'We'd best hush our mouths for the sheriff and his new friend.' Rodriguez added.

'And I couldn't imagine anyone nicer for you, sheriff. Not a bad-looking kid there!' complimented Luke.

Brett caught the last remark, and turned towards Mitchell. Luke was still fixing him with an admiring stare and, as Brett turned, Luke's eyes followed him. Brett found himself looking back, smiling clumsily. He was rewarded with a warm smile back, and a salute from the outlaw.

'C'mon, let's show a stranger in town some better hospitality, you three,' the sheriff pleaded lamely.

'Awww, sheriff,' teased Rodriguez. 'We'll let you show the new boy the town's hospitality . . .'

Again, the cell was filled with their mocking laughter. Rodriguez offered Josh his open arms, and the two began a mock dance. Luke watched as Josh's hands felt Rodriguez's arse-cheeks, squeezing them surreptitiously. Josh hummed a tune that Luke hadn't heard. It was melodic and poignant. Luke found himself tapping along gently to the sound.

Brett watched. He watched as Luke closed his eyes and tapped softly. As he saw Luke closing his eyes, Brett wondered if he looked like that while he was sleeping. He wondered if Luke closed his eyes while he made love. Or when he kissed.

The sheriff led Brett back into the office and brought in a spare seat.

'Sit yourself down,' he told Brett.

Brett sat on the plain stool, which was wooden and hard. He suspected that it belonged to Rogers, and that the sheriff did not have many visitors to the jail.

'I was glad you popped on over. Gets kinda tiresome, chatting to the boys over there.'

'I bet it does. Where's Rogers?'

'Oh, he'll be back in a minute or so. Two of them's being moved out, so we'll be having some tearful farewells in a few minutes. I'm gonna have to take them out myself, otherwise I'd take you out to eat.'

'I'll keep myself amused. Been over and chatted to Colm, earlier. He's a tongue on him, but he knows a fair bit.'

The sheriff laughed. 'Yep, I guess he does, in his own way.'

It had changed since last night. The sheriff looked down at the floor instead of straight up at him. Brett understood at once. Last night, this morning, in the privacy of his own home, Williams had wanted him. He'd needed their bonding, their intimacy, their lust. Now, in the strict confines of the jail again, with the responsibility of three prisoners only feet away, it had all become different. Brett was an incongruency, a part of his life that was now an uncomfortable reminder of something chaotic and uncontrollable for him.

Brett could see it. Perhaps the sheriff really did have to take the prisoners himself. Perhaps it was part of his job. Perhaps. Brett was sure that he could have left it to Rogers if he'd really wanted to. The sheriff could have found time to spend with him, he was sure. Perhaps it was better like this. An ending without an ending. As if nothing was wrong. As if nothing had happened.

Perhaps.

'According to Colm, I should be making out west as soon as I can. Beat the weather,' Brett said, returning to his conversation earlier that day.

The sheriff understood. 'So soon?' he played. 'I'll be sorry to see you go. A man like you could have found work round here. Maybe even be a deputy of mine.' It was a lie, and they both knew it. But it was a polite lie and it was meant well.

'Well, thanks all the shame, sheriff. I've had an interesting time here.'

This time, they did look at each other, and grinned. The memory of their passion was still wet with them.

Just to ruin the moment, Rogers barged in, bawling out 'SHERIFFFFFFF! I got everything fixed out there!' He saw Brett, and stopped abruptly. 'Er, howdy . . .' the embarrassed deputy offered.

'Hello, Deputy Rogers. Don't seem a moment since I saw you last.'

There was an uncomfortable silence. It was the sheriff who rescued it. 'What say we get these two sorted and take 'em out then, Rogers? No use hanging around when there's work to be done.' He gave the deputy his keys and his handcuffs and shooed him off towards the cell. Rogers mumbled something to Brett –

possibly an apology, possibly an insult – and shuffled off to do his duty.

'I'll be sorry to see you go, Brett. If you're ever in these parts again, I hope you'll look me up.' The sheriff seemed sincere, both in his sorrow and in his hope.

'I ain't planning on it, Sheriff. But if I'm around, you can bet I'll come down here. On the right side of them bars, for sure!'

'Well, if you want to spend some time just hanging out round here while I'm gone, I don't mind. It'll keep Rogers on his toes, and I bet Luke over there would be glad of the company. I have to warn you, though, I'll be gone the best part of a day.'

'Well, we are saying goodbye, I guess, then. But thanks for the offer of staying a while. I ain't never spoke to no real criminal before – I might learn a thing or two!'

'There's worse than Luke. He just got himself into a situation.' The sheriff gripped Brett's hand, wishing him farewell. They embraced briefly but meaningfully.

Rogers arrived at the doorway with the two prisoners shackled at their hands and feet.

'You be a good boy there, now, Luke,' Josh was shouting back to the cell. 'Don't be no trouble for the sheriff and our friend Rogers here.'

'We'll be seeing you, boy,' Rodriguez added. 'Nice meeting you!'

'Good luck to you,' Luke replied. 'And make sure the sheriff comes back in one piece!'

With the goodbyes finished, the sheriff handed over command of the jail to his deputy and led Josh and Rodriguez out to the waiting cart, both of them smiling breezily. Anyone would have thought they were out for a daytrip, rather than being shipped off to another jail somewhere. Brett watched the party leave, and Rogers take up his place in the sheriff's chair. He didn't say anything to Brett, so McKinley wandered over to the jail, calling over his back, 'Sheriff Williams said I could stick around a while, see what there is of the place.'

A noncommittal grunt from Rogers was the only reply.

Brett approached Luke's cell. It was a strange sight to see another man behind bars. Brett wondered how it felt to be locked away, to have no freedom. He saw himself in the jail cell, and tried to imagine how it felt to be a caged animal. He thought back to St Joseph's, to the restraints on him there. At least there was freedom there: the river, the outdoors. Here, there were three walls and a row of bars. Brett prized his freedom, and couldn't – didn't want to – imagine it being taken away from him.

Luke's eyes were still closed as he softly hummed the melody he had learnt from Josh. The man had a handsome profile and a strong physique. Brett imagined the sheriff standing where he stood, watching and desiring the outlaw. But Williams would have known that he was beyond his reach. Williams might have allowed his passion to get the better of him with a young stallion like Brett, but not a criminal. Luke was forbidden territory.

But not to Brett. To Brett, such danger was only a challenge. He thought back to the way Luke had looked at him, how their eyes had challenged each other. He had felt a stirring within himself then. It was sexual, there was no doubt about that – the quiver of his cock as he looked at Luke again emphasised it. Yet there was more to it than that. He found himself warming to the outlaw, in a way that he hadn't before for another man. Scott, Taylor, Williams – those three men had been like his brothers, but brothers born out of intense passion and lust. Luke seemed more of an equal, a partner. Brett wanted him, and Brett was going to have him.

He woke Luke with a cough. Luke's eyes opened with a start; he cast around the cell looking for the cause of the noise.

'Howdy.' Brett introduced himself again.

'Howdy yourself, and see how you like it,' Luke said. 'I reckoned you'd been told not be talkin' with the likes of us by the sheriff himself. You disobeying the chief's orders?'

'What the sheriff says and what I do are two different things. I'm not behind these bars remember.'

'Ah, you got one up on me, there.'

'You missing your friends already?' Brett asked.

'Short-term visit,' shrugged Luke. He grabbed his chest and grinned. 'Just another of life's heartaches.'

Brett's heart was aching. He was looking at Luke, knowing

that he wanted him. Slowly and surely, he was making sure it would happen. 'Oh, yeah? Wouldn't mind hearing 'bout some of those heartaches of yours.'

'You not got anything better to do? Rogers won't like you chatting to me. That's given he's still awake, back there.'

'I'm awake and I'm listening to you, Mitchell,' barked Rogers. Luke turned and saw that the deputy wasn't paying as much interest as he was making out, contenting himself with another cup of coffee.

'Might know he'd be listening in,' confided Luke in a low whisper. 'It true that you saw to it he was beaten black and blue? He's been sulking round here like a dog that's been kicked for licking the cream.'

Brett grinned. 'Well . . . let's say we had a disagreement.'

'Good on you! If I was out of here, I'd be disagreeing with him, that's for sure.'

'Sheriff told me you'd been stealing . . .'

'Yeah? That sheriff can't keep his mouth closed for more than a minute.' Brett suspected that Luke was flattered he'd been talked about. 'And that ain't half the truth, anyhow.'

'No? Well, why don't you tell me what the truth is?'

Brett pulled over his seat, which now seemed unusually comfortable, as he sat listening to Luke's story. The time passed without problem. Luke was a good storyteller, as good as Colm, but Brett sensed his story was truer. Luke didn't need to impress him; he was a prisoner, so they were separated in a way that he and Colm weren't.

He listened with pleasure as Luke spilt his life story, telling him all about the early days with Matt Wilmott. He listened as Luke spoke of the man, and knew that there was more to the relationship than was being expressed. The sheriff had been right, Brett was sure of that. The two men had been involved far more intimately than Luke was confessing. Brett wanted him to tell him everything, to share it all with him.

As Luke told his story, Brett also became convinced of something else. He was convinced that Luke was innocent of the charge against him, and that Wilmott had made it up. It just didn't make sense to him – how difficult could it be to steal from a drunk? Luke wasn't stupid. He could have done the act and been clean away long before Wilmott would suspect anything. No, Brett was convinced that Luke was in jail for no reason at all. He wanted him out. He wanted him out and with *him*.

Luke paused for breath. Brett looked at him and told him he believed him. Luke could barely look at Brett when he said it. There was an uncomfortable pause before Luke finally said: 'You believe me? You believe I didn't do it? That Wilmott made it up?'

'Yeah, I believe you. I reckon the sheriff does, deep down, too. You're in trouble, Luke, but there's gotta be a way out.'

'I've always been in trouble. Ain't nothing new about that!'

And Luke carried on with his story. Brett heard everything, spoken in a voice so low it was almost a whisper, in order that Rogers wouldn't overhear. The deputy wouldn't take as kindly as him to Luke's story, Brett knew, and would try to find a way to use it against him. Luke spoke of being orphaned, of growing up at St Mary's, of working night and day and travelling around to find casual work. Brett listened to the hopes and fears of this handsome rebel, and was intrigued.

Their close proximity was also having another effect on Brett. He was aware of the warmth of Luke's body so close to his, despite the bars. Occasionally, as Luke had been speaking, Brett looked over at him and sometimes they would catch each other looking. A shy smile would pass between them. Then Luke would turn away, face his own history, and carry on with the story.

Luke's hand on his shoulder through the bars brought Brett back to the present moment.

'And what about you? I've been jawing all this time, I ain't paid no heed to anything you might have to say.' Luke left his hand on Brett's shoulder, as Brett started to tell his life story.

For the first time, he shared everything about himself. He told Luke about his brothers, about his parents, about St Joseph. He told him about the dream lying out west for him. He told him about meeting Scott, about meeting Taylor, although he kept their intimacies to himself. At the same time, he knew he would tell Luke about that, too. Not now, and he wasn't sure when, but it would be shared between them. He felt, in that moment, they were going to share more moments like this one. Brett couldn't understand it, the intensity of his feelings, but he knew there was something more happening here than he could pinpoint.

Brett eventually got up, ready to stretch his legs after sitting down talking to Luke.

Luke looked at him, disturbed. 'You off?' he worried.

'Just stretching. Getting cramp sitting down there with you, Luke. Getting a little stiff.'

'Wouldn't want that, now, would we?' Luke, still sitting on the floor, looked over between the bars, between Brett's legs. 'Yeah, you seem like you might be a little stiff to me.'

'Oh . . .' Brett looked down at Luke, who was grinning up at him. 'You are something else!'

Brett blushed as he realised that he was indeed a little stiff – noticeably so. At the front of his trousers was a small mound. He let his hand rest on it and cover it.

'You needn't do that, friend. It happens to the best of us.' Luke grinned, and opened his legs. Running a hand down his right thigh, Luke traced the line of his own semi-erection.

Brett liked what he saw, and touched himself. He looked over to see Rogers, his head back, dozing lightly. An illicit thrill rushed through him as he felt Luke touch his extended crotch. The man's forefinger slipped down the length of his shaft, under his cupped balls, and between his thighs, back down towards his anus. He repeated the action with two fingers and then with his whole right hand. Each time, there was more of Brett's manhood to feel.

'Mm, you've a good touch, Luke. You sure it's just cattle you been taught to handle?'

'Old Man Wilmott taught me more than just handling cattle,' confessed Luke. 'We had ourselves quite a little school on his farm.'

Brett took the outlaw's hand in his own, and rubbed both against himself. It felt good to feel the two of them stroking his tool. It felt even better when Luke moved forward and ran his tongue lightly over the front of his groin.

Brett grabbed Luke's head, and remembered the sheriff pleasing him the night before. This was different, so very different. Luke had turned him on from the moment he set eyes on him, and now to feel his tongue close to his cock and balls was a dream come true. The two men moaned slightly as they felt each other.

Brett looked over again to where Rogers lay sprawled in the chair, certain that even the dopey deputy must have become aware of what was going on. Nothing, not even a sound, came from him. This was going to be good, thought Brett. This was going to be something else.

He pulled down the top of his trousers, enough to let his cock slip out and point directly at Luke's attentive face. He was pleased to hear the other man sigh with delight, and then feel a hand gently stroking his shaft. Luke kissed the tip, licking round the glans with his eager tongue. In a moment, he had the crown in his mouth and Brett shuddered with pleasure. He looked down as Luke feasted on his throbbing rod, as thick as the iron bars it was surrounded by. Watching such a man like Luke suck him through the bars really got to him, giving him the strongest erection he could remember. He wanted Luke as much as Luke evidently wanted him.

Brett grabbed the bars and began bucking his hips towards Luke's eager mouth. He rubbed the length of his erection over the man's face, until his hairy balls rested on Luke's chin, and then pulled back again so that his tip could rest between Luke's lips. It felt incredible to have his cock sucked from the other side of the cell as Deputy Rogers slept at the desk.

Now he began fucking Luke's face between the bars, using his hands to pull Luke deeper on to him. His hairy groin slammed into Luke's nose and upper lip, grinding his shaft deeper into Luke's throat. The pleasure was so intense, so sudden, that Brett had to pull back to stop himself from climaxing too quickly. Luke almost seemed disappointed as Brett pulled away slightly to take a few strokes on his cock.

'Something wrong?'

'No, nothing at all. Everything's perfect. Just making sure we don't peak too soon. Show me your cock. Let me see what you got there, Luke. '

Brett watched as Luke and slipped his pants down over his hips to reveal a firm erection, curling upwards. Luke licked his finger and ran it over the head of his knob, making it twitch under the deft touch. Arching upwards, the magical eye of his cock stared straight at Brett. Brett moaned as he let Luke kiss his tool while he stroked himself to full erection.

Brett looked over to Rogers, and grinned at Luke.

'I got myself a little idea. Seems strange I can't get in there with you.' He made his way over to Rogers, his stiffness up close against Rogers's face. He bent down and picked the keys carefully off the deputy's belt. Luke watched from the bars, continuing to masturbate. Brett mocked jacking off into Rogers's face, but returned to Luke, kissed him and placed the key in the lock. Quietly, ever so quietly, Brett unlocked the cell door as they continued to kiss.

Now, inside the jail, the two men were all over each other. Hands pulled at shirts, trousers, boots. Mouth against skin, tasting sweat and desire. Fingers groping, pulling, poking. Cocks, hard, throbbing, wet, sticky. Muscle melting into muscle. Their appetite was bottomless, an open chasm that couldn't be filled. Brett and Luke became as one, united in their passion there in the cell. Brett had never felt so alive with another man, never so equal and never so full of the need for physical release. He licked every tuft of hair on Luke's body, letting his tongue drift all the way down the navel, into the pubic forest that surround his tumescence. Kissing, licking his balls, licking all the way back up Luke's chest. He gently took each nipple in his mouth in turn, his teeth gently biting the erect buttons, as his hands clawed into Luke's back muscles. Then Brett was tonguing his way up to Luke's open mouth, where their tongues met.

Luke tugged on Brett's rampant cock, pulling the shaft between his legs and urging Brett to hump between his thighs. Brett felt Luke tighten his muscles around his erection, as he humped the firm flesh. The crack between Luke's thighs was a substitute arsehole, a forging of flesh for him to ream. Brett pushed his cock back and forth between the sweating limbs, soaked in their perspiration liquid. The natural lubricant oozed around his erection, while Luke's short hairs at the top of his legs provide added resistance and tactile arousal. Brett felt so intimate, even without being inside Luke; this was a pseudo-penetration.

The pace was picking up. Their bodies were hot, their rods stiff and ready to spill their boiling craving for each other. Humping more urgently, forcing himself between Luke's legs and letting his manhood rage up against his sweaty back on the other side, Brett leant heavily into and on to his lover, so that he could feel Luke's pulsating organ against his own skin. He wrapped his hands over Luke's, squeezing them on to the dirt floor.

'Luuuuuke!' he found himself crying out. 'I'm so nearly there. Take me over, take me over the edge . . .'

'Shoot it. Shoot that hot load; I'm right behind you,' urged Luke.

Hearing his lover's voice at the height of his own passion was more than enough for Brett, and he let his open mouth fall over Luke's. Brett felt the orgasm shudder through him, forcing his hot jism out of his bell-end and up over the mountains of Luke's arse-cheeks. Luke also groaned and Brett felt the fountain of his juice spraying his chest, up as far as his shoulders. More quakes soared through them as they continued to pump into each other, wetting each other with their steaming love-milk.

The two exhausted lovers lay gasping and panting on the cell floor. It wasn't enough to have shared the intimacy of orgasm, for then they tongued the cooling fluid off each other. Their salty kisses were lazy and sloppy, open-mouthed and open-hearted. Brett felt like he had broken down the bars of the jail itself. And that was when the idea came to him. The idea that would change his life. That would make him too an outlaw.

The idea to give Luke his freedom.

The words tumbled out. They came in a breathless whisper to Luke, an idea half-formed but there all the same. Luke looked at him in disbelief, expecting a roar of laughter to follow the plan, or for Brett to dress and leave before locking the cell. But Brett was serious.

'Escape? *Now?* But Rogers is . . .'

'Rogers is sleeping,' Brett stated confidently. 'And I thought I'd proved I'm man enough to handle him, anyway.'

'You're serious? You are, you're fucking serious!'

'You bet I am.'

'But Sheriff Williams . . . Aren't you his lover?'

He'd guessed, Brett thought. 'Don't you get it?' he answered. 'He *wants* you out! He set us up. He doesn't believe you should be behind bars, any more than I do. That's why he told me to stick around. That's why he told me about you in the first place.'

Brett thought Luke had stopped breathing for a minute.

'Let's do it. Let's fucking do it, Brett.'

'There's another thing,' Brett said cautiously

'More? You're crazy!'

'Well, the cell's gonna look kinda empty . . .'

'Empty?'

'With you gone, no one in it. Not much of a jail cell, I reckon . . .'

'No!' Luke caught on and couldn't believe the audacity of his new lover.

Brett grinned back at him. 'I need to finish this thing off, Luke. It's a man thing!'

They dressed quickly and stealthily, before creeping out of the cell. The two men stood either side of the chair Rogers was in. Brett held up his hand and mouthed the signal. *One . . . Two . . . Three!*

The two men grabbed the chair, and rushed it into the prison cell. Deputy Rogers was still snoring, asleep. Even the bumpy ride into the cell didn't wake him. Even the closing of the door didn't wake him. Even the key in the lock didn't wake him. By the time Rogers was awake, Brett and Luke would be a long way away from Independence, and Rogers would have to hope that Williams was getting closer. There would be no living this one down in the saloon bar.

The lovers gathered up their belongings, and what few provisions they could find in the jail. Brett stepped out first, checking that the way was clear for Luke to follow him. Grinning from ear to ear, Brett McKinley and the outlaw Luke Mitchell walked straight out of Independence, towards freedom.

132

Nine

They fucked for days. Luke and Brett were driven along by the new passion they had found for life and for each other. The men spent most of the early part of the night on the run, making headway while the darkness covered their movements. They made good progress, spurring each other on when either slackened a little. Luke taught Brett how to live off the earth, how to look after himself and survive while on the run. But if the nights were spent trying to escape the arms of the law, the early mornings were spent escaping into each other's loving arms, before they could safely sleep in some derelict barn or cave. It was exhilarating to be free of everything except each other and to spend their new found freedom exploring each other.

If they were worried about being recaptured, neither man let the other know. They seemed too full of excitement – yes, even romance! – to let such concerns get in the way. Brett wondered if he'd already found his gold: not the mineral in the mountain, but a rich treasure in his heart. He had sworn he would never feel this way about anyone. He had never wanted to be tied down, had never really believed that he was capable of loving or being loved. He had known that it was sex he wanted, but his relationship with Luke was becoming more complex than that.

He was getting used to sleeping with Luke like a pair of nested spoons, curled up against each other. Then, waking up and feeling his warm body pressed against him. The lazy morning kiss, sleepy mouth on mouth. The ritual of working off each other's morning hard-on, a low release that could take hours. Then, the moments of slumber that followed in the afterglow. Brett was also getting used to the smaller things: the glances they shared, their moments of intimacy and appreciation. The times when their bodies might touch by accident – hands, legs, shoulders brushing against each other in the course of an ordinary day. The sparks that would fly between them, until they lost themselves again in an act of passion.

There was more to it, too. It wasn't just the sudden and pleasurable sex. That might happen three or four times each day. He was sharing himself with Luke in a way that he hadn't done so with any other person he had lain with previously. The sex got better, more pleasurable, more intense as they learnt about each other and how to satisfy each other. Their time together was a school of sex, discovering new ways to enjoy each other. Taylor and Scott had been a rehearsal for the passion he now shared with Luke.

It wasn't just physical. They connected on so many different levels that it was a joy for Brett to spend time with Luke. Of course, they were sharing an illicit thrill anyway, what with the nature of their relationship and their escape together. Luke excited him, and Brett felt alive with him. Although Luke was elder by only three years, he had so much experience in those years. Brett still felt the anger rise as Luke spoke of Wilmott: anger on Luke's behalf, and anger that Wilmott had been a part of Luke's life for so long. He realised he was jealous of Matt Wilmott's intimacies with Luke, the hold he had had over his lover. The feeling was only tempered by the realisation that if it hadn't been for foolish Wilmott, Brett and Luke would never have met.

Although they spent so much time talking of their different pasts, it disturbed Brett that Luke didn't talk of the future. For him, it was everything. The past was nothing to Brett any more. Perhaps the future scared Luke. Perhaps he could only see himself being recaptured, or spending years on the run for a crime he hadn't committed. It was exciting to be so firmly in the present, in the moment of now, but surely it had to lead *somewhere*? If Brett so much as mentioned what might happen in the future, Luke would go quiet. Not sulk, or argue, or walk off. Just go quiet, as if he had no words to talk about it. Then, of course, they would make love, and it would be back to the glorious, ecstatic, moment of *now*.

Somehow, they were making their way west, closely paralleling the Oregon–Santa Fe trail. They steered clear of the main popular trails, and Brett tried hard to remember everything Colm had told him about the terrain. Although Colm had spoken quickly and excitedly, Brett could remember much of what he had been told. Luke had practical skills and a little knowledge of the area, so that together they proved a dynamic and successful partnership. They trusted each other and relied on each other. If either one of them made a mistake, calculated wrongly, there were plenty of ways in which they might end their journey abruptly. They were focused on survival, every sense alert.

After the heat of their passion had subsided, they would take it in turns to watch out as the other slept. Brett enjoyed these moments. The brightness of the day, the anticipation of being caught. And the soft breathing of his lover lost in sleep beside him. He would catch himself watching Luke's face twitching, maybe a grin, maybe a grimace. A kick, an opening and closing of his palm, some nonsense uttered without warning. Occasionally he would wake with a start, his eyes alighting on Brett's, then grin sleepily, and return to his slumber. Did Luke dream? wondered Brett, for he never spoke of dreams. And when Brett lay asleep and dreaming of Luke (as he had done the past few nights), was Luke looking at him and wondering the same things he now was? He thought – he *knew* – he did. Their love was mutual, shared.

The weather changed about a week after their escape. It became wet, chillingly so. By Brett's estimation, they must have been fifty miles or so from Council Grove, although it was difficult to tell for sure, the way they had criss-crossed the trail to Santa Fe. Every now and then, they had caught a glimpse of prospectors making their way forward – a sure sign that Luke and Brett were too close to the trail, and in danger of being detected. They would then cautiously wend their way further south of the immediate route.

The rain didn't dampen their spirits, however, or even their lovemaking. There was a freshness for Brett in feeling the cold wet rain break against his skin as he cavorted with Luke, an outdoor abandon that excited him. Their wet skin touching, the smell of Luke's wet hair, the coolness of his skin in the rain, all turned Brett on. And, after they both came, he watched the rain washing their juice off each other in a single stream of joy. The rain continued to pelt down on them as they danced together in the open country.

The journey was a mix of recklessness and caution. They were as reckless in their lovemaking as they were cautious about not being seen. Both men were wild and spontaneous in their acts of carnal passion. Neither wanted to relinquish his freedom and get caught by Rogers or Williams. They were each other's safety, protective of one another.

For a while, Brett totally forgot about his search for gold. He was so caught up in being with Luke that he didn't care about the trail out west, or whether he was following the right route. Luke was bringing him into the here and now, and it felt good. Nothing else seemed to matter to him, and Brett found himself filling his head with Luke's stories, his past, his knowledge. Brett realised he was falling head over heels for the outlaw, but didn't care. He was sure that the feeling was reciprocated.

Of course, neither of them had mentioned the word. Love. Neither of them would spoil the moment. If they labelled the feeling, it might disappear. It felt too precious at the moment to speak out loud, as if talking about it might betray what was between them, or poison it in some way. Perhaps there would come a time when the two might be able to express what was happening in ways other than their sexual intimacy, but that time wasn't yet.

It was early days. They were only just learning about each other, how to pleasure each other and how to care for each other. They were buddies. And they'd just found their freedom, together. It felt good to Brett, and he could see the happiness in

Luke. Although he was the older man, sometimes there was a childish playfulness in Luke that amused Brett. He was an open spirit, and that was what had appealed to Brett from the start. That and his obvious good looks. His body. And, yes, his beautiful cock.

Things couldn't be any better, thought Brett. A fine man, freedom, and the dream that still lay for them way out west. As he curled up with Luke, feeling him close against him, his soft breath on his skin, Brett thought that he had come home. He'd found a home when he thought he had none. Things were good for him. As they had made love only moments before, Brett found himself closing his eyes and moaning Luke's name. Even with his eyes closed, he could see Luke in his head. Brett had heard his own name being called in return, followed by the soft release of their passion joining them together.

If only it could last, Brett found himself thinking. If only it could last.

Ten

Sheriff Williams was pleased with himself as he rode the wagon back to Independence. Things weren't so bad, after all. He'd had fun with young Brett McKinley early that morning and also late the evening before. Now, there was a man of spirit, for sure. Williams laughed out loud as he remembered the sight of his deputy Rogers beaten and bruised at McKinley's hands in the bar. He'd had it coming to him for years: nobody could deny that. Ever since he'd started working with Williams, Rogers had had that snidey and unpleasant attitude, and had always rubbed people up the wrong way. At least the beating he got might suppress it for a few weeks, might make the man reasonable enough to live with. It would, no doubt, be a short-lived conversion. The old Rogers would be back within a month. He'd turn Rogers out if he could, but it wasn't all that easy to find a good deputy these days. Especially now, with so many of the young men off seeking an easy fortune in the gold hills of California.

Not like when Williams had started. Then, good law-abiding men were two a dime. Hadn't he had to work hard to get this position? To command the respect of the townsfolk of Independence? He'd done it all through his own hard work, and by showing that he was a fair but just man. Some of the decisions he'd made had been hard, but he'd shown he didn't take favourites, and that he was no harsher than he had to be in implementing the law. Once people realised that, knew that they could rely on him, they were good to him.

At least, he hadn't had favourites until Luke had shown up, and then he had met Brett. He admired Luke's style, his honesty, and was sorry to have to take him in. To keep him caged like an animal. He was a wild buck that should be out in the open. Yes, and, come to think of it, a handsome wild buck at that. Even Sheriff Williams was human, after all, and could be tempted by a handsome young outlaw.

Human enough to fall under Brett's spell. He didn't know how it had happened. One minute he was just being polite, kind enough to a stranger; the next, he was bent over his own cock with his hands cuffed behind his back! All for Brett. It made no sense, a man of his years suddenly falling for a guy in his early twenties. But there it was. It had been sudden, impulsive, and the sheriff knew that it wouldn't last for ever. Hell, he'd be surprised if McKinley was still there when he got back to Independence this evening. He'd dropped as much of a hint when he'd left. Brett wouldn't stick around for a fellow like him – there were too many opportunities out there for him.

Oh, but the passion had been good. It had been too long since he'd felt that way, since he had enjoyed sex so much. Since he had had any sex in fact. The past few years had found the sheriff on his own night after night, apart from odd sojourns to the bar to meet some buddies now and then. He tried to keep those events to a minimum, knowing that Rogers would be in the bar and, more often than not, in a state of intoxication.

Once he had found Rogers standing naked on the bar, inviting the women to inspect his genitals. The sight had been embarrassing, not only because of Rogers's paralytic state, but also because the size of his genitalia hardly bore investigation. Indeed, many of the women had fallen to the floor, laughing at Rogers's sorry specimen. Such an event only fuelled Williams's own belief that Rogers was in truth a virgin and also sexually inadequate, and so infatuated with sex because he had no experience of it.

This frustration with members of the opposite sex had turned into bitterness and desperation – a desperation to get laid, and a bitterness against those women who would turn him down. Williams had noticed that Rogers railed at all women: for being of easy virtue, for being uptight, for being married to the wrong men, for not being married at all. Williams let Rogers know that he had no time for such views, and that he should keep his thoughts in order. But Williams also knew that Rogers harboured such views and always would, unless the deputy found happiness with a woman – an event the sheriff thought most unlikely. He pitied the poor woman whom fate handed such a disaster.

But this was all speculation. There was work to be done when he got back. The sheriff had handed over Josh and Rodriguez to their new custodians in the south, and was determined not to leave Independence in the jurisdiction of Rogers for a moment longer than he had to. Josh and Rodriguez had been pleasant enough company. They spent their journey laughing and joking with him, and he had quickly guessed the intimate nature of their relationship. It wasn't unusual for guys to hook up with each other out here, no matter what people said. It seemed only right, he tried to convince himself, that a man should have some company, some warmth, some intimacy. Williams wanted to believe his own arguments, knowing that it was what he felt, too.

That it was what had drawn him to Brett McKinley.

What would happen to Josh and Rodriguez? The sheriff wasn't entirely sure. He didn't trust the law enough to allow them real justice, both of them being different enough from the average farmhand to engender irrational hatred. Yet they had seemed strangely happy, hopeful. He had wished them well as they left each other, and they had shaken their manacled hands with his. Josh had even thanked him for the hospitality! And then they had told him to see Luke got taken care of. 'A good kid,' winked Josh . . .

And soon he would be checking on Luke Mitchell to see how he was being taken care of in his absence. Soon, too, he would be handing him over to Matt Wilmott's cohorts. Unless, by some miracle, the kid could escape. Unless the kid could break down walls, melt iron bars, fly through roofs . . .

Or, more likely, Rogers would muck up and leave the jail door open. Or perhaps Brett had taken the hint he'd dropped after they had made love. About Luke not deserving to be locked up. About hanging around in the jail for him to come back . . .

He hoped Brett had understood. It was the only way that he could ensure justice. Not the justice of the letter of the law, but the justice of the underdog. The justice he had always worked for.

Sheriff Williams rode into Independence at dusk as the light was failing, unsure of what he'd find. As he entered the jail, he called out.

'Brett! Rogers! I'm back!' Interesting that he'd called Brett's name first, rather than his own deputy's.

'Hello?' He was in the jail and there was no sign of anyone.

Then an almighty howl filled the air.

'Sherifffffff!' Rogers screamed. 'Get me outta here! Get meeeeeee outtttttttta here!!'

Funny, thought Sheriff Williams. Rogers is calling from . . .

He had to contain his laughter. The sight of Rogers grabbing at the cell bars and imploring to be released was as funny a sight as he'd ever seen. It rivalled his naked dancing on the bar top! Rogers's face was tear-stained, his eyes red and swollen. He'd smashed the cups in the cell, ripped apart the papers that had been left in there with him. His clothes were ragged and dirty.

'What happened here?' Williams asked coolly.

'Those damned troublemakers! That McKinley and no good Mitchell. They escaped and locked me in here!'

'Escaped?' Williams raised an eyebrow. 'How did they escape, when *you* were guarding the cell?'

'They . . . They overpowered me. McKinley, it was, took a gun out, forced me in here . . .'

'Brett McKinley threatened you with a gun?' The sheriff had difficulty hiding the incredulity in his voice.

'That's what I said . . . They were in it together,' lied Rogers. 'But never mind them, sheriff! Get me out of here so I can go after them! I've been in here for hours already.'

'Well, I hope it's been instructive, Rogers. I always think you should know what it's like to step into another man's shoes. Especially one more unfortunate than yourself.'

'C'mon, sheriff, quit stalling and get me outta here!'

'Well, Rogers. You know I'd be only too happy to do that. But it seems I must have misplaced my spare keys. Now, you just hang on in there. If I'm lucky, I might find them straight away. But you know how bad I am at misplacing things. Could take half an hour, an hour: maybe more. But don't you worry, Rogers. It'll be my first priority to find those keys and set you free. Unless something important crops up in the meantime, of course.'

'*What?* C'mon, Sheriff, release me now! You must have the keys!'

Williams made a show of checking himself for the keys – unsuccessfully.

'Nope. Gonna have to look elsewhere for them. You just hang on in there, Rogers. Don't worry 'bout nothin'. We'll have you out in no time.'

The sheriff went off, as if looking for the keys, but in fact ended up making himself a celebratory cup of coffee. The way Williams figured it, while Rogers was still under lock and key, stewing, Brett and Luke would be putting distance between themselves and Independence. The more time he could earn for them, the better. This time, the sheriff's sympathies lay with the lawbreakers.

So it wasn't until an hour later, after Williams had a chance to burn the image of Rogers in a cell into his mind, that he eventually 'found' the keys. 'Don't know what I was thinking of, Rogers. There they were under my nose all the time.'

But Rogers wasn't listening. He had become so wound up while in the cell that when he was released, he was like a dervish, wheeling around with an unnatural manic energy.

'I'm going after them, sheriff. I'm gonna get them bastards, I swear it. I'm gonna make them feel my wrath! No one makes a fool out of me!'

It was only after Rogers had rushed out of the jail in search of his prey that Sheriff Williams allowed himself to fall on the floor laughing. He'd hardly been able to contain his enjoyment of the situation for so long. Raising his coffee cup to the air, he toasted the runaways. 'Here's to you, Brett McKinley and Luke Mitchell. Here's hoping you get what you deserve!' The hot coffee tasted damned good as Sheriff Williams drank it down with undisguised pleasure.

Eleven

The heat was getting to them now. It was becoming unbearably hot and it had been so for several days. After the rain came the heat. It suited Brett and Luke, who would parade in from of each other, bare-chested and bronzed. They delighted in each other's physique, watching themselves tan, while trying to avoid getting heat stroke. Their own strokes, however, were also raising the temperature.

Brett gazed as Luke chopped wood. They had traded food they had gathered, and Luke had managed to track and skin several beavers, so that they had acquired some of the tools they needed for survival. They had tried to deal with people they felt they could trust, some of the men that Colm had mentioned to Brett. Although wary of the man for other reasons, Brett figured that even if news got back to Colm of where he was, Colm would be discreet enough to keep the information from Rogers. He owed them that for Siobhan. Unless, he suddenly thought, they'd put a price on his head . . .

But Brett was too involved at looking at Luke's muscled torso to think much beyond the present. The sun beat down on his lover, causing rivulets of sweat to run along his flesh. On the wiry tufts of dark chest hair, the small wet beads glistened in the light, before following the trail down to his navel. The ripples of chest muscles lined Luke's stomach, centring on a thin line of black hair diving into his groin. Just above Luke's belt, worn low on his hips, the hairy bush of his pubic region just peeked over his trousers. As Luke reared up, ready to beat down on the wood with his axe, the expanse of visible flesh grew, teasing Brett with its desirability. Brett had lost count of the times he had licked, tongued, kissed, and touched that area between Luke's belly-button and the rich dark forest that surrounded Luke's treasure.

Using his hand to guard his eyes from the harsh gaze of the sun, Brett looked up at his lover. They took it in turns to chop, and Brett was taking an exhausted respite from the cutting. They'd been careful with fires but, in the cold of the night, it was necessary to have more than each other for warmth. The fire was necessary, too, for them to cook the meat they trapped and caught. Both men had become very competent hunters, particularly when driven on by hunger. Hunger was a strong motivator.

His eyes took in Luke's strong broad shoulders, his raised biceps, and then the dark curves of hair on his forearms. With Luke's arms raised high in the sky to get enough momentum to split the wood, Brett could see Luke's armpits, dusted too with dark hair. Luke hadn't been used to his tongue exploring them, had pulled away at first as Brett kissed his hidden spaces. Luke had soon come round to the feel of Brett's warm tongue over his body, though, kissing, licking his warm crevices. Luke was becoming used to doing the same for Brett, neither man afraid now of shocking the other with their insatiable hunger for each other.

Luke caught Brett looking up at him. He grinned, although the sun behind him prevented Brett from seeing anything other than the broad flash of a smile. 'How you doing there, partner? You recovered enough, yet?'

'Just watching, Luke! Kinda getting used to seeing this man o'mine toiling away.'

'Well don't get too used to it, McKinley. They had you spoilt on that farm of yours. I'm gonna make you work your clothes off.'

'Is that so?' Brett sat up, his hand drawing in the dust between his legs. 'You reckon you're man enough to do that, huh?'

'You bet your sweet ass I am,' boasted Luke, dropping the axe for a while.

'You like my sweet ass, don't you, partner?'

'Happen I do. You've got a sweet juicy ass there.'

'Yours ain't bad either, Mitchell. A nice firm ass you got, there. Mighty tempting to a man like me in this heat.'

'You're all talk, McKinley. Quit fooling around. We got work to do.'

Brett felt betrayed by the refusal, but Luke continued. 'Maybe, when I'm done here, you can have a piece of my sweet ass. I might treat you to some of my hot cock, too, *if* you're a good boy and let me get on with this work!'

Brett licked his lips, and gently rubbed his groin. 'I'll be waiting for that. I'm holding you to your promise, buddy.'

Brett contented himself with foraging for berries in a nearby wood. The leaves gave him some shelter from the heat, and he was more than successful in gathering enough fruit to make a hearty meal. He enjoyed this self-sufficiency, being able to hunt and gather for their meals, for the two of them to live without recourse to the large town of Independence or somewhere like his hometown of St Joseph. He had enjoyed every meal he'd had to share with Luke, nothing very fancy, but enough to satisfy their hunger and maintain their other voracious appetites.

When Brett returned from the foraging, Luke seemed to have finished chopping the wood. He was leaning over the smashed wood, and placing it into a small hearth he had prepared with a few boulders from nearby. They had picked a good space, fairly secluded, and not easily accessible from the path farther down the canyon. It was slightly cooler here than out in the space of the rocky chasm they had left for somewhere more secure. However, the heat was still more than enough to tire Brett from the relatively simple act of berry hunting, and he was secretly hoping that the chopping hadn't worn Luke out too much. Even the most athletic of men could be drained in this heat.

'How'd you do?' he asked Luke.

Luke wiped the sweat from his brow, slightly breathless from the activity. 'I'm fine. All worked up. Thought I'd lost you in that wood, for a minute. How long does it take to pick a few berries, young Brett?'

'As long as it takes you to get your breath back, Luke.'

'There's plenty of breath left in me, don't you worry about that. Enough to fill you for sure. You wanna taste my hot breath, buddy? Feel me fill your chest . . .'

And they fell on each other, kissing. Brett felt Luke panting into his mouth, the heat from his lungs entering his own. Their sweat-soaked mouths tasted salty together, a bitter spice suddenly added to the cauldron of their sweet lovemaking. Their bodies melted into each other against the heat, their own passion as hot as the sun above.

'I always keep my promises, Brett, you know that. You're gonna get what I promised.'

'I know, Luke. I knew it when you promised it to me. I trust you.'

They fell apart for a moment, silently eyeing each other up. Brett unbuttoned his shirt slowly as Luke watched. His hands reached for his nipples, tweaking them slowly as Luke looked on. He imagined his own hands were Luke's, caressing his chest, his hardening nipples, circling the pink buttons sensitised by the hot sun.

Luke joined him, fastening his mouth on Brett's chest. His tongue seemed cool on Brett's burning skin, moving over the eroticised mound of flesh. Then the warm wet probe kissed its way up Brett's chest, over his collarbone. It stopped just at the bottom of his neck, moved upwards slightly to the uprising of his Adam's apple. There Luke let his mouth cover Brett's throat, his tongue wetting Brett's sudden vulnerability. His throat rose and fell as a guttural sound of pleasure escaped from him. Then Luke kissed his way up his throat, tonguing the sweat off him, covering his cheek in soft but wanton kisses.

Luke found Brett's mouth waiting for him, open and panting. Again their kisses became full and open, their tongues becoming one. Brett felt Luke's moist warmth flick over his teeth, round his mouth, then wrap round his own tongue. As he opened his eyes, he saw Luke looking into his own. Then they fell apart again, as Luke ducked away from Brett and made his way towards the basket of fruit that Brett had gathered.

Brett watched Luke scoop some of the fruit into his hands, licking a few of the red berries on his tongue. He brought the basket over to him, and offered his berry-covered fingers to his lover. McKinley took the outstretched fingers on his tongue, tasting the sweet liquid dripping from them. He licked them clean, savouring the squashed fruit in his mouth before kissing Luke and sharing the sticky sweetness. Luke let his fingers slip in and out of their mouths, both men feeding on the remaining ripe juices.

Brett grabbed another handful of the fruit, and brought his fingers to Luke's hot lips. He bruised the fruit against them, letting the sweet river flow down his chin. He gently licked at his lover's reddened lips and mouth, lapping up the thick liquid. Gently he would flick the fruit with his tongue, then guzzle with his mouth at Luke, sharing nature's bounty between them. The taste of the sweet juice drove them on, tasting it off each other, thirsting for the luscious liquid. Brett's mouth cleaned Luke up, until all that was left of the handful of fruit was its delicate perfume on their breath.

'Mm . . . You taste good – good enough to eat.'

'Yeah . . . Let's eat each other, buddy. Let's taste the juices.'

Now Luke was rubbing some of the abundant harvest over Brett's naked chest, rubbing the stuff in until he was covered in a sweet sticky goo. Brett closed his eyes and felt Luke feasting upon him, taking the food into his mouth and licking the trickles of escaping juice from his chest. He would alternate between eating the fruit and kissing Brett hard and full on the mouth, so that Brett too could savour the sweet sensuous salad. Luke devoured the luscious fruit, rubbing the juice into Brett's sweat so that he could mop up the exotic cocktail with his tongue. Brett relaxed so that Luke could enjoy the taste of him, and the sublime juice of the ripe fruit.

When they kissed next their bodies were sticky together, stained red flesh awash with the berry aroma. Their hands, still covered in the juice, grabbed at what remained of their clothes. Brett felt the front of Luke's trousers, his hard organ stretching against the material of his pants. He also felt Luke's hands over his own growing erection, as they had been so many times before. He felt Luke's fingers warm against his throbbing rod, feeling them grab its width and then trace its length from his balls to the moistening tip. He wanted to feel Luke's mouth on it, feel him take the length deep into his throat and nurse it there until he exploded with passion.

At the same time, he could feel Luke's penis growing in his hand and he slipped his hand down the front of Luke's britches. He moaned as he found Luke's hot cock, the soft skin of his organ silky to touch. Slowly he wanked the length of Luke's manhood, kissing his mouth as his hand filled with flesh. Luke grabbed Brett's own knob, until they were rubbing against each other, still partially clothed. Their blood rising, the two men continued to fist each other off. For days now they had been practising how to pump each other expertly, and Brett felt they had now perfected it. Luke responded to Brett's deft touch by moaning into his ear, and tickling Brett's sweating hairy bollocks.

'Yeah, pull on that meat. You are sooooo good,' urged Luke.

'You're so fucking hard. I love feeling that monster in my fist,' moaned Brett. 'It feels so good and hard.'

'You're so stiff, too. I'd love that length inside me, Brett. Charge into my hole and ride me fast and hard.'

It was the first time they'd talked like this. Neither man had penetrated each other with anything other than fingers or tongues until now. Brett had secretly desired it, to seal their union with such intimacy. He had never been sure what Luke's response would be, or if he wanted it, too. Now they both wanted the moment of utmost intimacy and sharing.

'You want me, Luke? Inside you? You want me to fuck you?'

'Yes, Brett. Fuck my ass, Brett! Fuck me!'

Brett was so hot for Luke now. He kissed him, harder than they had ever kissed before. He turned Luke over, so that he was on his hands and knees in the dirt. Then he started kissing the nape of his neck, licking the sweat from the line of his hair. He let his tongue slide into Luke's right ear, following the shapes and coils of his cartilage and skin, before lightly biting his lobe. He continued to gently chew on the soft plate of skin, feeling Luke

arch into him. His hands embraced the other man's chest underneath him, stroking and caressing his hairy front.

His hand slipped, running along his abdomen, round the hips
and resting at the top of Luke's hairy, muscular thighs. He felt
the shape of the muscles, then travelled upwards and fumbled at
the belt. 'Help me out Luke. Let me give you what you need.'

Luke was keen to shed his second skin, and helped Brett strip
him off. When he was finally naked, Brett took some time to
savour the naked man's form. He let his hands wander over
Luke's sweating back, feeling the muscles relax and ripple under
his touch. He took some time to massage the sweat into the skin,
using the natural lubricant to soothe and relax his lover. He kissed
the vast expanse of tanned bronze skin, rubbing his stubbled face
against it. He rained his kisses down on Luke, kissing all the way
down the spine, down further to the top of Luke's muscular
buttocks.

Brett kissed Luke's left buttock first, a soft kiss planted lightly
on the hairy flesh. It was followed by another, then another,
travelling gently inwards towards the dark crack in the centre.
Just as he was about to honour Luke's inner sanctum, he turned
his attention to the other arse-cheek. Again, kisses rained down
on the tender expanse of flesh, until Brett's kisses became soft
nibbles. Their trajectory was still unerringly inward, driven by a
frenzied lust that Brett hadn't experienced before.

Brett's hand slipped further down beneath Luke's spread thighs.
There he found Luke's heavy hanging balls, instinctively grabbing
and squeezing them. The milking motion produced the desired
effect, and Luke's cock twitched hard upright against his belly.
Brett buried his face against the hairy testicles, softly nestling
them one by one in his open mouth. He treated them as gently
as bird eggs, letting his tongue flick over their outline in the hot
fleshy sack that protected them. He stroked Luke's stiff dick as he
sucked on his lover's nuts, feeling them tighten with pleasure
under his tongue.

Brett let his tongue slip behind the balls, slobbering over their
base. He tongued the mound at their root, leaving a wet trail of
his own saliva as he pleasured Luke. He let his strong nose nuzzle
against Luke's hanging testicles, rubbing against them softly, only

to be replaced by his eager searching mouth. Again, his hand ran along the entire length of Luke's hard shaft, pulling on it and making it throb further.

Luke moaned as he felt Brett's tongue on him. 'Take those balls in your mouth. Suck my balls.'

Brett obeyed the instruction, sucking again on Luke's balls.

And then he drew back. Suddenly he grabbed Luke's arse-cheeks and opened them up with his hands. Then, without further ado, his tongue was snaking its way towards Luke's hot arsehole, landing at its entrance with a gentle lapping. Brett felt the wrinkled hole react to the pressure of his adoring tongue, while at the same time Luke gasped in disbelief and pleasure. Brett's tongue poked into and around the sphincter, relaxing the sensuous muscle with his wet probe. He let his tongue slip into Luke's arsehole, then around the hairy entrance, and then follow the line of his crack up and down.

Brett was enjoying rimming his lover's anus, tonguing that secret and intimate hole. It became a fecund altar upon which he prostrated himself and whose inner sanctum he explored. With each licking motion, Luke moaned louder and longer, opening himself wider for Brett's ministrations. Attending to his partner's desires caused Brett's own cock to harden considerably, and McKinley began to rub at his own hard rod as he tongued away at Luke's sweaty arsehole.

'Mm, your tongue in my hole feels so good. My ass is so soft and relaxed, Brett. It's so hot for you. I'm ready now. I'm ready for you.'

'You like my tongue in your ass, Luke? You like me going down on you like that?'

'Yeah, it feels real good. It makes me so horny for you.'

Brett lifted his index finger to Luke's mouth, indicating for him to lick it. Luke moaned and took the finger deep into his mouth, as if it were Brett's cock that he was sucking on. Brett slowly withdrew his finger, and then placed it at the tip of Luke's arsehole. Slowly he slid it inside, and felt his lover arch back on to the digit, accepting it inside his warm relaxed hole. He slid it in further, until his finger was engulfed by Luke's anus, and gently moved it in a soft dance of ecstasy. He slid the finger out slowly, then in again, making Luke moan over and over. For a third time, Luke slipped the solitary finger up and into the other man's backside, before adding a second finger to the first penetration. He felt Luke's arse muscles fighting to accommodate the new width, then relaxing as they accepted the new intrusion.

Again, Brett inserted the two fingers, and then a third, testing how relaxed Luke was actually becoming. With a groan, Luke relaxed into it. The second time, all three fingers thrust into him. Slowly but surely, Luke was moaning with pleasure and Brett could feel how relaxed his sphincter muscles had become through his desire. He continued to finger Luke's sexed-up arse until he began to beg for Brett's cock.

'Please, I'm there. I want you inside me, Brett. Fuck me with your cock. Ride my ass with your hard shaft.'

Luke's coarse calls turned Brett on further and, as he kept his fingers inside Luke, he spat down on his throbbing organ. He rubbed his own hot spittle into his erection, and spat again at Luke's arsehole. He let his fingers knead the lubricant into Mitchell's relaxed sphincter. A lazy river of his spit ran down the crack of Luke's arse and down his outstretched thigh. Now it was Brett's turn to moan with desire, to want to enjoin with Luke in this last intimacy.

Brett slowly rubbed his knobhead against Luke's rear. The thrill of anticipation ran through them both. He let the rubbery tip of his glans massage Luke's flesh, throbbing against its comfort. The full shaft rested at the base of Luke's cheek-crack and with one thrust, it slipped along the length of the hairy rift between the soft fleshy mountains either side. Another thrust and Brett felt Luke tightening his cheeks to provide tension to the manoeuvre.

And then his wet tip was at the entrance to Luke's hole. He grabbed his lover's shoulders, and bent his head down to Luke's, kissing him hard on the lips. Maintaining the oral contact between them, Brett slowly pushed his cockhead into Luke's arsehole, resting the tip just inside. He could feel the sphincter contract to accommodate his plump crown, welcoming him into Luke's private nest. The two men moaned in unison, a low guttural sound that escaped into each other's suckling mouths.

Sure of the motion, and confident that Luke was relaxed

enough for him, Brett slowly inched his dick further into Luke, feeling his lover open up for him. He knew it was a tight fit, and that it was the trust between them that allowed Luke to take his thick girth. Inch by inch, his full length penetrated Luke's hole, until Brett was fully inside him. They stayed like that for a moment, savouring the feeling of being fixed together, fitting so tightly into each other. Brett's cock throbbed in Luke's hot flesh, every heartbeat echoing through them. It felt like they were stuck in time itself, as Brett softly open kissed his willing partner. This was going to be a ride like no other thought Brett McKinley as he felt his hardness deep within Luke's softest part. This was going to be the ride of a lifetime.

Brett began to fuck Luke gently, thrusting motions pressing him deeper into his lover's backside. He groaned as he felt his cock slipping in and out of Luke, his hard shaft stiffening with excitement. Feeling Luke beneath him, he ran his hands over his chest and legs, smothering his back in lustful kisses. He let his swollen knob push right up into his lover, then pulled it back so only the head rested within the warm heaven of Luke's anus. He continued to use slow full strokes to ease his cock into Mitchell's tight hole.

Gradually, the pace quickened a little. His stroke became more certain, more powerful. Deeper and faster he fucked Luke. The feel of his lover's muscled rear tightening around his thick prick urged him on. As hot as it was in the sun, it didn't match the heat he was feeling in his groin, and the heat of Luke's own fiery cauldron. His hardness contrasted with the softness of Luke's inner flesh, although their amour was mutual.

Brett let the pace pick up naturally, as he felt Luke pulling him in deeper, urging him to take him harder and quicker. They found a rocking rhythm; Brett's jerks were regular, long and fast. Luke moaned as he took him, sinking his cock deeper and faster, their exertions causing them to sweat and groan more in the heat of the sun.

Now Brett was fucking Luke furiously, his whole body shaking as he slammed into his lover's deep arsehole. Their balls met with each thrust, and Brett used his right hand to wank Luke's cock as they mated. He could feel Luke enveloping his hard meat, pulling him inside, and driving his orgasm closer. He could also feel Luke's cock quicken at his touch, his own masturbatory attentions becoming long fast strokes.

Their journey was almost finished and, with the end of the trail in sight, Brett felt his body thrusting hard and fast into Luke, unaware now of the other man's moans of joy and ecstasy. He was fucking without control, banging into Luke. He could feel himself approaching the point of no return, and thrust his mouth hard on Mitchell's.

'I'm comming. You want it inside you?'

'Yeah, shoot your load in me. I want to feel you spurt inside. I want to feel your river of joy flow into me.'

It was more than enough, to know that Luke wanted him to explode inside him. A couple more final thrusts, and Brett felt himself shudder, his cock forcing itself as deep as he could manage in Luke's willing frame. With a final moan, he climaxed inside his excited lover, hot spurts of come showering out of his cock. He shuddered with the momentum of each hot jet, and was joined by Luke's own ejaculations as the erection took off in his hand. As he came inside Luke, spurts of hot sticky ejaculate spat out on to his hand, covering him in Luke's jism.

The two men let the final judders of their dying orgasms run through them, clinging tightly to each other. They panted like wild animals in the heat of the day, melting way into each other's flesh. Brett felt contented, as he lay on top of Luke. Their bodies rose and fell with their breathing, in tune with each other. He rested his head against the nape of Luke's neck, feeling the hot flesh beginning to cool. He purred like a cat that had sipped at the cream, softly nuzzling his nose against Luke's earlobe. Luke replied with a satisfied soft moan.

They spent a few minutes like that in the afterglow of their lovemaking. They often would become lazy in each other's arms after their erotic exertions, but this time more so than usual. They savoured the closeness they were feeling, and the joy they had just experienced.

Eventually, and with deliberate slowness, Brett nestled his mouth at Luke's ear. 'Next time,' he drawled dreamily, 'I'll let you fuck me.'

'Mm, that sounds like fun,' his lover enthused. They kissed tenderly. 'Promise?'

'Promise.'

He returned the kiss. Brett closed his eyes and imagined Luke fucking him. He felt his cock quicken at the thought and wondered if Luke would fuck him gently, or hard and fast. He rolled off Luke, on to his back, and looked over.

Luke squinted back at him, a grin breaking over his face. 'I guess this means we're married, huh?'

They both laughed, and then drew together for a kiss. The moment was sweet but also painful – they had declared something for each other. It wasn't possible, it wasn't rational, but it was so clearly what they both felt that it hurt. Brett felt Luke's hands pulling him on to his face, the first kiss becoming a second, a third. Their sweat- and dust-covered bodies rolled once more into each other, not simply out of desire this time, but out of a need for the reassurance of each other's warmth.

The words wouldn't come for Brett. He wanted to say it, but couldn't. He had never told anyone he loved them, let alone another man. Even though the time felt right, and it was certainly Luke that he loved, the sounds from his throat were only moans and not the words running through his head. Brett told himself that he was just being sensible, that he had only been with Luke for a short time, and couldn't possibly know what his feelings for the man were.

But he did. Brett loved Luke. He loved him so much he thought his heart would break. He was so happy he could die, yet felt so churned up and anxious inside that he couldn't understand it. Instead, he brought his hand up to Luke's face, stroking the soft bristle that had emerged in the last day or two. He ran the back of his hand against the stubble, aware of every small hair against his skin.

'I need to take a piss,' he confided to his lover. It wasn't romantic, but it broke the silence.

'Need a hand?' Luke joked back.

'I think I can handle this on my own.'

Luke looked down at Brett's limp penis. 'Looks like you might need two hands, anyhow,' he remarked.

Brett lazily got up and dressed himself again. As he headed off for the woods, Luke laughingly called after him. 'You're gonna need to get some more fruit, too! '

Brett laughed and entered the wood. He quickly pulled out his penis and began to urinate. He watched the golden stream arch in the air and hit the floor, causing first a small puddle, then a trickle as it washed away down the dirt. He seemed to piss for ever, and felt a sense of relief afterwards. The river of his urine was drying in the heat even as he finished making it. He shook the last drips of urine from his knob, and did his trousers up again.

Brett turned away from his makeshift urinal, and went looking for the fruit bushes where he had gathered the fruit only a short while before. Who knows, he joked to himself, maybe they would enact the whole scene again, feeding off the fruit on their naked flesh. This time he would take Luke inside him, allow his mate to fuck him. Brett began feeling horny again, and went about his task with a renewed fervour.

A cool wind began to blow, the heat taken off for the moment. On the wind, Brett thought he heard voices: but, knowing only Luke was around, he dismissed the idea. The vicious whispers continued, background chatter to the flutter of leaves in the trees. McKinley busied himself with gathering the fruit, stopping occasionally to satisfy his own hunger. Sex with Luke always left him with a strong appetite, and the sweet fruit satiated him well.

But he was troubled when he thought he heard voices again. At first, with the slight breeze, Brett thought he could have been mistaken, that it was simply the movement of air through the natural instruments of the wood. As a child, he would often imagine the trees speaking to him, a strange conversation with nature. Well, apart from anything else, it helped ease his loneliness, and was a welcome escape from his brothers.

This wasn't the woods talking to him, though. There were very definitely voices carried on the air. One of them he could recognise as Luke's. Although he couldn't hear what was being said, he could identify the forced calm in Mitchell's voice. He suddenly had a very real sense of danger. The other voice was fast, a higher pitch, with an urgency and instability. He'd heard the voice before, he was sure. He couldn't quite put a name to it.

Then, with a fright, it came to him. He'd heard the voice only too recently.

Rogers!

Rogers must have caught up with him. Brett knew they had only bought themselves some time by locking Rogers away, although he had secretly hoped that the deputy might have given up on coming to look for them. He had been wrong, and the deceptively stupid deputy had managed to track them down. Or – more likely – stumbled upon them.

He would be mad. He would be angry and, when Rogers was angry, he would be dangerous. More than that – they were criminals, he was the law. And it was just them against him. Rogers would want revenge. Not just for the escape, for being locked in the cell, but also for the beating Brett had given him. That was worrying. Very worrying.

Brett stealthily walked to the end of the wood. He crouched behind a bush, nervously pulling the leaves aside to see what was going on. Ahead of him he could see Luke, dressed, and standing off Rogers. He could see that the deputy had his gun drawn, and aimed at Luke. The two men were angrily shouting at each other. Brett strained to hear the conversation.

'So you got out. How long did Sheriff Williams keep you in there, huh? Bet he wasn't keen to let you go.'

'Shut up, Mitchell. You think it was funny to pull a trick like that?'

'Yeah,' Luke said. 'I thought it was goddamn funny. Near enough laughed my head off.'

'Really? Well now I got the chance to blow your head off.'

'Awwww, but deputy, I'm willing to come easy.' Luke held his hands up.

'I don't care what you're willing to do, Mitchell. The way I see it, you're just a lousy criminal. Ain't no one gonna miss you if you don't come back alive. What do I care? In fact, I reckon it'd suit me if you were dead.'

'That wouldn't sit too well with Sheriff Williams, Rogers.'

'Hell, that old fool wouldn't know. I can cook up a story to cover my ass right enough. It's your ass that's in trouble now.'

'Enjoying it, Rogers? Playing the big man now?'

'Oh yeah, I'm loving it. Every minute of it. 'Course, I might like it if you were to beg. You fancy begging for your life, Mitchell?'

Brett could see the sneer on the deputy's face.

'Not much. Not to vermin like you, Rogers.'

'Watch your mouth, you scum. I've just said you can beg for your life. Now I reckon I'll have to change my mind. And there was me thinking that I was being a reasonable man.'

'You're not man enough, Rogers. Everyone knows how Brett kicked your ass in that bar. You'll be the laughing stock of Independence. Nothing you do against me can stop folks laughing behind your back. Maybe some of them will do it to your face, too.'

Brett saw the deputy getting angry. Even more than usual, his face turned ugly. He could see Rogers looking around. He could see him holding his gun up and aim it at Brett's beloved Luke.

'Any last words, you loser?' Rogers gloated.

'Fuck you,' said Luke.

'Awwwww, no last message for your pretty boy? Where's he, then? Your little boyfriend, where's he got to?'

'Leave Brett out of this,' Luke started angrily.

'So it's true, then. I knew he was a cocksucker soon as I set eyes on him. You too, for that matter. '

'We're both more men than you could ever be, Rogers.'

'He around, then? Your sweetheart? Where is he?'

Brett saw Luke shrug his shoulders. 'Beats me,' came the reply.

'Oh, I'll find him. Just 'cos he can throw a few punches in a bar don't mean he can get the better of me. I've time enough for him. Time enough to see that he never gets to live that crazy dream he had of getting gold out west. '

'He'll get there, Rogers. Nothing you can do to stop him. He's a great guy. And a great fuck.'

Brett found himself grinning, despite himself. Even with Rogers holding a gun against him, Luke was able to boast about McKinley's sexual prowess.

'You disgust me.'

'The feeling's mutual, deputy. Believe me.'

It was as he stepped forward that Brett realised that he'd made a mistake. He'd only meant to steady himself a little better, and avoid the risk of cramp. But underneath his foot, the dry twigs snapped loudly and broke the silent air. The noise seemed deafening to him, and it was more than enough to cause Rogers to look over in his direction.

'That you, McKinley?' he heard Rogers shout. 'You there, you lousy cocksucker?'

Brett was unsure about what to do. Was there a way that he could save Luke? His own gun was in their camp, so he couldn't simply shoot at Rogers. *Blast!* There must be something he could do.

'McKinley? You gonna come out or you gonna watch me shoot your boyfriend from behind these bushes? Either way, you're next, boy!'

Brett didn't reply. If he could buy some time, maybe he could resolve this. He couldn't lose Luke like this! He just couldn't.

'You coward, McKinley. Not even man enough to face me down!'

'Don't listen to him, Brett! Save yourself!' Now Luke was calling to him.

'Shut the fuck up, Mitchell!'

'Run now, Brett. You can make it! I'll see you in the west, partner!'

'I said, *shut the fuck up!*'

There was nothing to do. He couldn't help Luke. He could help himself. Even with the tears stinging his eyes, Brett turned around and ran into the woods. He ran faster than he had ever ran before, until his heart was beating so fast it nearly ran ahead of him. He kept running, running away from the only thing he had ever truly loved in his life. Even as he was running, his thoughts were with Luke – he had betrayed his lover, deserted him. He'd decided to save himself and let Luke die alone.

Brett McKinley ran for his life, and didn't stop. Not even when he heard the sound of gunshots ringing in the air behind him.

Twelve

The shots rang out again and again.

BANG! BANG BANG!

Luke's bleeding body falling to the ground, slowly, slowly, ever so slowly . . .

The handsome face, draining of life, turning to Brett, calling for him to help. That godawful scream of the banshee running around his head.

At the side, the figure of Deputy Rogers, laughing caustically, mocking them both. The laughter echoed with the gunfire, a raucous cacophony that stabbed at the air. The figure seemed to grow, its shadow getting larger and larger as Brett continued running away, gasping, panting, a pain in his chest. Still the laughter, the gunshot, the ever increasing shadow enveloping him. The ghostly dark figure became thick, a black fog that engulfed, feeding off him and suffocating him . . .

Brett screamed, the suffocating fog waking him from his sleep. He had been having the same nightmare for nearly three months. He'd seen Luke die before him dozens of times and each time the pain was worse, the demise in greater and gorier detail than the last. Sometimes he would see Luke twitching in pain on the ground; others, Rogers would be turning the gun on Brett himself.

He still couldn't quite remember what had happened. The

shots had urged him to run on, not daring to look back, to see his lover's corpse on the ground. The pain, the loss, and the fear, had all driven him on to run faster and harder, away from the scene and away from the danger. He never wanted to see Rogers again, never wanted to hear about Independence.

He had run for hours on end. When he stopped, exhausted, he was overcome. The tears welled up and burst out of him, leaving him sobbing by the roadside. His dream was gone. It was empty. Without Luke by his side, there was nothing. His loss was absolute. Not only had Luke died – part of Brett had, too. And it was the best part of him that had been washed away with Luke's life.

Brett couldn't remember how long he had just sat there crying. It was the first time he had shed a tear since he was a boy, since he had been kicked by a horse and broken his leg. His father had told him then that no man would cry over such a thing. Well, he was no man, now. He didn't want to be the sort of man his father wanted him to be. Cold, loveless, lifeless. What sort of man was that? He might as well be a wagon, rolling on but feeling nothing, doing nothing but following the path it was being led down.

He kicked at the earth beneath him. He railed against the sky. He spent two days in a rage, breaking anything he came across as he continued to travel westwards. The rage was senseless, a pure flame of anger that burned as bright as the sun in the sky. Thank God, he had thought afterwards, that he didn't come across another living being during those dark days, or he didn't know what would have happened.

He also didn't know how he had survived. Something innate had taken over, for it was only a shell that had carried on walking, eating, breathing. Brett McKinley seemed to have disappeared, become nothing. In his place there was a mirage, an empty husk that managed to put one foot in front of another, push food into his mouth when he was hungry and defecate at the right moment. It wasn't much of an existence, to feel so alone in the world. At times, it felt as if he was the only person in the world.

Sleeping was the worst part. Where once he had snuggled into Luke's warm flesh, now the wind howled round his desolate form. When he woke suddenly in the night, hoping to be comforted by his lover's warm embrace, the empty sky ridiculed him. And over, and over, he thought to himself in the hollow silence, I never said I loved you. You never knew. And then, again, the tears would come.

I never said I loved you.

I love you, Luke.

How simple it seemed to be now. Just a few words. How hard would it have been to say them then? What a fool he was. To let the moment pass so quickly – the moment that he could never get back now. The moment that he wanted to live in forever, which would never – could never – happen now.

Those first days, he had completely lost any sexual desire. He couldn't bear to think of it, the loss too immediate. When, after a few weeks of complete celibacy, he had lazily found himself masturbating, it was about a man who he had never seen or met. The man was just a fantasy, an erotic image to help him get through what needed to be done. There was no passion, no intimacy: simply an act of sex with an imaginary partner who had no history, no past. No connection with Brett, or with Luke.

The weakness in him eventually became replaced with a desire to survive, to get through the dreadful ordeal as best he could, and to live on. He managed to get from day to day, a little more aware of what he was doing, a little more purposeful. If only to keep Luke's memory live, he wanted to fulfil his own dream. He wanted to reach California, to dig the mines, to make his fortune. In some way, Luke might be with him. Isn't that what he had said?

You can make it! I'll see you in the west, partner!

The words haunted him. The last words he had heard Luke speak to him. Words that spoke of the confidence Luke had in Brett. Words of hope, that they would be together again. *Partner.* Words of love. They echoed in his head nearly as often as the damned gunshots, but where the shots kept him running away, the words gave him something to run to. Some thing, but not someone.

So he'd carried on westward. He became a loner, shying away from people, making contact only when he needed to trade the skins and meat he had tracked and hunted down. Mostly he tried to get by off the land as he moved on. People only brought him trouble. People were nothing but trouble.

Until he had got to Snake River. He had known the dangers, known about the quicksand after the heavy rains, and had managed to steer clear of such a catastrophe. He knew how the place got its name, and that it harboured all manner of serpentine menaces. Colm had warned him about such dangers, but Brett knew he had elaborated the stories. Colm had once spoken of how he had saved a man's life by grappling with a rattlesnake, claiming to have bitten the snake itself and then eaten it afterwards.

Yet such warnings hadn't prevented Brett from falling prey to nature's legless hunters. It was as he was picking his way along the canyon that he happened to grab at a rock. In the heat of the day, a rattlesnake had taken to hiding under it to escape the burning sun. The stone had come away in Brett's hand, and all of a sudden he felt the cool scales under his fingers. He pulled back immediately, but had already disturbed the reptile from its slumber. Dazed and exposed, it had lashed out in the only way it had known how, and had sunk its teeth into his flesh. The pain of the bite had been simple enough, a sharp attack on his right hand. It was over as quickly as it had happened, accompanied by a raspy breath and rattling tail.

It was afterwards that he had felt the effects. The shortness of breath, his whole nervous system becoming damaged. He thought it might be the shock of having been bitten, the strange dullness that was passing through him, the effect on his heart.

Brett didn't know what would have happened to him if it hadn't been for Reverend Morgan. Well, that wasn't entirely true, although he didn't want to admit the awful truth. The Reverend had saved his life. Seeing him there, lying prostrate in the heat of the sun, the Reverend had ridden up and seen the snake scooting off in the dirt. Morgan had immediately dismounted and checked over the supine figure and found the small puncture wounds.

Brett hadn't felt the Reverend's mouth on his hand, had hardly been aware of what was happening. Morgan had sucked at his wound, trying to draw out the poison and save his life. When the blood was flowing again, Morgan had pulled out his neckerchief to create a tourniquet, to staunch the bleeding. He had picked Brett up – not an easy feat in itself – and taken him to his horse, throwing him over the saddle. In his dazed state, Brett though he could hear Morgan introducing himself, saying something about God being with them now. And, on the way to the Reverend's house over the hill, he had heard the soft murmuring of prayer.

He had been aware of the tending of the bite, but must have slipped into unconsciousness shortly after arriving at the Reverend's sparse wooden cabin. When he had awakened, some days, later, he became aware of how empty the room he was in was. For a moment, he thought he must have been captured by the law and imprisoned, but later realised that this wasn't some strange cell: merely the lean dwelling of a man with few worldly goods. The only decoration in the room had been the crudely carved wooden cross on the wall opposite his hard bed. A couple of clean light sheets lay on top of him, but there was nothing else to identify this room. A small, narrow window in the wooden logs gave a view out to a clearing, beyond which stood a pine forest.

He had lain there for an hour, awake but not knowing where he was, before Reverend Morgan finally looked in on him. Brett peered up at the man's bespectacled face, a big smile beaming from ear to ear.

'You're awake, then? I thought we might have lost you, but the Lord is good!'

'I'm not sure I remember much.' Brett had struggled with the words, his throat dry and tight, a weakness still hampering him.

'Don't worry. You'll be fine, now. Do you remember what happened to you?'

'Sssssnake . . .' was all that Brett could manage.

'Yes, you were bitten. It was by God's good grace that I happened to be along that way. The Lord seemed to tell me what to do, for I have never helped in such a way before.' The priest then went on to tell Brett about his miraculous escape, about the days he had spent in his company, and the prayers that he had said over the young man to bring him to health.

Brett had been unsure how to respond to Morgan's kindness at first. His words seemed so strange to hear, after Luke's erotic coarseness. Yet there was an appealing gentility in Reverend Morgan, and he was attractive in a sensitive and feminine way – his short wavy blond hair tight against his high cheekbones and tight red lips. Bright blue eyes – almost angelic in their intensity – stared from either side of a small flat nose, slightly snubbed upwards. Light freckles dotted his face, like soft red paintmarks on a canvas. His frame was wiry, not as well built as Luke's masculine musculature, but with more of a boyish vulnerability.

'You're a priest?' Brett could have kicked himself for stating the obvious.

Morgan grinned. 'Only just – I'm just starting my vocation. I'm sort of starting over.'

'Good start,' Brett complimented him with an effort. The very act of speech was tiring him.

'I seek no thanks. You're welcome to whatever hospitality I can afford you. As you can see, though, I have not much to offer.'

For someone who had saved his life, the Reverend seemed unduly apologetic.

'You've done more than enough,' spluttered Brett. 'Really, you have. You don't know anything about me, yet you saved my life . . .'

'You've a kindly face, that much I know,' said the Reverend sincerely. 'And you've been terribly ill. I was in the right place to help you.'

His kindness touched Brett, and in it he sensed a vulnerability. As the days wore on, Brett and Reverend Morgan began to get to know each other better, each man opening up a little to the other. To Brett, the Reverend seemed keen to talk, to have somebody close to him. No one called by the house, and the only thing in Morgan's life seemed to be the small services he conducted at the local chapel. It was clear that attendances were small, that Morgan's district was pretty much out of the way. However, that didn't stop him from spending hours poring over his Bible and attempting to write an impassioned and enlightened sermon.

Occasionally, the Reverend would test his sermons out on

Brett. McKinley actually enjoyed listening to the man orate, his voice filled with fervour and encouragement. Morgan would often anxiously look over to see how Brett was receiving the message, and somehow Brett had always managed to give the correct impression. He nodded gravely in the right places, smiled and laughed and applauded in the right places. Each time the reaction was appropriate, Morgan's face would light up in glee.

Then, after the service, Morgan would tell him all about what had happened, sharing his joy at this comment or another. Even though he had never met them, Brett was beginning to feel as if he knew some of the Reverend's flock – the Brown family with the young children who never seemed to be healthy; the old spinster, Ma Proctor, who didn't appear to have a good word to say about anyone (except the Reverend, of course!); young Mary Stone, who was worried by her fledgling adolescence and the sudden attentions of Mack Glover – a tearaway, even by Morgan's own admission. Simple people and simple problems, Brett often told himself, and wondered if Morgan could even guess at his own past.

He had thought about telling him. Every day, when Morgan brought in a breakfast for him, he had thought about saying that he was on the run, confessing what had happened. But somehow the words had never been spoken, and now McKinley thought that it was better that way. He saw his near-fatal snake bite as an awakening, a call to forget about Luke, and his past life, and to create a new life now. It was a sort of baptism, he told himself, almost beginning to believe what Morgan himself had told him. There was a reason behind him nearly dying, and a reason for being saved from death. It wasn't entirely clear what the reason was, but surely part of it must be to give him this new life. Where else would he get a new start like this?

Reverend Morgan had been patient, caring, kind. He was attractive. He had accepted Brett into his house. He had made sure Brett had recovered from his fever and sickness, had prayed over him morning and night. Brett couldn't desecrate such purity with his own simple truth. He would become the person Reverend Morgan believed him to be – honest and hard-working. He had seen the admiration on Morgan's face when he had spoken of his work at the farmstead, had realised that these were the qualities the priest had been taught to commend.

Today, waking from the recurring nightmare, Brett couldn't quite work out if the dream was a way of saying goodbye to Luke, or of walking away from him. Luke is dead, he told himself, I need to create a new life and move on. Even as he said the words, his heart felt heavy, even though the rest of him was yearning to get up and do something for once.

Brett went with his body's sense of itself. He washed early, savouring the cold water on his naked flesh, and began making Morgan's breakfast – a complete reversal of roles, for once. He knew that the Reverend prayed for an hour first thing in the morning, and that he would have time to prepare the bread and coffee they shared each day. By the time Morgan sauntered into the kitchen in his black cassock, Brett was seated at the table, grinning over a mug of coffee.

'Brett! Why, it's good to see you up and about!'

'I was getting awfully lazy in that bed all the time, Reverend.' Brett grinned at the holy man, 'I thought it was about time I started earning my keep!'

'Earn your keep? Why, good man, I appreciate the sentiment but, I've said often enough . . .'

'That may be so, Reverend: but for a man like me, I only value something when I work for it. I have to earn it, see? For me to believe that I deserve it. I don't take charity.'

Morgan paused. He understood, and meekly accepted the coffee and roll of warm bread Brett had made. 'It's good,' he said, and Brett grinned in appreciation of the praise. 'You got plans, then? I mean, you still ought to take things easy, you know. Can take a man a long time to get over a thing like that. Maybe you should take things one step at a time.'

'I can manage, Reverend Morgan. I was just wondering what chores you might have that need doing. Reckon I can manage most things.'

'Well, now, I spent so much time here on my own, I can't rightly think of things for other people to do. I tend to do things as and when they need doing. If I see something needs fixing, I fix it. If I feel hungry, I cook. If I've got time on my hands, I pray.'

'That sounds good enough for me. I'll take a look round in a while, see what's broke and what could do with fixing. Can't guarantee 'bout the praying, though,' he added sheepishly.

Morgan laughed. 'I hadn't realised how much I missed having company round the place. It's good to have someone to check me out. I spend all this time praying for other people, yet I know nothing about them!'

'You've got that lot down at the chapel, don't you? I thought they were pretty friendly with you?'

'I don't mean to be uncharitable, Brett, but it's a pretty one-way relationship. They need me to feel good about themselves, so they make sure I get what I need. But they don't really think about me, Brett.'

'I thought Old Ma Proctor had invited you over for dinner next Sunday?'

'That she has – so she can moan about the new land, the prospectors, the hunters, the folks who never visit her . . . despite the fact there's always someone in the house whenever I go over.'

'I thought you loved this job. Didn't you tell me it was all you over wanted to do?' quizzed Brett. Again, he saw the chasm of vulnerability and loneliness opening up in the young Reverend Morgan.

'The Lord has been good to me, Brett. He really has. I've had a happy family; I was blessed as a child. Some might say spoilt. I've always felt I should share that good fortune. That can only be why things have been so good for me. When people talk to me, they can only ever see the problems, the way that we're challenged by the Lord's will. Yet I can only see the good fortune in everything we do, everything that happens to us.'

Brett listened to Morgan speaking. He was conscious of the heavy sighs, and the smile he gave apologetically at the end of every sentence.

'And it all seemed so certain at first. That was my mission – to share with everyone how good it all was. To ease the pain, or make some sense of it, anyhow. And it was easy, to begin with. I could find the inspiration; I could sing my song loud and clear. And yes, it did feel like the Lord was working through me, Brett. I felt that I was doing the Lord's work.'

'You said "did",' noticed Brett softly. 'You don't feel that now?'

'I'm getting tired of being so alone, Brett. Of feeling like an outsider, everywhere I go. Of people always being polite with me, and not knowing what they really think or say when I've gone. Sure, sometimes they like to confess to me. But that's feeling like a burden, now. Sometimes I just want to share some of that, unburden myself the way that they unburden themselves on me. And I don't have anyone, Brett. I can't do that, they way that they can. Sometimes it feels so . . . lonely. I feel so alone.'

Brett found himself putting an arm round Morgan, cradling him in his arms. He could feel the blood coursing through his veins, much stronger than he had felt for days, nearly weeks.

'I understand, Reverend. We all feel that way, sometimes. Like you just want to be part of something more than yourself.'

He felt the Reverend move into him, slightly shaking. It was then that Brett realised the man was crying. It was a soft, blocked whimper, tentative and careful. The wave of sadness flowed over him. Brett continued to hold him, and pulled him closer so that he could feel his warmth against him. There was no embarrassment about the union, merely a willingness to share this moment together.

Brett stroked the Reverend's hair, wiped his tears from his eyes. Here was the man who had cared for him while he had been sick, and now Brett was caring for him. Now he was providing the support and love that had been missing from the reverend's life as a minister. He lookd down at Morgan, whose lip was quivering slightly. In fact, Brett realised that the whole of Morgan's body was trembling.

Brett pulled Morgan up so that they were face to face. He stroked the other man's face lightly, running his thumb down the salty river of a tear that trickled along the left side of his face. 'It's all right, Reverend, to feel like this. Trust me.'

The kiss was soft, but assured. Brett leant his head into Morgan's; their lips met and fastened to each other. Brett felt

Morgan acquiesce to the first intimacy, but there was no resistance as their lips met. Sure of himself, and of Morgan's feelings, he kissed him again, a little harder, and a little more certain. The Reverend moaned slightly and eased into Brett's strong grasp. McKinley cupped his face in his large hands, pulling it into his passionate kiss.

There was no going back, now. The floodgates were open, and Morgan was aching to be filled with McKinley's passion. They were now vessels for each other's emotions, falling on each other with deep kisses. It was Morgan who opened his mouth and urged McKinley to explore it with his tongue, sucking him into his open orifice. Brett, eyes open, watched Morgan closing his eyes, and moaning with unremitting desire, a longing born out of years of loneliness.

Brett fumbled with the large, ornate black buttons of Morgan's cassock. He let his hands pull the heavy, oversized garment up towards the top of Morgan's soft hair-covered thighs. The feel of Morgan's downy muscles under him excited Brett, knowing that this was a new territory, one which no other man had explored. He could hear the soft moans of Morgan as he allowed himself to be mapped, his fertile plains to be exploited by Brett's searching fingers.

Brett steered clear of the obvious route, wanting to postpone the moment of intimate connection with his new lover. His hand moved up over the fine fair hair of Morgan's chest, not as muscularly a sculpted chest as Luke's had been, but broad enough, and heaving under his touch. Brett took it slowly, so that every inch he covered sent another sensation rippling through Morgan, until he found the erogenous zone of his nipples, gently rubbing his thumb against first the left then the right. The touching brought gasps from his lover, then moans of ecstasy.

Soon the fingers were replaced by Brett's warm mouth, his wet tongue flicking over the nipples, lips and teeth closing softly over them. He sucked the erect projectiles into his mouth, running his hand down towards the soft trail of hair from Morgan's belly to his crotch. He moved his oral attention back to Morgan's mouth, now gasping in heavy pants of desire. This must surely have ended the loneliness Morgan had felt for so long!

Morgan was supine, not quite believing what was happening to him. Brett let his right hand drop down to Morgan's burning groin, feeling the stiffening form awakening from its celibate history. Morgan pushed his mouth on to Brett's as McKinley's hand closed over the hardening cock, slowly stroking it from base to tip. He masturbated Morgan, wondering how many times the minister had tossed himself off in his loneliness. How many times had he ejaculated into his own palm to break the lonely days and nights with some ecstatic relief?

Morgan's cock was average-sized, a turgid six and a half inches, but thick in the girth, with a plum-shaped red head, surrounded by soft pliable foreskin. The ooze of juice from his hole gave each long stroke a wet slapping sound, a soft squelching sound-track to their lovemaking.

'No one's ever . . . I haven't done this . . .' spluttered Morgan into Brett's right ear as he was being slowly masturbated.

'I know . . . Enjoy it . . . I bet it feels great, huh?'

'Oh, for sure . . . So good to have your hand on my cock like that.'

Brett softly kissed Morgan's neck, licking the length of his sweaty collarbone. Morgan's skin was soft, burning with desire, flushed red all over. The blood pumped into his cock, making it throb with every touch of Brett's masterful hand. Brett grabbed it hard, and worked it quickly, wanking Morgan's dick faster and faster. His other hand reached down to cup Morgan's lightly hairy bollocks in his hand, and Brett gently tugged at the sac as he stroked the hardened knob.

Meanwhile, Morgan unfastened the buttons of his cassock completely, so that the heavy material fell away at the centre, the curtains of fabric parting to reveal his naked flesh. McKinley was filled with desire at the sight of Morgan's exposed manhood and bowed his head down to the altar of Morgan's church of flesh. He looked up at the disbelieving Reverend, whose eyes half closed in sweet anticipation of the pleasure Brett was offering.

'Oh, yes . . . Taste me, kiss me. Brett, suck me . . .'

Brett held the fat cock in front of his face and pulled the heavy foreskin right back, exposing the throbbing glans. He flicked his tongue out so that it just made contact with the wet flesh, accompanied by a long groan from his lover. Then he rested his tongue under the throbbing crown, letting the dripping pre-come collect on his tongue. It was fresh and salty, a hot liquid ejected from inside Morgan's excited body. Brett lapped it up, tasting the other man's desire. He was the first man to explore this juicy elixir, and he savoured each moment.

Brett ran his tongue over the whole soaking head, spreading the hot juices all over the sizzling flesh. As Morgan gasped with the intensity of pleasure Brett was giving him, McKinley covered the cockhead with his lips, encasing it in an envelope of attentive warmth. Struggling to cope with the girth, Brett moved his mouth over the length, taking more and more of the hard cock into his willing mouth, down the full extent of the pulsating flesh. Morgan's manhood seemed to fill Brett's entire mouth, and he could feel the inexperienced man trying to send his thick arrow of desire into the back of his throat, almost making him gag. Grabbing the base of this eager monster, McKinley was able to control its movements and urges so that it accompanied his own course of action.

Brett unfastened his own pants, and pulled Morgan on to the floor with him. He was excited himself now, a full erection breaking out from his groin. He grabbed Morgan's head and pushed it towards his dick. He wasn't going to be the only one sucking hard cock! He wanted release, too. When he felt Morgan's soft tongue gently probing his erection, he gasped also. Gone now was the polite religiosity – Morgan's true hunger was revealed at once. In a matter of moments, the gentle probings had become long, welcome sucks on his pole, a feeling he hadn't experienced since leaving Luke. Morgan was a natural cock-sucker, feeling his way along the underside of the penis, then tonguing the base, the shaft, the head. Brett's erection grew in accordance with the sucking he was receiving from Morgan's virginal mouth.

The men sixty-nined each other, eagerly slurping on their thickened tools. Their thrusting became syncopated, matching each other's movements exactly. Both men were eager for their orgasm: Morgan for his first time of ecstatic joy, and Brett desperate to relive the moment after so long a gap. It wasn't clear who was dictating the pace, as both men sensed each other's desire for fulfilment.

When Brett heard Morgan's moans become loud warnings of impending discharge, he began bucking wildly into his partner's sucking mouth. He wanted them to come together, for Morgan to experience the communion that only mutual orgasm could bring. Brett could feel the heaviness of his own release building in his groin, awaiting sensational release.

'C'mon, let's go there together,' he urged Morgan. 'Let's come together, Morgan. Suck me harder'.

'I'm ready, Brett. Take me all the way . . .' Morgan's voice was broken, hoarse, filled with pre-orgasm tension. A tension that was soon going to be relieved.

The sucking quickened, blood forging its way through their engorged veins, and Brett felt the swell of spunk rising in him. He thrust twice more into Morgan's wanton mouth, the last a long heavy stroke, and kept his throbbing cock inside as he erupted. He clamped down on Morgan's knob as he orgasmed fiercely, the hot white liquid spurting into Morgan's willing body, as his lover swallowed his semen. Spurt after spurt ensued, matched by Morgan's first virginal spray into Brett's thirsty mouth. Morgan's body wracked itself in ecstasy as Brett tasted the hot salty prize of his attentions.

They lay for a while, licking and sucking each other, until both men were limp, finished. It was Morgan who broke their coupling, to kiss Brett full on the mouth – a deep, long kiss, during which McKinley tasted his own sperm on the Reverend's tongue.

'I can never feel alone now. You have given me a divine experience; one I can never forget. My angel!'

Brett wasn't sure if he felt embarrassed or comforted by the Reverend's words. He was pleased to have relieved him from the prison of abandonment and loneliness, and to have connected in this almost spiritual way. He felt the warmth of him as they held each other afterwards, and thought of how he had felt with Luke. That had been special, for him: that had been his moment of heaven. But it was over. Luke was dead, and he had found a new companion to share himself with. The feeling wasn't as intense, but Brett was sure he could grow to love Reverend Morgan, in a different way. His life had been saved, and he must atone for that with his fidelity to Morgan.

Morgan, his new lover. Not a replacement for Luke, as no one could be, but someone to share intimacy with, to pleasure and to take pleasure from. And it was only as Brett contemplated their future together that he realised something – he didn't even know the Reverend's first name.

Thirteen

The mist cleared in the canyon, revealing the morning's chilly welcome. The wagons were parked in their familiar horse-shoe shape, a protective and comforting gesture that created a strong defence against unwanted intruders. The white canvas of the upper deck of the wagons lent an eerie embryonic feel to the womb-like construction, increasing the feeling of security and protection. A slight wind buffeted the material, blowing through the myriad nooks and crannies, as horses neighed and awoke, having slept through the night but not quite rested. The animals always seemed restless in convoys like this, as aware of the wolves and bandits and Indian scouts as their human counterparts.

The humans slumbered on, the women and children safe within the confines of the wagons, while the menfolk lay blanketed around the embers of last night's fire. Smoke still rose from the makeshift hearth, hot nuggets of wood still orange in the brittle cold of the morning. The acrid stench of burning wood still hung in the air, the smoke still strong enough to sting the eyes of anyone fool enough to be up this early in the morning. The smoke formed a light haze around the encampment, a ghostly film that mixed with the last of the mist. Its smell was slightly reassuring, the definite creation of human hands, a sign of cultivation and creation.

The only such sign in this rocky wilderness. There wasn't a

homestead or outpost anywhere around for miles, just the long canyon with its steep rocky walls on either side. The ground was hard and barren, although tumbleweed seemed to follow the convoy wherever it went. The light wind guided some through the camp, softly rolling it like some child's toy through the horseshoe and out the other end.

For weeks the wagons had been fighting to beat the rocky trail, to find something else which would prove that this was indeed a trail and not some dead end. Rumours of the Ned Clements Trio, a fearsome band of outlaws led by brothers Ned and Lance Clements, had swept through the voyagers quickly, and laid over the trail a cloud of fear from the beginning. The Clements Brothers and their cohort Deadeye Pete were notorious for their vicious and unprovoked attacks on travellers. The legend surrounding Deadeye Pete was that if you looked into his eye, you might as well consider yourself a dead man – hence no reliable description of him for the local sheriff to respond to. Rumour had it that the officers of the law were in the Clements Gang's pocket anyhow, receiving a sizeable amount from each ambush.

There had been no sign of the gang thus far on the trip. However, that didn't stop the nervous glances, the heightened sense of alarm following every unusual sound or movement. Fear was the worst companion on a journey like this, slowing every-thing down immeasurably. The convoy moved forward slowly, carefully, trying to reach its goal before the weather gave out and late summer passed all too quickly into the depths of winter.

The party was made up of many different characters, seeking to make their way back west. There was the Farrell family, Will and Emily, with their ten-year-old son Douglas, who had come up from Arkansas seeking to make their fortune. They were friendly young folk, in their early thirties, hard-working and kindly. There was also Old Man Russell, the unacknowledged leader of the group, who had been a hunter and tracker at the beginning of the century. He had a fierce temper when chal-lenged, but his general judgement was clear and articulate.

And then there was Luke Mitchell, the angry young rogue and outcast of the group. Luke had joined the caravan halfway through its journey, and hadn't made much attempt to explain himself or his journey. He hadn't been keen on talking to anyone and mostly kept himself to himself. Of course, the rumours had spread through the camp about him – that he was a spy for the Clements gang; that he had been thrown out of his house by his wife, who had found him cheating on her; that he was a criminal of some kind trying to escape the law.

The last allegation he had chosen to ignore. That it was true did not bother him, but he felt it best not to respond to such stories – just in case word got back to Sheriff Williams. After Rogers had found them on that auspicious day, Luke had been running ever since. He hoped against hope that his warning to Brett had been heeded, but couldn't be certain that his young lover had escaped, or was still alive. He just hoped that he was.

Luke had been caught by surprise by Rogers, and he kicked himself daily for allowing that to happen. He had been getting dressed, still a little too drunk on his lovemaking with Brett to be fully in charge of what was happening. Rogers had crept up behind him, and it was only when he heard the familiar snigger that he realised what was happening. Turning round, he had been faced with Rogers's ugly sneer, and the Colt pistol only yards from his face. He remembered Rogers's opening line:

'Remember me?'

And his own response:

'I reckon so. You're the jailbird from Independence, right?'

They hadn't got off to a good start, and it got worse from there. He remembered Rogers's anger, his taunting, his threats. He remembered being told to beg for his life, and feeling that he was already dead. He sincerely believed that Rogers would shoot him dead, and make up some lie to cover his back when he got back to the sheriff. Luke had gambled on the fact that Rogers wanted both him and Brett, and would try to use him to get at McKinley. By not answering his questions directly, Mitchell hoped that he could buy himself a little time to think through the situation.

Until Brett had been seen by Rogers. He had called him over and, even though there was no response from McKinley, Rogers had known that he was there. He had fired two shots into the wood thicket, a ridiculous waste of ammunition. But it had given Luke his chance to rush at Rogers, taking him off guard. Fortunately, it had been easy to knock the gun out of Rogers's hand, and to force him to the ground. They had tussled, but Luke was the better man by far in a one-to-one hand fight. It hadn't taken long to subdue the surly deputy. He had taken out his own anger against himself on Rogers, beating against him in his fury. Many of the blows hadn't even connected with Rogers: Mitchell had just wanted to release his pent-up frustration.

He had thought about killing Rogers. He remembered getting up from the fight and picking up the deputy's gun. He remembered the hot metal in his hand, warmed by the sizzling sun. The sweat had made it slippy in his hand. He had fired a warning shot in the sky, and looked at Rogers lying on the floor. The deputy had looked up pitifully, begging for him not to shoot. His life, his death, in Luke's hands. He had felt the anger welling up. The sense of injustice at being imprisoned in the first place, the way he had been treated by Matt Wilmott. He thought of the way Rogers had treated him in the cell, the ritual taunting, the verbal abuse. He thought of Rogers threatening to kill him only a few moments ago.

And then he thought of Brett.

His lover. His companion. His partner. They had had only a few days together, a few sweet days of passion. Now those days were gone. Rogers had split them apart, torn them asunder with his arrival. In order to save Brett's life, Luke had had to give him up. Rogers could have done no worse an act. But what would have been achieved if he were to kill him now? One more dead man. Luke had told himself he was no murderer. He had never killed another man, and would not do so.

'You know I could kill you. You know that?'

'Yes . . . please . . . no . . .' begged Rogers.

'I'm not going to, Rogers. Not because I don't want to. I hate you enough, and I never knew that I could hate so much. But I want you to live, knowing this – I'm an innocent man, Rogers. I never stole, I never killed: I just tried to get by. You understand that?'

'Yes . . .' Rogers had croaked, too weak to speak in anything other than a hoarse whisper.

'I want to hear you say it, Rogers. Tell me I'm innocent.'

'I believe you. You . . . are . . . innocent.'

The words had sounded like a chorus of angels from heaven.

'Good. At least you're listening. Now here's the deal. I don't care enough about you to kill you. You don't mean anything to me, Rogers, dead or alive. But I guess your life means something to you. Right?'

'Yes . . .' Rogers said weakly.

'So you want to stay alive. I'm going to leave you here. Then you're going to make your way back to Independence. You're going to go straight there. You're going to forget any crazy plans you might have about me and Brett. You're not going to come looking for us because, as far as you are concerned, we are dead. We're history. And that's what you're going to tell anyone who asks. Understood?'

Rogers had nodded in acquiescence.

'That means no one's going to come looking for us again. Ever. We're free men because we're dead men, in the eyes of the law. Is that clear?'

'Yes . . .'

Luke had looked at Rogers. Could he trust him? Would Rogers come after him or Brett just as soon as he could, when the cuts and bruises had healed? Luke hadn't been too sure. On balance, though, he had believed that Rogers would do what he was told. He wasn't the sharpest tool in the box, but he wasn't that stupid. This way, at least Rogers could save some face – could maybe even make up his own story of the fate that befell Luke Mitchell and Brett McKinley. At least, this way, the two men had a fighting chance to make a new world for themselves – together or apart.

He had turned his back on Rogers and walked. He had gone off in the direction McKinley had taken, part of him thinking that Brett would be standing there, waiting to congratulate him on how brave, how remarkable he had been. How he had sacrificed himself for his lover, shown his true love for him. For that was what it was – he did love Brett McKinley. He had felt it the first time he had laid eyes on him in Independence, had known that this was a special man. He thought of Rodriguez and Josh, of their relationship, and wondered if they had shared as deep an affection as he now felt for Brett.

But there had been no Brett waiting for him. There was no happy ending this time. Brett had fled, just like Luke had told him to. Luke had told him to go, to leave him, to follow that damned dream about goldmines and freedom. This was the price he had to pay. He had killed their love, just as surely as he could have killed Rogers. He had paid the price for Brett's releasing him. His debt to him had now been paid in full. McKinley had given him his freedom, and he had saved McKinley from the deputy's manic hatred.

In the woods, he had come across a man's bootmark in the dirt. He had bent down to look at it, and recognised the imprint as Brett's. Feeling ridiculous but unable to stop himself, he had touched the footprint with his right hand, stroking it as the last lingering proof of Brett's place in his life. He gathered the dry dirt up in his hand, and watched as it trickled through his fingers. He had wiped Brett away. He'd erased his place in the world, now nothing more than his memory of their coupling.

And so Luke Mitchell had walked away from Rogers, away from the woods, away from Brett. He had walked until he fell in with a caravan of wagons meandering their way across the canyon. Thinking that this journey was as good as any, he had joined them and become part of the group heading westward. He remembered telling Brett that he would see him out west, although he didn't quite believe that they would ever meet again. What did Luke mean to Brett? A quick fuck? Some outlaw who would only bring him trouble? He had nothing to offer – no wealth, no authority or power. Brett had his whole life ahead of him, and a man like Luke could only hold him back.

The convoy wasn't all bad. Luke had heard early on about the Clements brothers, and wasn't worried about the rumours, the way that other members of the group were. He knew he could handle himself and, if the worst came to the worst, he would get away from the convoy – the gang would have no need to follow a lone man like him. After all, he had no money, nothing of worth for them to steal. He knew that the Clements brothers were pragmatists who did what they had to do. Deadeye Pete sounded another matter, but nevertheless Mitchell was big enough to take care of himself.

Luke wasn't afraid of anything now. He had already faced his demons. After all, wasn't he dead anyway? Hadn't Luke Mitchell been killed in some dreadful catastrophe, according to Deputy Rogers of Independence? What possible fate could be worse than death? Mitchell smiled to himself as he stretched in the morning air. He liked these early morning moments, when there was no one around but himself. He wandered over to the edge of the encampment, looking out across the canyon trail. There was nothing but rock for miles, apart from the trickle of water which had once been a river accompanying the trail out west.

Luke wandered down to the water, washing himself in it. He let the chilled water run over his face. The icy feeling jolted a memory – Brett telling him how he often masturbated in the river at home, how he enjoyed the sensation of his burning flesh in the cool stream. Luke wondered where Brett was now. Had he made it out west? Had he been killed by a gang like the Clements Brothers? By the Clements Brothers themselves? Had he become an outlaw himself? Did he think about Luke at all?

Luke picked a stone, smooth and tactile, and skimmed it across the water. It bounced a couple of times over the running stream, and crashed over the other side. He picked up a harder, rougher piece of flint, and smashed it against the wall of the canyon opposite, watching it splinter as it broke. He smashed another stone against the wall, just for something to do. If only he could while away his hours doing such empty things as smashing stones against a canyon wall!

Returning to the encampment, Luke began to stoke the fire. He looked around for pieces of dry wood, found a few branches washed up by the river's shore, and added them to the fire. He skilfully arranged the branches so that the fire took off, and warmed himself against the flames. The previous night, they had sat around the same fire, singing campfire songs and telling stories late into the night. He had kept his distance, as usual, from the group, but had appreciated the company. It had made him feel part of a family, that he belonged. It was a passing feeling, for he knew he didn't belong anywhere, with anyone, but it had been good to feel that way for a moment.

He almost felt he had belonged when Brett had made love to him. The last time, when Brett had fucked him, had taken him fully, had felt like home. He longed now for Brett inside him again, to feel his strong arms around him, Brett's lips on his, bearing down on him with unbridled passion. Luke crouched in front of the growing fire, wrapping his arms around him to comfort himself, to remind him of how it felt to be held.

Glancing about, Luke checked that there were no figures on the mountain ridges, looking down on the sleeping party and waiting to jump them. Mornings were a dangerous time, more dangerous than the night-time. They would take it in turns to watch through the night – Luke was just finishing his watch now – but it was easy to feel tired in the morning, to lose concentration. Luke would be glad to kip down when the men awoke with the rising dawn and, looking in the sky he saw that the moment would be soon. His solitary watch would soon be finished.

The ridges were safe; there was no movement, no indication that they would be attacked this morning. The silence always seemed eerie, ominous, a calm before a savage thunderstorm. He didn't want to feel complacent, but suspected that the Clements Gang were after other prey, for today at least. Mind you, there was no obvious wealth in the group – even if he was a criminal (and Deputy Rogers had said he wasn't!) Mitchell would have wanted to rob people with a more obvious gain than this lot. He'd want such risk to be worth his while.

Luke stretched out in front of the fire, and lay on his back, his head on the ground. Knowing the party was safe enough for the time being, he allowed himself to catch up on his rest. As he nodded in and out of sleep, Luke missed the warmth of Brett next to him, the feel of the younger man's body against him. He hadn't quite got used to sleeping alone again, but supposed that he would. It was all a matter of time, he told himself.

He hadn't realised he'd fallen asleep until he was woken up by voices talking softly. They were low and lazy voices, and Luke struggled to recognise them. In his hazy awakening, Luke knew that he recognised them, but couldn't quite distinguish them, and connect the voices to faces. In the end he realised that the voices belonged to two of the men from the encampment – a huge relief, as he worried what would have happened if the voices and belonged to Deadeye Pete and the Clements boys. But he had checked, he reassured himself, he had made sure the camp was safe. Still, he didn't want to be seen sleeping on duty, so he crouched up before the men would see him lying down.

The two men were the other side of the wagons, and Luke recognised the youthful Will Farrell and one of his closest friends, Dirk Barrett. Dirk was a few years older than Will, in his mid-thirties, a broad-shouldered blacksmith who was joining his wife out west. Luke hadn't had much to do with him, but had seen him sharing a pipe with Will every now and again. Will was an enigmatic fellow, popular in the camp because of his hard work and sense of humour – he was the perfect counterpoint to the dour Old Man Russell. He had strawberry-blond hair, wild green eyes, and a lean build. Beside Dirk, who was much taller and heavier than Will, they seemed an odd couple. Dirk had developed a large belly from years of drinking too much beer, hanging over his belted pants. Shirtless, his dark shoulder-length hair met with the clouds of dark hair along his shoulders and back, giving the impression that he was closer to animal than human.

The men were sharing a morning pipeful of tobacco, a ritual that Luke had noticed them indulging in most mornings. Will took long slow lungfuls of the tobacco smoke before passing it to his friend, who tended to puff in shorter, quicker intakes. Will was dressed only in his pants and vest, and Luke approvingly noticed the soft curve of his penis under the cloth. Dirk, only in his pants, was scratching his groin; when Dirk moved his hand, Luke couldn't fail to notice how well-endowed the large man was. It almost looked like he had stuffed a large thick sausage down his pants! Luke imagined him fucking his wife with such a monster pole and hoped for her sake that she could accommodate Dirk.

Without attempting to, Luke found that he could overhear

their conversation quite easily. The men occasionally broke out in raucous laughter, and then caught themselves on the verge of waking the sleeping dozens around them. They talked easily and intimately, a sign that their friendship had been close for many years.

'I tell you, Will, I'll be glad when this damned journey is finished. I'm missing my Louise something terrible right now,' Dirk confided.

'It's not long now, Dirk. You'll be with her soon enough. You can manage till then,' Will reassured him.

'I'm not so sure 'bout that, now! I'm feeling like a dog with no bitch these days, and it's taking its toll on my old fella down here.'

The two men laughed, as Dirk grabbed again at his crotch.

'Well, it's not enough to have the wife near to you, Dirk, I can assure you of that. Last night, I was feeling horny as hell and ready to get down to it. I called my Emily over, I whispered sweetly in her ear like a good man should, and she plain turned me down! Muttered something about a headache and how I was constantly seeking her attention, these days. '

'You must pester her too much, Will. I reckon you wear her out!'

Luke saw Will grin broadly. 'Well, it has been known. I'm a pretty mean animal when I get it up.'

'I know the feeling, my friend. Mornings are the worst, too. Waking with a raging hard-on, nowhere to take it. Thought my loins were on fire, this morning.'

'A man needs certain things, that's for sure, Dirk. I reckon I'm gonna take myself a leak. The morning air's getting to me.'

Dirk watched Will walk away from him, past a rocky outcrop. Luke saw him looking over at his friend, and then watched Will join him. Knowing that men never piss together, Luke wondered what was really going on. He knew that both Will and Dirk were not lovers in the way that he and Brett had been. He was sure they had never sucked each other's cocks or that either of them had been fucked like he had. Yet there seemed to be something sexual in the tone of their conversation, an understanding of each other's needs. Luke had heard Will fucking his wife, only a few nights before, and knew that she did indeed approve of his passion – and that Will was as good a lover as he boasted. He also knew from the groans and shouts of ecstasy that Will's attentions were certainly with the fairer sex, and that he had expertise in pleasing them.

Luke found himself getting aroused as he thought of Will fucking Emily, his hard length inside her. Luke felt his own cock begin to stir, and moved closer to the rocks Will and Dirk were standing behind. He could hear their heavy breathing, fast movements coming from the other side of the rock. Gathering up his courage, Luke stood up and turned round the corner.

'I just came over for a leak . . .' He heard himself starting an excuse and stopped short. Will and Dirk were standing opposite each other, cocks in hand. The two men were wanking in front of each other, watching each other pump their hard meat. The men grinned at him, not in the least embarrassed at the state he had caught them in.

'Come to join us?' invited Will cheerfully. 'It's our early morning work-out.'

'Only rule is,' explained Dirk, 'no touching. OK?'

Luke couldn't believe his luck. He'd have gladly touched, sucked or licked either man's throbbing erection, but watching and playing would make a good second best. He looked them over as they masturbated. Will's cock bent slightly, but was a handsome size, although it was dwarfed by Dirk's nine-inch red-headed monster. Dirk lovingly fondled it, one hand playing with his hairy balls as the other stroked up and down his dripping length. Will looked on as his mate tossed himself off, pulling on his own firm manhood.

Luke fished out his own member, half erect already from watching the two men touching themselves. He planted himself between the other two, grinned at them, and started slowly stroking himself in front of them.

'You got yourself a nice pair of snakes there, fellas. Your wives must be pleased to see you at night.'

'Not as often as I'd like, Luke. And your dick ain't bad, either,' complimented Will. He stopped stroking for a moment, gently teasing his foreskin right over the tip of his penis, milking out a drop of pre-come. He let it drip on to his finger, and then rubbed it into his hard flesh.

'Mm, I'm leaking some nice juice already, here,' he boasted. 'Shame Emily isn't here to lick that up for me.'

Luke would have offered, but he'd been told the rules of the game.

'You're lucky, Will. My Louise won't do anything like that.'

'You don't know what you're missing. There's nothing quite like having your cock sucked. Am I right, Luke?'

'Sure, Will. Having a hot pair of lips over your bell-end is as good as it gets.' He thought of Brett sucking on him, and quickly hardened. He pulled on his erection in long lazy strokes, afraid that if he came too early, the men might suspect he was wanking over the fantasy of sucking them both off.

'I'm really hard, now. It ain't gonna take me long to ride this baby home.' Will's erection curved out to prove his point, his hand full of it.

'I'm not far off myself, this beauty is pumped full of blood, and I can feel the fire in my balls rising as I pump it.' Dirk's commentary on his pleasure-seeking turned Luke on, and he stroked faster on his own length.

'You had it recently, Luke? Been sowing your wild oats, I bet – that dick of yours must have seen some action, I reckon.'

'Oh yeah,' grinned Luke, thinking back to the sex he had shared with Brett, 'few weeks back, now. It was good, though.'

'Hope you gave as good as you got,' Dirk joked.

'Oh, yeah,' replied Luke, thinking of Brett fucking his willing arse. 'I gave some, too.'

Luke watched Will as the other man's face creased with desire; Will was pleasurably playing his instrument the way he clearly liked it best – a twisting pull, so that he moved the skin round and up his shaft. Dirk's style was different; he used his clenched fist to fuck, making love to his own warm hand. Luke preferred to alternate his strokes between slow movements and then fast jerks, so that he could bring himself to the point of orgasm and then stop just before boiling over.

He felt so turned on, jerking off with the two other men, sharing their libido in this way. This was as close as he could get to sex with them, as much as they would allow their curiosity to wander. Taking his cue from the other two men, he quickened and slowed as they did, as if they were all wanking in unison, taking it in turns to dictate the pace of their masturbation. Luke longed to watch the other two men shoot their load out in the open, watch the fountains of jism shoot up into the sky and splatter to the ground at his feet. He could hear them breathing coarsely; no conversation passed between them now as they concentrated on reaching their destination.

The three men were so wrapped up in releasing their tension that they did not notice a fourth figure joining them, until Old Man Russell was within their jerk circle.

'Morning, lads,' the sixty-year-old greeted them. 'Thought I'd pop out for a leak first thing. Glad to see you've been waiting for me.'

Luke realised then that this was a regular routine for the three men, and remembered that he had seen the three of them disappear other mornings, too. They'd been wanking themselves off all this time! Luke felt a fool for not realising what had been going on earlier.

'We've got ourselves a newcomer, Russell. A pretty mean weapon he's got, too.' Dirk grinned at Luke as the men looked over at his impressive erection. Luke waved it at them, and pulled his skin right back to make the bloated head stick out at them.

'Nice of you to join us, Luke,' Russell said as he pulled out his own erection, already fully hard. The wrinkled foreskin gave way to a juicy red head, and Luke found himself hoping that his own cock would be in such good condition when he hit sixty.

'Hope you've given yourself a head start, Russell, because I'm going to find that sweet moment pretty soon.'

'Oh yeah, Will, don't worry about that. I've been playing this baby for a good half-hour. Seemed a shame to hit the moment on my own, so I thought I'd come join you.'

They went silent, concentrating on balling themselves off, their hard dicks seeking release. Luke surreptitiously looked over at Will, eyes closed, grunting occasionally, his cock twitching in his hand. Then he looked over at Dirk, eyes fixed on on his cock as he copulated into his fist, watching his erection penetrate the orifice he had created in his palm.

It was Old Man Russell who came off first. Without warning, a jet shot out of his erection, up into the air, and fell on the floor. The hot come sizzled into the dirt, followed by another jet, and finally a third. Only then did Russell moan in relief, shaking the remaining semen from his cock and wrist.

He was followed by Will, who roared out that he was coming, a hot jet surging out of his knob. The force was so great, the jettison so strong, that the first rain of sperm fell on Luke, covering his own hand. It was enough to trigger his own orgasm, and Luke also roared as he shot his load, letting his dick spit out his joy juice, mixing with Will's and Russell's on the floor. Finally, Dirk let out a high pitch squeal, and his jism joined theirs after arcing out of his hard tool.

The three men took a while to recover, relaxing back against the rocks. Luke lay down on the floor, watching their semen mingle together in front of him. Will pulled out his pipe, filled it with tobacco, and lit it up. He passed it to Russell, who took his puff and passed it on to Dirk. After having taken a good smoke of the pipe, Dirk turned to him and offered the pipe.

'Reckon we'll be seeing you of a morning again, Luke?'

Luke took the pipe, and puffed away. He felt his body cooling after coming with the other men. He wished he'd been able to taste Will's hot juice, having to be contented with the warm splash of his juice as it hit his hand by accident. But there would be other mornings to wank of with Will and his mates as the convoy made its way out west. He turned to Dirk and winked. 'Reckon you will, Dirk. I reckon you will!'

Fourteen

————————

It had been a long haul, but Brett had arrived in Sutter's Mill in October, despite all the events that had almost stopped him from getting there at all. He was glad to arrive before the winter set in. He didn't fancy being on the trail in the cold winter months. Many had perished in the freezing cold, from starvation, exposure, or disease. It was a harsh journey once you were travelling beyond September.

Brett had been sorry to leave Reverend Morgan, but knew in his heart that he could only stay with him a while. It was after he had fully recovered that he finally realised that he could not replace what he had with Luke, and that it was unfair and unrealistic of him to expect that. Morgan had taken it badly, and Brett knew he had hurt him when he left. The Reverend had tried to be Christian about it, talking about forgiveness and the love between men, but even so Brett had detected the resentment and sense of betrayal.

Yet his heart had felt stifled. The novelty of helping around the chapel had worn thin very quickly, and Brett realised he couldn't hack being a handyman for the Reverend. He needed to be useful on his own account, have a sense of purpose in what he was doing. Had he really come so far to give it all up for a comfortable life with Reverend Morgan? Brett realised then that he had to face up to the loss of Luke, and had to come to terms with it. He needed to reassess his priorities and decide what it was he wanted to achieve, to do with his life.

Yes, Morgan had been good and kind, and had saved his life. Had Brett asked him to? Did that mean they were married for life? Did that mean he had to give up his dream? Brett had decided not, and in a long evening of tears and honesty had persuaded Morgan to see it that way, too. He wanted to leave as friends, but was prepared to leave anyway, should the minister not understand his reasons. Fortunately, Morgan had accepted the hard and painful truth.

Brett felt good after he'd made the decision. He felt he was back on the trail again. From leaving Morgan to arriving at Sutter's Mill had been a long arduous journey, particularly as the chill set in, but he had finally made it. He'd travelled light, although Morgan had given him nearly everything that he had needed. He'd made good progress, had covered much ground in the six weeks or so after leaving Morgan. He'd been more wary of snakes, that much was certain, and had been cautious of large groups of men. He'd steered clear of the major towns and encampments, until he finally arrived out in California.

He'd staked his claim, and was surprised how easy it had been for him to follow the dream. The piece of land he had been digging around in was now his! He wondered what he should call it, should it become a town. If he struck gold, it would be a prospector's dream: not only finding his wealth but calling a town after himself. McKinleyville? Brettsville? Neither seemed quite right – more thought needed on that front. Of course, it would help if he could actually find some gold, let alone mine it successfully!

Back to the search, thought McKinley. He had already spent days scouring the ground and the river in search of the elusive treasure. Now, he had decided to panhandle the stream that ran through his territory, and was in the process of checking through the minute pieces of grit and stone that landed in the bottom of his netted pan. It was a meticulous and soul-destroying task, every panful reinforcing the disappointment and despair of the last. He gathered this panful up, and sat down on the riverbank to fish through the debris.

Much the same as the last load: plenty of tiny grit and some large pebbles, which were easily discarded. Then he picked up his eye glass and looked in detail at the stone pieces, hoping that one of them would glint in the sunshine, a yellow golden gleam that would announce the discovery of gold in his river. Every panful brought this strange mixture of despair and hope, but it was the hope that Brett knew he must cling to, if he were to succeed.

His fingers moved quickly over the small pieces in front of him, separating them so that he could look closely at each small fragment, not wanting to miss that one piece that would tell him he had struck it lucky. Having cleared the pan of the debris, McKinley threw it down in disgust, failing again. Would he never find what he had come looking for? Was he just deceiving himself? Hadn't hundreds of men come out here expecting the same easy fortune, only to be disappointed and become some of the debris of alcoholics and gamblers that Brett had passed as made his way through Sutter's Mill? Was that his true fate?

Brett cupped his hands and drank the cold water from the stream, using it to wash over the despair on his face. He lay back in the October chill, the sun bright overhead but the air biting. He liked this time of the year, anyhow – the way the leaves found their true colours in falling from the branches, the fiesta of golds, reds, lush browns, oranges. He liked the abundance of fruit at this time, gathering it and drying it for the winter, as he had learnt to do from his mother back at St Joseph. The nuts, the harvest that had to be gathered in before the chill really set in.

Brett wondered if his brothers and father would have finished the harvest by now. Would they manage without him? Of course – they were all too proud to let it be known that he was that important to them. Despite their laziness, they would have managed somehow – and perhaps they had learned a valuable lesson with his leaving. Perhaps they would all become more responsible in the future. He thought briefly about contacting them, letting them know that he had arrived safely, and where he was. He decided there was time enough to do that, and he'd prefer to let them know when he had discovered the gold he instinctively knew was here under his feet. That would show them that he had been right, all along.

The autumnal breeze caressed Brett's skin, making him feel slightly dozy and lazy all of a sudden. He decided to take a break, and unpacked the lunch he had made himself. Having only recently arrived, Brett was still living in a makeshift shelter resting against the side of a mountain, and Brett knew that before winter set in he needed to build himself something more sturdy. He had been looking about for little caves, something which would at least protect him from the elements and wouldn't blow away in a sudden gust of wind. He'd heard there were earthquakes, too, in this part of the world, another danger he wanted to guard against as much as possible.

It was a simple lunch: bread, cheese, and an apple that he had picked himself. He drank it down with water fresh from the stream, enough of a meal to keep him satisfied until late in the evening when he normally had his main meal. McKinley remembered the meals he had shared with Luke, both men having a hearty appetite – for food as well as for sex. If only Luke could be here to share this, to see that at least he had followed the dream, that he had worked hard at it, had had some success. Brett McKinley had got back in the saddle, had got back on the trail, had made it out west.

He would work the stream until the light failed, around seven or eight in the evening if he was lucky. Darkness wasn't a good time to be out prospecting – not only because of the wild animals that still roamed these mountains, cougars and the like, but because of the wild men and bandits who were looking to make an easy claim. Greed was a strong motivator, and drove men to desperate actions. Just as the prospect of gold had attracted young men like himself, it had also attracted bands of outlaws eager to become wealthy themselves.

Sometimes Brett would seek out the company of some of the other prospectors, and have a drink with them. Some had been lucky; most had not – but these were still early days in the gold rush. More prospectors would turn up every week, with the same hopes and dreams that Brett had. He had been surprised once recently to catch a glimpse of Colm, drinking with some of his buddies in a corner of the local saloon. He had quickly got away, still unsure of Colm's loyalties, and not quite sure of what Sheriff Williams and Deputy Rogers had planned for him. Did Colm know that Luke had been killed? What had Rogers told the folks back home? Brett wondered if Colm would even remember him, but steered clear, just in case. It was better to be safe than sorry.

He hadn't made any close friends, as yet. Most of the men were territorial about their prospecting sites, which McKinley could understand. He'd seen the fights breaking out over disputed ground, the swaggering of men who had found gold, and the jealousy of men who hadn't. He felt lonely at times. He would have liked the raucous company of men he could trust, men he could laugh and joke and drink with. And he knew, deep in his heart, that he still missed Luke. Part of him questioned what had happened that day months ago now, whether Rogers really could have killed Luke. Somehow, part of him told him that Luke was alive.

Luke – alive? It couldn't be possible. And even if it was, the chances of them ever meeting again were extremely remote. The land was growing; there were all sorts of opportunities available for a man like Luke in this new America. Maybe he was languishing in some jail somewhere, or maybe he had been executed. Brett put Luke out of his mind again, although he could feel his heart leap every time he thought of him.

After finishing his brief lunch, Brett continued scouring the stream for signs of hidden treasure. Every moment he hoped for that one nugget which would guarantee him his fortune, but which never seemed to arrive. His hands were bruised and bleeding by mid-afternoon, cut from the tiny fragments of rock that he had been searching through. He had more luck catching fish, as the stream was teeming with them. Just as a break from the interminable prospecting, he allowed himself to sport with the fish, catching a nice couple of specimens – something to grill over his fire, later that evening. Brett watched them flapping in the air as he threw them on to the bankside, before swiftly killing them. He popped them in a small canvas bag, and continued sifting through the river.

He hadn't expected to be disturbed by another human being

all day – it was bad form among the forty-niners to disturb one another when they were working. It was also considered a tactic used by tricksters and cheaters trying to put miners off their task. So when he heard a voice calling out to him, he was taken unawares. However, the disturbance was welcome, a break from the monotony of the river search.

'Hey, there,' said a half-remembered voice. 'Now this must truly be heaven if I'm looking at the dead raised again!'

Brett turned around, and saw the figure of a man approaching him. He recognised the lazy gait, the confident swagger in the step. Colm! He had caught up with him after all.

'Colm!' he said cautiously. 'What brings you to these parts?'

'Oh, I happened to be passing through, thought I'd come see what all this fuss is about; thought I'd get some trading down here.'

'Well, it makes a change to see a familiar face.' Brett was wary still, not quite sure how to play the scene with Colm until he knew more about it. He got straight to the point. 'Rogers and the sheriff still after me?'

'What's the point in chasing the dead? Deputy came back saying you and Luke had both been killed in the mountains, that he'd come across your corpses half eaten by mountain cats and vultures. Reckoned he'd recognised you from that wound he gave you on your arm with the bottle. Must admit, I thought it was a pretty weak story, myself.'

Brett laughed. 'Well, let him believe it – suits me! Though, as you can see, it don't quite ring true.'

'So you both managed to get away from the grasp of Rogers, hey?'

'What?' Brett was sure he must have misheard what Colm had said. He latched on to the word immediately. 'Both?'

'Sure. It's good to know you and Luke got the better of him.'

'Luke? You've heard from him? You're saying Luke's alive?'

Colm grinned. 'Hey listen, I'm not saying as I approve of you two fellas – criminals and all, but I can't help admiring you for getting one over on Rogers. I pissed myself when I heard he'd been locked in the cell, I'm telling you I did!'

'Luke's alive?' repeated Brett incredulously.

'Luke? Well, sure! I agreed to help him out. I said I could do it . . .'

'You've seen him? You've spoken with him?' McKinley didn't want to believe it. He didn't want to raise his hopes too high, only to have them dashed from under him.

Colm's grin grew bigger. 'Yeah, I've spoken to him. I told him I'd find you. Told him I hadn't lost my tracking skills. And find you I did!'

'Where? Where is he, Colm? Where's Luke now? How do I . . .?' His words were gushing out, almost incoherent with anticipation. 'I've gotta know, Colm, please tell me . . .'

'Hey, hold on, fella, give me a chance. When I said I knew I could find you, I guess I should have been saying we.'

'We? Who is we . . .? You mean Luke's with you? He's here at Sutter's Mill?' Brett was nearly collapsing with the news.

'Hell, closer than that!' Colm turned and called over his back. 'Mitchell! Get your sorry ass over here – someone here's looking to meet you!'

Disbelievingly, Brett turned to look in the direction Colm had called. He looked to the skyline, the sun half blinding him as it lay bright against the sky. A silhouette appeared, a tall and muscular silhouette that Brett recognised instantly. Unable to control himself, he ran shouting at the figure of the lover he had presumed dead.

'Luke! Luke, you're alive!' He ran into his lover's arms, letting Luke pick him up and swing him around and up into the air. Now he could feel Luke's arms around him, the warmth of his embrace, he knew it was true – Luke was alive, and was with him here at Sutter's Mill.

'I told you I'd see you out west, partner! I keep my promises, Brett: you should know that!' Luke grinned broadly at Brett, his face as handsome as ever, his eyes bright with delight.

Colm, a little embarrassed by the fervour of the men's reunion, decided that this was an apposite time to break away. 'I'll give you guys some time to, er, get reacquainted, shall I?'

'Thanks for everything, Colm! Thanks for helping me find young Brett here.' Unable to resist, Luke ran over to kiss Colm on the cheek.

The Irishman was taken by surprise by the response, blushing slightly as he pulled away. 'Yeah, well.' Colm punched his hat, and grinned conspiratorially at Brett. 'Maybe I'll see you in the town for a drink, hey?'

'It's on me, Colm! Least I can do!'

'I'm holding you to it, McKinley! And not just the one!'

Colm made his way over the ridge, leaving the two men in shocked silence.

'So . . .' began Brett, not knowing where to begin.

'So . . .' repeated Luke, holding Brett's shoulders in his out-stretched arms.

And then they were kissing, long hungry kisses they thought they'd never have together again. There was time to be made up, passion to be shared again. Brett felt Luke pull him to his heaving chest, drawing him in close.

'I've missed you, Brett,' Luke spoke softly, rubbing noses with his, nuzzling against his new-found lover.

'Me, too,' Brett returned. 'I've been fucking crazy for you, Luke. I thought . . . I thought he'd killed you . . .'

'Being away from you nearly killed me, Brett. I love you. I had to find you again.'

They kissed, a long slow kiss that dispelled the months of separation.

'I love you, Luke. I never got to say it before . . . and when I thought you were dead . . . I wanted to say it. I want you to know it.'

'I did, Brett. I always knew.'

Luke took Brett's hand in his and walked him down to the stream. 'So this is yours? This is McKinley's, huh?'

'It's ours. If you want, that is.'

'Oh, yes, I want. I want it all . . .' Luke was kissing Brett's neck, hot passionate kisses that followed the trail of his flesh round to the nape, down into the back. They fell into the water, letting it course around them, as they pulled at each other's clothes. They tore their tunics and breeches off, smothering each other in love bites, letting the water cool the bitemarks with its chilled current. They lay on the river bed, letting the stream run round them, tonguing and touching each other's burning flesh.

Brett kissed Luke's chest, letting his tongue lap at the water running over his hairy belly and nipples. His hand stroked his partner's flesh, trembling with ardour and release. Luke responded by running his hands through Brett's wet hair, down over his shoulders, massaging them in his dripping hands. Their lips met again, as Brett looked longingly into Luke's eyes, his hand resting on Mitchell's thigh under the water.

They kissed again, Brett rubbing his hand against Luke's upper thigh, reaching for his groin, to feel the hard curves of his cock once again. The familiar feel of Luke's erection jumped to his touch, as Brett stroked Luke's wet knob. At the same time, he felt Luke reaching for his own cock, stroking his hard penis under the water. He straddled Luke, and they began skin-fucking in the water, its natural lubrication slipping between them. They took it in turns to hump each other, wrapping their legs around each other, gyrating their burning flesh into each other. The frottage was exciting them, cock against hard cock, rubbing against each other.

Brett thrust his cock between Luke's thighs, feeling the warmth as Luke closed his legs against his dick, the hard length slipping between them and up the crack of Luke's arse. Then Luke turned him over in the water, so that he was on top, with Brett on his back, Luke slipping his weapon between Brett's muscular legs. Each stroke was strong and dominating, Luke controlling the fucking motion. Devoid of speech for the time being, they communicated only with their desire for each other, a physical communion that neither man thought they would experience again. Luke snatched Brett's hands in his, arching them above Brett's head. He felt Luke thrusting between his legs, pinning him against the bank of the stream, banging him against the bank with each additional thrust.

Brett felt the heat of Luke's manhood between his legs, the shaft rubbing against his hairy muscles, the tickle of Luke's hairy balls beneath him. He struggled lightly against Luke's arms pinning him down, but Luke held him firm, continuing to exploit the territory between his legs. The two men were gasping at their pretend fucking, harsh gasps amid mouthfuls of chilled water as Brett turned his head into the current. He felt Luke's mouth on him, kissing the front of his neck, his collarbone, his chest. Their reunion was nearly complete. They were going to take each other to orgasm again, after so long a break.

'Luke thrust his wet mouth into Brett's ear, tonguing the lobe forcefully. 'I'm going to come. I want to shoot my load, Brett.'

'Yes, let's fucking come together, Luke. I want you to shoot!'

They kissed, Luke continuing to rub forcefully against Brett, their hard dicks meeting, manhood rubbing against manhood. Luke grunted loudly, pinning Brett into the riverbank, thrusting his heaving body against him, fast hard strokes that excited Brett with their passionate urging. Luke looked at Brett, then raised his head and roared into the autumn air. Brett felt the sudden rush of hot spunk washing over him under the water, and let himself relax into his own long awaited orgasm. He looked back up at Luke, roared his lover's name, and felt his cock stiffen and issue its seed up into the driving current.

Luke continued softly thrusting, but releasing his grip on Brett, and falling limp on to his lover's chest. Their last spasms continued to send milky white liquid into the river. Brett watched his semen mix with Luke's in the water, long strands of viscous fluid that marked their lovemaking's success. They lay in the water, holding on to each other, making occasional contented noises. The stream flowed over them, easing their limbs with its soft lapping. They cooled quickly in the babbling stream, feeling each other's skin lose the ferocious heat of desire.

Brett was so horny, now he was back with Luke, he couldn't stop there. He wanted more, to feel his lover's desire again; as soon as they were back on the ground, he let his mouth roam over Luke's naked body. Luke allowed him to roam over his musculature, his manhood already beginning to twitch under Brett's expert tongue. McKinley lapped up the remaining drops of semen, tasting his lover's juice for the first time in many months, savouring its bitter rarity. His mouth closed over the limp form of Luke's penis, gently encouraging it to stiffen and harden. He looked up into Luke's eyes, bobbing his head up and down the shaft as Luke spread his legs wide apart and relaxed back, enjoying the attention he was receiving.

He stroked Luke's hairy balls, moving his mouth down and

over each precious egg, snaking his tongue between Luke's arse-cheeks, letting his tongue tease the wet sphincter with his warm tongue. The water had cooled its burning, and the muscles closed in as Brett ran his tongue over them. Luke reached down, forcing Brett's head in between his arse-cheeks, demanding that Brett rim him fully. Brett was only too happy to comply, to show his lover the attention he deserved.

Brett returned his attention to Luke's hardened rod, taking it full in his mouth and enjoying the gasp of surprise from Luke as he did so. He dug his nails into Luke's thighs as he deep-throated him, almost gagging on the size of it. He could taste the pre-come already issuing from the cock-hole, and lapped it up with his tongue. Luke completed his entry into Brett's willing mouth, his balls resting against McKinley's chin. The feel of his soft flesh against him again urged Brett on to suck his lover's turgid tool deeper into his mouth.

He wanked the hard cock into his warm mouth, delighting in the nectar that leaked from it. He smothered the wet tip with his kisses, removing it from his mouth and ravishing it with his lips. He kissed his way up to Luke's face, kissing the eyelids closed in ecstasy, down over Luke's nose, on to his lover's lips.

'I want you to fuck me, Luke. I want you to fuck me with your hard cock like I did with you. I want to feel you inside me, I'm so horny for you. I want it now. Fuck me. Fuck me, Luke!'

'I want to fuck your sweet tight ass. Feel how hard my cock is for you.' Luke pushed Brett's hand down on to his cock, throbbing with the thought of penetrating Brett. Brett stood up, and watched as Luke instinctively held his hard cock in his hands, lying back on the ground. 'C'mon and ride my cock. Sit down on me, Brett; take it inside you.'

Brett lowered himself down over Luke's stiff tool, feeling the wet end against his quivering hole. He teased himself with the feel of the rubbery head, and then lowered himself over the first inch. He gasped as he fought to accommodate it, relaxing his sphincter to allow Luke inside. It felt really good as he allowed another inch inside, gently enticing Luke to push it further. Crouching over his lover, Brett held himself with half of Luke's dick inside him, making sure that he was in control of the fuck.

He held the base of the shaft, then sank down on to the entire length. An unintentional groan escaped from him, and then he felt Luke softly thrusting in and out of him.

It was soft and gentle lovemaking, as Brett sat on his lover's chest, Luke's cock thrusting into him. Luke grabbed his hips, bucking him up and down on the hard pole. Brett reached behind him, tugging gently on Luke's balls, which resulted in Luke thrusting up deeper into him. He had the whole of Luke's weapon in him now: not an easy feat, but it felt comfortable, intimate, loving. He heard Luke panting underneath him, felt his thrusting as he quickened the pace and began to fuck Brett more forcefully.

'Turn over, Brett. Let me fuck you from behind,' urged Luke.

Brett eased himself off Luke's rampant member, which stood stiff and upright, throbbing in the cool air. He knelt on his hands and knees, preparing himself for Luke's assault.

Brett twitched as he felt Luke guiding his cock between his legs, and started stroking himself in anticipation. He trusted Luke to be as gentle as he could, but also wanted to feel the force of his lover's passion driving into him. He heard Luke spitting into his hand, heard the squelch of saliva on rubbery cock, felt the nuzzling of Luke's cock against his arse. Luke pulled away, then rubbed himself against Brett's entrance again, this time rubbing the cock head into his warm arsehole.

Then he was penetrated; Luke's knob slid inside his soft cavern. Deeper his lover plunged, until the full length was embedded within him, and then Luke began fucking more earnestly. Brett moaned and lowered his head, as Luke took control of the situation and began shafting in and out of Brett. Short sharp strokes pummelled Brett's insides. McKinley allowed it to happen, allowed the urgent thrusts to wrack his body with pleasure.

Brett started to play with his dick, determined that he would come with Luke, that they would forge their alliance together. He felt his backside exploding with the filling it was receiving, and his own erection throbbing with excitement.

'Oh yes, Luke, give it to me. I've wanted this so much since I last saw you.'

'I've dreamt about fucking you like this, Brett. Come on, make me come!'

The two men renewed their exertions. Luke pinched Brett's nipples, started jerking his lover's cock in his hands. They moved together, Luke banging into Brett as he moved back to impale himself on Mitchell's erection. Brett felt Luke quicken the pace, felt the fast thrusts into him, and speeded up his own wanking. They moaned together, knowing that their moment was soon to arrive. Brett allowed Luke to fuck him more forcefully, feeling his cock sliding in and out, feeling it fill with blood and ache for release.

Luke kissed Brett hard on the mouth, letting out a groan that echoed round the canyon. Brett felt his cock spasm inside him, felt the last intimate thrusts as Luke ejaculated. He forced himself back on the man-spear in his arse, milking it of juice. Then Brett reared up with Luke still fucking him, thrusting his own cock forward as he felt his own climax arriving. He felt Luke's hands join his on his dick, four hands reaching over the stiff member, tossing it off. Luke played with Brett's hairy balls, causing them to shrink upwards, preparing for climax. Brett turned his head to kiss Luke once more on the lips, glad that his lover had joined him once more. Their lips met, encouraging Brett to spend himself fully.

'Come on, Brett, come for me. Shoot your hot load now; show me how much spunk you got left in those tasty balls of yours.'

Luke's coarse words sent him over the edge, his cock ejaculating semen in spurt after spurt. Luke continued pulling on Brett's discharging penis, the erection fully maintained. As Brett finished coming, sobbing with delight, and falling back against Luke's chest, Mitchell rubbed his spunk-covered hands into Brett's chest. He smeared his lover with jism, rubbing it into the skin, moving his hands up so that he could massage the last remaining drops into Brett's shoulders.

Brett fell forward, feeling Luke slip out of him, and the strong hands began to massage him more conventionally. He felt Luke's hands over him, comforting him with the reality of their existence. Luke was finally back with him, close against him. Luke lay on top of him, covering Brett with his naked body. His flesh felt warm, snuggled up against Brett. He felt Luke's face against his own, their cheeks rubbing against each other. Slowly, Brett turned and kissed his lover, receiving a tender kiss back full on the lips. He rested with Luke on top of him, the heavy weight giving him a feeling of succour and security that he hadn't felt since their parting.

The men lay together, savouring their reunion. The separation had been painful for both of them, not knowing where the other was and what they were doing. But, with the help of Colm, they had come together again at last. Brett raised himself first, sitting up and tracing a line across the sweat on Luke's skin. They smiled at each other, content to play gently after their bout of lovemaking.

Brett sauntered down to the stream, to be joined moments later by Luke. Luke washed him down, scooping up the water and running it over Brett's flesh. They cleansed each other of sweat and love-juice, joyful at being together again. It was as Luke was soaking him with water, playfully drenching him, that Brett happened to look over at his pan, and saw the sparkle in the October sun. Fearful of overexciting himself, he broke away from Luke's grasp and strode through the water to the bankside.

'Hey . . . what're you doing?' Luke responded disappointedly. He didn't understand why Brett wanted to break off his loving embrace

Brett didn't turn round to him, but peered down at the debris in his pan. He grinned excitedly at his returned lover and beckoned Mitchell over. He grabbed at his lover's arm to steady himself.

'See?' he said, trying to contain his excitement. 'See, Luke?'

Brett held up the pan close to Luke for him to study, but his lover pulled a frown and looked quizzically back at Brett. 'I can't see nothin' but dirt,' he said.

'Dirt? You fool, Luke! Can't you see it? It's gold, Luke! Gold!' He pointed out the two tiny nuggets of dirt-covered gold, enough of the shine emanating from them for Brett to be certain of his discovery. 'We've done it, Luke: we've found it! We've found gold!'

Luke's face broke into a broad grin, then he clapped his lover on the back, and hugged him close. 'Clever lad,' he congratulated Brett. 'I knew you'd make it! I knew you'd do it.'

'Not me,' interrupted Brett McKinley. 'Us. We did it. We made it. And now we're home, Luke! This is ours. This is our land!'

Brett triumphantly raised the pan to the sky, for Luke to hold on to. They put it safely to one side, and grinned at each other, already beginning their dance of desire. Cradling the tiny nuggets in his fist, Brett embraced his naked lover. The heat of the trail hadn't diminished for them with its journey's end. It was now, reunited and living Brett's dream for real, that the true heat of passion between Luke Mitchell and Brett McKinley was only just beginning.

IDOL NEW BOOKS

SUREFORCE
Published in November   Phil Votel

Not knowing what to do with his life once he's been thrown out of the army, Matt takes a job with the security firm Sureforce. Little does he know that the job is the ultimate mix of business and pleasure, and it's not long before Matt's hanging with the beefiest, meanest, hardest lads in town.

£7.99/$10.95

ISBN 0 352 33444 4

THE FAIR COP
Published in December   Philip Markham

The second world war is over and America is getting back to business as usual. In 1950s New York, that means dirty business. Hanson's a detective who's been dealt a lousy hand, but the Sullivan case is his big chance. How many junior detectives get handed blackmail, murder and perverted sex all in one day?

£7.99/$10.95

ISBN 0 352 33445 2

HOT ON THE TRAIL
Published in January   Lukas Scott

The Midwest, 1849. *Hot on the Trail* is the story of the original American dream, where freedom is driven by wild passion. And when farmboy Brett skips town and encounters dangerous outlaw Luke Mitchell, sparks are bound to fly in this raunchy tale of hard cowboys, butch outlaws, dirty adventure and true grit.

£7.99/$10.95

ISBN 0 352 33461 4

Also published:

CHAINS OF DECEIT
Paul C. Alexander

Journalist Nathan Dexter's life is turned around when he meets a young student called Scott — someone who offers him the relationship for which he's been searching. Then Nathan's best friend goes missing, and Nathan uncovers evidence that he has become the victim of a slavery ring which is rumoured to be operating out of London's leather scene.

£6.99/$9.95

ISBN 0 352 33206 9

DARK RIDER
Jack Gordon

While the rulers of a remote Scottish island play bizarre games of sexual dominance with the Argentinian Angelo, his friend Robert — consumed with jealous longing for his coffee-skinned companion — assuages his desires with the willing locals.

£6.99/$9.95

ISBN 0 352 33243 3

CONQUISTADOR
Jeff Hunter

It is the dying days of the Aztec empire. Axaten and Quetzel are members of the Stable, servants of the Sun Prince chosen for their bravery and beauty. But it is not just an honour and a duty to join this society, it is also the ultimate sexual achievement. Until the arrival of Juan, a young Spanish conquistador, sets the men of the Stable on an adventure of bondage, lust and deception.

£6.99/$9.95   ISBN 0 352 33244 1

TO SERVE TWO MASTERS
Gordon Neale

In the isolated land of Ilyria men are bought and sold as slaves. Rock, brought up to expect to be treated as mere 'livestock', yearns to be sold to the beautiful youth Dorian. But Dorian's brother is as cruel as he is handsome, and if Rock is bought by one brother he will be owned by both.

£6.99/$9.95   ISBN 0 352 33245 X

CUSTOMS OF THE COUNTRY
Rupert Thomas

James Cardell has left school and is looking forward to going to Oxford. That summer of 1924, however, he will spend with his cousins in a tiny village in rural Kent. There he finds he can pursue his love of painting – and begin to explore his obsession with the male physique.

£6.99/$9.95   ISBN 0 352 33246 8

DOCTOR REYNARD'S EXPERIMENT
Robert Black

A dark world of secret brothels, dungeons and sexual cabarets exists behind the respectable facade of Victorian London. The degenerate Lord Spearman introduces Dr Richard Reynard, dashing bachelor, to this hidden world.

£6.99/$9.95   ISBN 0 352 33252 2

CODE OF SUBMISSION
Paul C. Alexander

Having uncovered and defeated a slave ring operating in London's leather scene, journalist Nathan Dexter had hoped to enjoy a peaceful life with his boyfriend Scott. But when it becomes clear that the perverted slave trade has started again, Nathan has no choice but to travel across Europe and America in his bid to stop it. Second in the trilogy.

£6.99/$9.95   ISBN 0 352 33272 7

SLAVES OF TARNE
Gordon Neale

Pascal willingly follows the mysterious and alluring Casper to Tarne, a community of men enslaved to men. Tarne is everything that Pascal has ever fantasised about, but he begins to sense a sinister aspect to Casper's magnetism. Pascal has to choose between the pleasures of submission and acting to save the people he loves.

£6.99/$9.95   ISBN 0 352 33273 5

ROMAN GAMES
Tasker Dean

When Sam visits the island of Skate, he is taught how to submit to other men, acting out an elaborate fantasy in which young men become wrestling slaves – just as in ancient Rome. Indeed, if he is to have his beautiful prize – the wrestler, Robert – he must learn how the Romans played their games.

£6.99/$9.95   ISBN 0 352 33322 7

VENETIAN TRADE
Richard Davis

From the deck of the ship that carries him into Venice, Rob Weaver catches his first glimpse of a beautiful but corrupt city where the dark alleys and misty canals hide debauchery and decadence. Here, he must learn to survive among men who would make him a plaything and a slave.

£6.99/$9.95   ISBN 0 352 33323 5

THE LOVE OF OLD EGYPT
Philip Markham

It's 1925 and the deluxe cruiser carrying the young gigolo Jeremy Hessling has docked at Luxor. Jeremy dreams of being dominated by the pharaohs of old, but quickly becomes involved with someone more accessible – Khalid, a young man of exceptional beauty.

£6.99/$9.95   ISBN 0 352 33354 5

THE BLACK CHAMBER
Jack Gordon

Educated at the court of George II, Calum Monroe finds his native Scotland a dull, damp place. He relieves his boredom by donning a mask and holding up coaches in the guise of the Fox – a dashing highwayman. Chance throws him and neighbouring farmer Fergie McGregor together with Calum's sinister, perverse guardian, James Black.

£6.99/$9.95   ISBN 0 352 33373 1

THE GREEK WAY
Edward Ellis

Ancient Greece, the end of the fifth century BC – at the height of the Peloponnesian War. Young Orestes is a citizen of Athens, sent to Sparta as a spy. There he encounters a society of athletic, promiscuous soldiers – including the beautiful Spartan Hector.

£7.99/$10.95   ISBN 0 352 33427 4

MORE AND HARDER
Morgan

This is the erotic autobiography of Mark, a submissive English sadomasochist: an 'SM sub' or 'slave'. Rarely has a writer been so explicitly hot or so forthcoming in the arousingly strict details of military and disciplinary life.

£7.99/$10.95   ISBN 0 352 33437 1

BOOTY BOYS

Published in September Jay Russell

Hard-bodied black British detective Alton Davies can't believe his eyes or his luck when he finds muscular African-American gangsta rapper Banji-B lounging in his office early one morning. Alton's disbelief – and his excitement – mounts as Banji-B asks him to track down a stolen videotape of a post-gig orgy.

£7.99/$10.95

ISBN 0 352 33446 0

EASY MONEY

Published in October Bob Condron

One day an ad appears in the popular music press. Its aim: to enlist members for a new boyband. Young, working-class Mitch starts out as a raw recruit, but soon he becomes embroiled in the sexual tension that threatens to engulf the entire group. As the band soars meteorically to pop success, the atmosphere is quickly reaching fever pitch.

£7.99/$10.95

ISBN 0 352 33442 8

---------------✂------------------------------

Please send me the books I have ticked above.

Name ....

Address ....

....

....

.... Post Code ....

Send to: **Cash Sales, Idol Books, Thames Wharf Studios, Rainville Road, London W6 9HA.**

US customers: for prices and details of how to order books for delivery by mail, call 1-800-805-1083.

Please enclose a cheque or postal order, made payable to **Virgin Publishing Ltd**, to the value of the books you have ordered plus postage and packing costs as follows:

UK and BFPO – £1.00 for the first book, 50p for each subsequent book.

Overseas (including Republic of Ireland) – £2.00 for the first book, £1.00 for each subsequent book.

We accept all major credit cards, including VISA, ACCESS/MASTER-CARD, DINERS CLUB, AMEX and SWITCH.
Please write your card number and expiry date here:

....

Please allow up to 28 days for delivery.

Signature ....

---------------✂------------------------------

WE NEED YOUR HELP . . .

to plan the future of Idol books –

Yours are the only opinions that matter. Idol is a new and exciting venture: the first British series of books devoted to homoerotic fiction for men.

We're going to do our best to provide the sexiest, best-written books you can buy. And we'd like you to help in these early stages. Tell us what you want to read. There's a freepost address for your filled-in questionnaires, so you won't even need to buy a stamp.

THE IDOL QUESTIONNAIRE

SECTION ONE: ABOUT YOU

1.1 Sex (*we presume you are male, but just in case*)
Are you?
Male ☐
Female ☐

1.2 Age
under 21 ☐   21–30 ☐
31–40 ☐   41–50 ☐
51–60 ☐   over 60 ☐

1.3 At what age did you leave full-time education?
still in education ☐   16 or younger ☐
17–19 ☐   20 or older ☐

1.4 Occupation _____

1.5 Annual household income _____

1.6 We are perfectly happy for you to remain anonymous; but if you would like us to send you a free booklist of Idol books, please insert your name and address

_____

_____

_____

_____

SECTION TWO: ABOUT BUYING IDOL BOOKS

2.1 Where did you get this copy of *Hot on the Trail*?
- Bought at chain book shop ☐
- Bought at independent book shop ☐
- Bought at supermarket ☐
- Bought at book exchange or used book shop ☐
- I borrowed it/found it ☐
- My partner bought it ☐

2.2 How did you find out about Idol books?
- I saw them in a shop ☐
- I saw them advertised in a magazine ☐
- I read about them in _____
- Other _____

2.3 Please tick the following statements you agree with:
- I would be less embarrassed about buying Idol books if the cover pictures were less explicit ☐
- I think that in general the pictures on Idol books are about right ☐
- I think Idol cover pictures should be as explicit as possible ☐

2.4 Would you read an Idol book in a public place – on a train for instance?
Yes ☐   No ☐

SECTION THREE: ABOUT THIS IDOL BOOK

3.1 Do you think the sex content in this book is:
Too much ☐   About right ☐
Not enough ☐

3.2 Do you think the writing style in this book is:

        Too unreal/escapist ☐   About right ☐

        Too down to earth ☐

3.3 Do you think the story in this book is:

        Too complicated ☐   About right ☐

        Too boring/simple ☐

3.4 Do you think the cover of this book is:

        Too explicit ☐   About right ☐

        Not explicit enough ☐

Here's a space for any other comments:

SECTION FOUR: ABOUT OTHER IDOL BOOKS

4.1 How many Idol books have you read?

4.2 If more than one, which one did you prefer?

4.3 Why?

SECTION FIVE: ABOUT YOUR IDEAL EROTIC NOVEL

We want to publish the books you want to read – so this is your chance to tell us exactly what your ideal erotic novel would be like.

5.1 Using a scale of 1 to 5 (1 = no interest at all, 5 = your ideal), please rate the following possible settings for an erotic novel:

        Roman / Ancient World ☐

        Medieval / barbarian / sword 'n' sorcery ☐

        Renaissance / Elizabethan / Restoration ☐

        Victorian / Edwardian ☐

        1920s & 1930s ☐

        Present day ☐

        Future / Science Fiction ☐

5.2 Using the same scale of 1 to 5, please rate the following themes you may find in an erotic novel:

Bondage / fetishism ☐
Romantic love ☐
SM / corporal punishment ☐
Bisexuality ☐
Group sex ☐
Watersports ☐
Rent / sex for money ☐

5.3 Using the same scale of 1 to 5, please rate the following styles in which an erotic novel could be written:

Gritty realism, down to earth ☐
Set in real life but ignoring its more unpleasant aspects ☐
Escapist fantasy, but just about believable ☐
Complete escapism, totally unrealistic ☐

5.4 In a book that features power differentials or sexual initiation, would you prefer the writing to be from the viewpoint of the dominant / experienced or submissive / inexperienced characters?

Dominant / Experienced ☐
Submissive / Inexperienced ☐
Both ☐

5.5 We'd like to include characters close to your ideal lover. What characteristics would your ideal lover have? Tick as many as you want:

Dominant	☐	Caring	☐
Slim	☐	Rugged	☐
Extroverted	☐	Romantic	☐
Bisexual	☐	Old	☐
Working Class	☐	Intellectual	☐
Introverted	☐	Professional	☐
Submissive	☐	Pervy	☐
Cruel	☐	Ordinary	☐
Young	☐	Muscular	☐
Naïve	☐		

Anything else? _____

5.6 Is there one particular setting or subject matter that your ideal erotic novel would contain?

_____

5.7 As you'll have seen, we include safe-sex guidelines in every book. However, while our policy is always to show safe sex in stories with contemporary settings, we don't insist on safe-sex practices in stories with historical settings because it would be anachronistic. What, if anything, would you change about this policy?

_____

_____

SECTION SIX: LAST WORDS

6.1 What do you like best about Idol books?

_____

6.2 What do you most dislike about Idol books?

_____

6.3 In what way, if any, would you like to change Idol covers?

_____

6.4 Here's a space for any other comments:

_____

_____

_____

_____

Thanks for completing this questionnaire. Now either tear it out, or photocopy it, then put it in an envelope and send it to:

Idol
FREEPOST
London
W10 5BR

You don't need a stamp if you're in the UK, but you'll need one if you're posting from overseas.